HERA'S REVENGE

Wendy Dingwall

HERA'S REVENGE

An Yvonne Suarez Travel Mystery

Wendy Dingwall

 Canterbury House Publishing

www.canterburyhousepublishing.com
Vilas, North Carolina

Canterbury House Publishing, Ltd.
www.canterburyhousepublishing.com

First Printing April 2011

Book Design by Tracy Arendt

AUTHOR'S NOTE:
This is a work of fiction. Names, characters, and incidents are either the product of the author's imagination or are used factiously, and any resemblance to actual persons living or dead, business establishments, events, or locales is entirely coincidental.

Library of Congress Cataloging-in-Publication Data

Dingwall, Wendy.
  Hera's revenge : an Yvonne Suarez travel mystery / by Wendy Dingwall.
    p. cm.
  ISBN 978-0-9829054-2-5
  1. Travel agents--Fiction. 2. Americans--Greece--Fiction. 3.
Murder--Investigation--Fiction. I. Title.
  PS3604.I475H47 2011
  813'.6--dc22
2010051557

For information about permission to reproduce selections from this book write to:
Permissions
Canterbury House Publishing, Ltd.
225 Ira Harmon Rd.
Vilas, NC 28692

DEDICATION

To my mother, Margery, who passed on to me her love of reading, especially mysteries, and who during my youth, kept me stocked with Nancy Drew novels, and later Agatha Christie mysteries and many others. I dedicate this, my first mystery novel to you.

CAST OF CHARACTERS:

Yvonne Suarez
Travel agent, tour leader and mother who wants to lead the perfect tour for the sake of her clients—and her sanity.

David Ludlow
Owner of L&L Software who designs banking software and has a design on Yvonne's heart if murder doesn't get in the way.

Beverly Nystrom
Paralegal/secretary who would do anything for fame and fortune and the attention of a man like David Ludlow.

Evelyn Malcolm
An observant chronicler of a long awaited trip to Greece with her husband, retired Dr. Richard Malcolm.

Dr. Richard Malcolm
A doting husband, he wants a trouble-free trip for his wife, but sees danger around every corner.

Cynthia Forsythe
A hairstylist on the prowl, she and her co-worker Mark Rogers seek excitement, romance and escape from a mundane life.

Mark Rogers
Recently "outed" gay hairstylist, he searches for acceptance and romance.

Melissa "Missy" Johnson
A strong-willed young woman, who at the peak of her career pins the hopes of her marital future on their second honeymoon.

Todd Johnson
Who, now that they are financially secure, finds that his dream of being a father is slipping away, but he wonders, will a romantic trip be enough to change Missy's mind?

Janice Armstrong
Wife of loud-mouth Bill Armstrong, delicate lady appears to be accident prone.

Bill Armstrong
Retired blue-collar worker who strives to out-do his wealthy art-collector friends, the Fontinellis.

Rosanna Fontinelli	An exotic woman who uses her feminine wiles to get what she wants from everyone, including her husband, Nicholas.
Nicholas Fontinelli	The kind of man you hardly notice in a crowd unless he is with his flirtatious wife and prize possession.
Aristotle, a.k.a. Ari	A humorous tour guide, he knows all the best places to find the treasures of Greece.
Demetrius Maverickos	Business partner of David Ludlow, he minds the business while David travels.
George Maverickos	Demetrius' brother, zealously oversees the finances of the lucrative family business.
Loukas Maverickos	Demetrius' father, the head of family-owned Maverickos' Antiques with several touristy locations, he affords his family a luxurious life.
Alexis Maverickos	Matriarch of the Maverikos family, her strong influence in their lives is evident the very first time you meet her.
Damian	Mysterious acquaintance of Bill Armstrong and Nicholas Fontinelli.
Inspector Michael Trakas	Pompous Athens police detective.
Inspector Stavros	Firm, but kind-hearted, Santorini police detective.
Christy Gianetti	Six-year-old daughter of Yvonne and Gino Gianetti appears to be adjusting to her parents divorce.
Nancy Suarez	Yvonne's British mother who can be the rock in times of distress with a demeanor of cool reserve.
Eduardo Suarez	A transplanted Cuban Aristocrat who would do anything to keep his family safe.

NATIONAL MUSEUM OF ATHENS

SPRING 2003

"**W**here the hell is Peters?**"** As was his habit, the curator of the National Archaeological Museum arrived at 7:30 sharp to begin his morning rounds. He entered between the massive stone columns that framed the grand foyer, mentally preparing for the public and tour buses arriving at 8:30, the appointed opening time. Peters, the night watchman, usually greeted him before he arrived at the monitoring station. This morning, however, there was complete quiet. Perhaps he had gone to the toiletta. The curator glanced into the systems monitor room, noting that all the screens were blank. Of course, this explained it. Peter has gone to check the electrical systems.

The curator proceeded to his office, certain that Peters would meet him there to report. During Dr. Daedalus' thirteen years as curator of the National Archaeological Museum of Athens, no major problems had occurred. A few overzealous tourists crossed into prohibited areas or out-of-control children knocked over rope stands, but they were brought into line immediately. This morning would be no different.

Fifteen minutes passed and still no Peters. The curator decided to begin his rounds as usual and check out the electrical station when he arrived at area B, the Byzantine era. The stairs that led to the electrical systems were across the room.

Dr. Daedalus always started his rounds with the same route the tourists most often took. "The museum, set up chronologically, started with area M for Mythology, or as he referred to it, the "Godliest room," the area with the oldest artifacts. The earliest mythological gods and goddesses, the Titans, were the most powerful of gods. According to ancient teachings, they spawned many of the more human gods that came later. The Titans were the curator's favorite because, like their stories, many of their artifacts were bigger than life. He breezed through area M and saw that everything was as it should be.

Entering the Byzantine room, he maneuvered between some larger statues of Apollo to check on a glass display case that held smaller artifacts and his penchant, a small golden statue of Hera, the original symbolic Mother, wife to Zeus and Mother of detested god of war, Ares.

The statue of Hera—the bronze dagger—where were they? Panic began to take hold—the two objects were missing from the case. He hurried back to his office and telephoned the police. "There's been a robbery here at the National Museum. Please hurry!"

As other employees arrived, they were sent to guard and prevent the visitors from gaining entrance. When the police, arrived the curator was waiting to lead them to the display case in the Byzantine room. "Peters, the night watchman is missing and the security screens were off when I arrived. I think he may have gone to investigate." The curator led them to the door of the electrical room. "Nothing like this has ever happened during my tenure!" His fear that the disappearance of the night watchman was somehow connected to the theft was confirmed when the police found the faithful watchman Peters lying dead on the floor of the electrical room, a bullet hole in his head.

YVONNE

SPRING 2003

Yvonne Suarez stared at her computer monitor. She squeezed her eyes shut, holding them tight a few seconds to clear her blurry vision, opened them and shifted her focus to the high-rise she could see through the plate glass window of the travel agency. The Galt Ocean Mile on A1A in east Fort Lauderdale shimmered through a wavy mist in the afternoon glare. Tourists found the city beautiful, Yvonne knew that nothing was quite what it appeared in this dazzling city sandwiched between Miami and Palm Beach in sunny south Florida. She thought of her ex, Gino—the man she married was nothing like the man she had fallen in love with.

Yvonne wondered how the evening would play out with her mom as babysitter and her six-year-old daughter Christy. She caught movement out of the corner of her eye. A man stopped and looked in the store front window bringing with him rain clouds and darkness that blocked the sun. He stared at the poster advertising her custom tour of Greece. After a moment he reached for the door handle to the agency.

Ay, Dios Mio. Why, do they always arrive at closing time? Is it possible? Could he actually be interested in my tour? I only need one more passenger to complete the group, and it's coming down to the wire. But if he is interested in my tour, I could fill the last spot, so the difference won't be deducted from my commission check.

She studied the man as he entered the Pinkerton Travel Agency. Average height, bald—he had sandy blond hair around the sides, but was completely bald on the top. She guessed him to be in his mid thirties. He wore a white shirt, sleeves rolled up, and his dark slacks (well-cut and expensive) were slightly crinkled from the day's wear. Not here to buy a tour, a corporate type, here to book a last minute business trip. Yvonne's heart sank.

The man stood and gazed around the office. All the agents, who'd been working at their computers or talking into their head-sets, turned to look at this latecomer. Closest to the door, Yvonne turned in her seat to face him. "Hello, may I help you?" His shocking blue eyes and pleasant smile caught her off guard.

"I'm looking for Yvonne Suarez. I'm David Ludlow. I stopped by to pick up my airline tickets and hotel confirmations for my trip to Austin, Texas."

Exhaling with an air of professionalism, she reached out to shake his hand. "Oh, Mr. Ludlow, it's nice to meet you. I'm Yvonne. Please—have a seat. I'll get your travel docs."

He shook her hand firmly, but not too tight. Good, she thought. He's strong but not macho. Yvonne sprang up from her chair and walked quickly back to the ticketing center. Finding the tickets already collated she placed them with his car and hotel reservations and returned to her seat, and handed them to David. "Please double-check your documents to be sure everything is correct."

David glanced at the itinerary. "I hope you don't mind my dropping by, but I wanted to meet you in person. My last travel agent frequently booked things backward." David's forehead creased. "I must admit I've been impressed with the way you put together my last-minute, often complicated routings and still manage to get me free upgrades along the way. Besides, I always like to put a face with the voice on the other end of the phone."

Yvonne's cheeks turned bright red and she fought to regain her composure. "It's a treat for me too, when I can meet a client in person." She took a second appraising look. Feel free to stop in anytime, she thought, but said instead, "And—thank you for the kind words. It's nice to be appreciated." She reached for her pen and started tapping it on her note pad.

David hesitated a few moments. "I confess I have another reason for being here. You know, my company—well—that is—I develop software programs for the banking industry. Apparently, the stress and pressure of the job has dictated a vacation. My doctor assures me that if I don't take some time off what appears to be a minor heart condition could become much worse. I hope you'll have a suggestion or two. When it comes to business, I know exactly where to go, but for pleasure, I'll need help."

Yvonne stared at the pad on her desk. Do I really want the responsibility of deciding where he goes? What if he has a heart attack and dies—I would feel terrible. But, maybe... "Mr. Ludlow, tell me what kind of physical activity you could handle? What about walking, climbing stairs and so forth?"

"Please, call me David." He thought for a moment. "Um... I don't think normal activity like walking or climbing stairs would be a problem as long as I could rest every now and then. In fact, the doctor wants me to exercise. He said it would help strengthen my muscles. He believes this will lessen the stress on my heart."

Yvonne pushed back her chair to face him. "Can you stand a little culture along with your relaxation?"

"What do you have in mind?"

"How would you like to be part of a small group tour I'm leading to the Greek Islands? It will be a nice mix of couples and singles. Coincidentally, I have one spot left rounding us out to a baker's dozen."

"Did you say that you're leading it?" David's eyes widened. "That sounds good to me, though, I suppose I should ask how much it will cost and how long I should arrange to be away?"

Yvonne reached into her standing files and pulled out a thick folder. "Here, take this brochure. It has all the details of the trip, and the contract lists the financial information. Please review everything as soon as possible—final payments were actually due a month ago. Don't worry. I'll work it out with the travel vendors. Just let me know right away." Yvonne returned her tour envelope to its designated space. "I know it's probably sooner than you planned to leave, but I wouldn't want you to miss this great trip. You'll love Greece." Yvonne took a breath and continued, "In addition to the sightseeing there will be many leisure breaks. Some of the most interesting and beautiful places in the world are located in the Mediterranean on the various Greek Islands." She leaned in closer to David, "If you agree that it's a go, I can take your credit card payment over the phone and courier the documents to you right away. The tour is set to depart two weeks from tomorrow. The flight leaves from Fort Lauderdale airport in the afternoon. There will be a change of planes in New York at JFK and we will arrive in Athens the following morning." Satisfied that he was serious about joining the tour, Yvonne gave David her best closing smile and waited for his reply.

"Thanks, Yvonne, the trip sounds great. I'll read the information tonight and call you from Austin tomorrow afternoon." Unaware of all the eyes turning to watch him, David left.

Now why in the world did I invite David Ludlow to join my group? So I could keep an eye on him to be sure he doesn't have a heart attack? He does have a great phone voice—and now that I've seen him in person.... Not that he would necessarily be interested in me anyway. Wait until he gets a load of Beverly. She's sophisticated, and well-off. Besides, I don't need another man in my life. In ten years when Christy is 16, I might be ready for another man. Ay...If today is any indication, David's presence is going to challenge my resolve. Just meeting him once, I got all jelly-bellied. It's too bad about his heart condition, but all the more reason to lay low.

"Earth to Yvonne." Debra Pinkerton, owner of the agency and mentor to Yvonne interrupted her thoughts. "It's after six. Don't you think you'd better be on your way home?"

"You're right. I can't afford to be late picking up Christy again." While waiting for the computer to shut down, Yvonne straightened her desk.

"Before you go, tell me about that hunky guy you were just helping."

"David Ludlow from L & L Software. Remember, he was referred to me by Jan at Kasper Electronics. He's a good account, travels regularly and is pleasant. In fact, I'm even planning his leisure travel now. I think he may join my group to Greece in two weeks. Yvonne stifled a grin. "I'll know tomorrow."

"That would be nice. He might make a good companion for one overworked travel agent I know." Debra's husky voice dropped to a sexy purr. Tall and willowy, she placed her hands on her hips and shifted her weight to one side, reminding Yvonne of a slinky toy.

"You know, Deb, I'm not about to fraternize with a client. But you're right about one thing, I gotta go."

Yvonne grabbed her purse and headed for the door. Debra turned to the other travel agents in the room and continued talking. "Gee, I must have hit a nerve. I wonder how she'll act after a two-week vacation with that good-looking client. Come on, guys and dolls—time to close up. Let's make like travel agents and cruise on out of here." Yvonne couldn't help but chuckle at Debra's corny sense of humor.

Traffic was stop-and-go on Federal Highway. Yvonne could only think of the old saying, "Hurry up and wait". Her neck and shoulders ached. Her body reacted to the stress of getting to the after-school-care program before the closing deadline. Her life was filled with deadlines. In the travel industry deadlines were set for all bookings and occurred throughout the day. If clients didn't pay deposits or final payments on time, bookings were cancelled and re-bookings, if available, were necessary. This meant double the work, not double the pay. Arriving late to pick up Christy meant she'd receive nasty looks from the daycare workers, and the fine of a dollar for every minute she went past the 6:30 deadline. She knew the fine was necessary, or some parents would abuse the situation, but it seemed harsh for the occasional mishap that was bound to happen to anyone.

While she sat in her air-conditioned car waiting impatiently for the bottle neck to open up, she willed herself to relax. Since her divorce she no longer needed to account for every waking moment or walk on eggshells fearful of upsetting Gino. She warmed to the sun beating in the car window on the passenger side. Within the hour there would be an incredible sunset with shades of golden peach overlaid with pink and purple hues. It would settle serenely over the city's new decorative cement-and-glass skyline, she could watch it from the back porch of her townhouse. She hoped she'd be home in time to enjoy it. She loved watching the sunset and relaxing in the shade of the lush and fragrant tropical landscape of her small back yard. Palm trees, banana plants, bird of paradise, pin-wheel jasmine and lariope-grass surrounded her home like a cocoon. "I will slow down and enjoy 'being'."

Christy was working a puzzle with her after-school friend Angie when Yvonne arrived. They were the last two children waiting to be picked up, and Cindy, the sitter, hovered nearby anxious for their departure. "Hi, Sweetie, did you have a good day?"

"Yes, Mommy, see the finger painting I did? It has you and Grandma and Grandpa in it!"

"Wow! It's beautiful, Christy." Yvonne breathed a sigh of relief. Christy was getting used to her smaller family. "Gather up your stuff. It's time to go home." Christy grabbed up some papers and stuffed them into her backpack. She waved good-bye to her friend Angie and Cindy, the day care worker.

Yvonne parked her car in the driveway in front of her townhouse, climbed out and opened Christy's door to help her from the car seat. "Christy, stop dawdling. Mommy's got yoga class tonight."

"I want to go with you, Mommeee." Christy whined as she set her jaw and secured her little fingers to the seat belt.

"When you're older we'll be able to do yoga together."

"When will I be growed up enough, Mommy? I'm already six. Shouldn't that be old enough to do everything like you?

"I'm afraid not, Sweetie, now hurry up. Nana's going to be here shortly, and we need to get you some dinner." At the thought of food, Christy unclicked the seatbelt and gingerly climbed out of the navy-blue Camry that Yvonne had acquired in her divorce six months before.

Christy finished eating her dinner just as the doorbell rang. Nana let herself in through the front door.

Nancy Suarez was not your typical grandmother. At fifty-two she was slender yet shapely. Her straight blonde shoulder-length hair always looked neat. Her striking blue eyes and cultured English demeanor gave her an air of someone refined and well-traveled. She was the perfect complement to her husband, Eduardo, one of Miami's wealthiest Cuban aristocrats, and she could easily pass for Yvonne's older sister.

"Hi Mom." Yvonne wiped up the mess left by Christy at the kitchen table. "Thanks for helping out. Christy's regular babysitter had a school program tonight and couldn't be here."

"That's fine, Hon. You know I'm always glad to have the chance to watch her, and just so you know, Dad and I are all set to be here while you're in Greece. We've got all kinds of fun outings planned to keep her busy so she won't be missing you too much." Nancy hugged Christy. "I thought we'd take her to Disney World for a couple of days, and then there's the beach and the Discovery Museum. It will be such fun. We can hardly wait."

"Yea!" Christy squealed.

"Oh, Mom, I don't know what I would do without you and Dad. I just know Christy's going to love being with Nana and Papa while I'm gone. But, don't spoil her too much. Remember, I will have to bring her back to reality when I return.

"I guess I better get going. Christy should be in bed by eight. She finished all her dinner so I told her that she could watch her favorite Dora the Explorer video before her bath. Then, if she's been very good she can have a bedtime story. I should be home around nine-thirty."

Yvonne felt a twinge of guilt as she found herself leaving to indulge herself. "Come on, Pumpkin, give me a goodbye kiss and just for something special to look forward to—tomorrow night we'll go to the beach and play in the sand until the sun goes down."

"I love you, Mommy. Will you come an' kiss me goodnight when you get home?"

"Sure I will, Sweetie." She blew Christy a kiss on her way out the door.

The last two weeks had been a blur as Yvonne prepared for their trip to Greece. The time finally arrived for the tour participants to gather for their flight to Athens. Yvonne made the necessary introductions and everyone chatted, excited about their upcoming tour. They related stories in a good-natured manner about the harassment imposed by the airline security checks.

"We still have an hour and a half before the flight departs. Boarding will begin in approximately 45 minutes. Are there any last minute questions?"

"I have a question," said Bill Armstrong, one of the retired passengers. "What's the terrorist forecast? Should we be worried?" He looked around to see if all the other passengers were focused on him and his very important question.

"Oh, Bill, why did you have to bring that up? We're having such a good time. Please don't spoil it." Bill's wife bit her lip suppressing any further comments.

"Actually, Janice, that's a valid question." Yvonne looked directly at her and the other tour participants. "Most travelers have similar concerns these days, and, what we are finding is, due to heightened security and fewer people flying, most flights have never gone smoother. I think you will also find that in the Mediterranean and Europe, the people are so happy to have our tourist trade that they will be rolling out red carpets wherever we land."

An hour later, with the exception of the Armstrongs and the Fontinellis who had upgraded to first-class, the group sat in their economy class seats waiting for lift off.

DEPARTURE

DAY 1

During lift off Yvonne felt slightly nauseous. Was it due to the motion of the plane, the excitement about this opportunity to spread her wings or the apprehension about leaving Christy.

Since her divorce Yvonne challenged herself to do things. Before she had lived in fear—she might make a wrong move or say the wrong thing to upset Gino.

I've finally done it. I'm so excited I can hardly stand it. Here I am on a plane to Athens leading my own group with an itinerary I specifically designed, to bring pleasure and memories that people will have for the rest of their lives. Yet, I still have this nagging doubt about leaving Christy... God, of all times I need to be professional and here I am tearing up. I've left her before when I've traveled, though not for so long, and she's been okay. I'm sure she'll be fine. The teacher said she'd been a bit unruly lately and seemed out of sorts. What's going on? Why hasn't she told me what's the matter? Christy promised to behave better in school. I hope Mom and Dad won't have any problems for this two-week period. Between school and weekends having fun, she probably won't even miss me.

David interrupted her reverie. "Yvonne, thanks again for squeezing me in at the last minute."

"I'm sorry that you got stuck sitting next to me, but it was the last seat available, in our allotment."

"Don't apologize. I was hoping that I'd be sitting near you."

As Yvonne tried to control the blush coming to her cheeks, she fought back a stammer in her voice. "Thank you." Now what do I do? I can't be distracted from my responsibilities as tour leader to flirt with my client. I need to steer him in another direction. Why did I inherit more of my father's Latin blood than my mother's cool reserve? I have to stay cool. I let my emotions rule my heart once, and it was a disaster. It can't happen again.

David studied her face and softened his tone. "You've grown quiet. Have I offended you?"

"No—of course not. I was just going over details in my head. It's what I do." *Ay Dios Mio*, why did I snap at him like that? Yvonne wriggled in her seat in an effort to relax her demeanor.

"Excuse me. I didn't mean to interrupt your work." David backed off, making the challenge he felt rising in him stronger by the minute. "Perhaps when you get a few minutes, you could give me the stats on my new traveling companions? I'd like to know a little something about the people. After all in the next two weeks we're going to be in close proximity with each other. "

She agreed to fill him in on some general information about their traveling companions. It would be a safer course of conversation.

"The two senior couples who upgraded to first-class are the Armstrongs and the Fontinellis. They are life-long friends and have traveled together many times. I believe they were business partners as well, but I'm a little unclear as to their business, something about real estate or investments. All I know is they are retired and financially able to travel in style frequently."

The stewardess interrupted Yvonne to ask for her drink order. Yvonne ordered ice water while David ordered a martini. As the stewardess served their drinks, David nodded his head for Yvonne to continue. "The young married couple three rows behind us are Todd and Melissa, Missy for short, Johnson. This is a second honeymoon to Greece. They're celebrating their tenth wedding anniversary. The platonic couple seated behind the Johnson's are Mark Rogers and Cynthia Forsythe. Mark, as you will probably be informed by him at some point, is gay. When he came out of the closet a few years back, he became adamant about letting everyone know this. I'm assuming he does it so that he can find out if they accept him as he is or not right away. Cynthia owns a local beauty salon and she and Mark became fast friends after she hired him. I believe they are both hoping to find romance in the Greek Isles."

Yvonne gathered her thoughts while munching on some sweetened peanuts and then took a long drink of her ice water.

"Seated further back is a very lovely client of mine, Beverly Nystrom. Every year she takes a wonderful trip out of the United States for her vacation. Last year she did a tour of Western Europe, this year she agreed to be part of my tour to Greece. She's a paralegal in a prestigious law firm. She confided in me that the pressure is enormous in her job, so she allows herself a nice vacation once a year as a well earned reward. I find her to be an interesting and intelligent person. I will introduce you to her when we arrive in Athens and you can see for yourself what a neat lady she is."

David rustled in his seat, "I didn't realize matchmaking was also part of your job description."

The twinkle in David's eyes revealed he had seen through her not so subtle attempts at playing cupid. "Why, I have no idea what you are talking about."

"Okay, play it your way. If Ms. Nystrom is so wonderful, why is she traveling without a companion?"

"Well, it could be the fact that she is a capable woman who doesn't need a man on her arm to feel secure." Yvonne sat up a little straighter in her seat.

"Oh, so you're saying she's probably a control freak?"

"I wasn't saying anything of the sort!" Just then, Yvonne realized he was pushing her buttons and enjoying every moment of it. She took another long drink of water and began again in her frostiest tone. "Are you interested in hearing about the remaining members of our group?"

The glint in his eye caught her attention. "Yes, by all means continue."

"The last couple is Richard and Evelyn Malcolm. It's their first vacation without children in twenty years. It's also their first time out of the United States. Evelyn has always dreamed of going to Greece, but I get the impression that Richard is just along for the ride and to humor Evelyn." Yvonne stifled a yawn.

"Well, that should do it. If you don't mind I think I'll get some rest before dinner arrives." Yvonne turned her face toward the window and closed her eyes but rest eluded her.

Her mind raced. Would her first test as tour leader be successful? Could she handle the problems that were inherent with any overseas trip? Would Christy be okay without her? Was this trip to Greece a means to escape the overwhelming responsibility of being a single mom? Self-doubt crept into her mind as thoughts shifted to her first trip to Greece with Gino on her honeymoon—the beginning of a downward slide ending in a failed marriage.

Divorcing Gino Gianetti had been difficult and scary. Though he was charming to most people in public, privately his cold and violent temperament had ruled Yvonne's life. Their divorce was a test of wills, and ended with her bearing more emotional scars than she wished to acknowledge. Still, since the divorce, Yvonne had gained back her strength of character, returning to her old exuberant self, the independent young woman she had been before Gino wore away her self-confidence. And, here she was, traveling on her own—leading a tour to Greece. She smiled and thought— what a fun job.

Later that evening Yvonne chatted leisurely with David. She learned that he preferred baseball to football, that he enjoyed Andrew Lloyd Webber musicals and that he had traveled to England numerous times to enjoy them in their original settings. He mentioned that his business partner, Demetrius Maverickos, was Greek and had relatives in Athens. He intended to look up his parents and introduce himself and offer regards from their son. David also confided that he'd been married to an emotionally unstable woman. Her paranoia became unbearable, so after a few years of marriage counseling with no improvement, he had divorced her. Yvonne could relate.

The evening and the flight went smoothly. Everyone slept as well as was possible on a moving plane. With stomachs full from all the meals offered, time passed quickly. They arrived at the Athens Airport at nine fifteen the following morning eager to start their tour.

Yvonne led her charges like a mother duck leading her flock. She was determined to be the first at the baggage claim area to coordinate the retrieval of their luggage and a smooth passage through customs.

She was waiting first in line when the conveyor belt began to move and a red light flashed announcing the impending arrival of luggage. The flaps in the opening began to push upward and a pair of feet, then legs and finally a whole body lying prone on the conveyor belt appeared. Moving in a circular motion along the conveyor belt, a man wearing a maintenance uniform began to circle where luggage should be in front of the dismayed travelers. One by one they saw the dagger sticking out of his chest, and the red stain growing around the knife wound on his shirt. Then, a dazed Yvonne heard the screams.

ATHENS

DAY 2

Two burly security guards herded the travelers away from the conveyor belt. Three other guards rushed through a nearby door headed towards the loading dock. In the distance the sound of sirens approaching gave way to an influx of Greek police.

Bill Armstrong had stopped in the restroom and missed much of the hoop-la. He found the tour participants in a room that had stray luggage strewn around and four customer service representatives waiting to help with lost and damaged baggage issues.

"Great! I wonder how long it will take us to retrieve our luggage and get on our way now."

Yvonne's protective instincts kicked in. Armstrong's arrogant attitude only made the situation worse. "Please, Mr. Armstrong, let's stay calm, I'll go check with the authorities to see when we can leave."

When Yvonne stepped through the door, two security guards blocked her way. "Excuse me." She addressed the guard whose uniform had the most impressive insignia with a matching cap. "Can you tell me how long it's going to be before we can get our luggage?"

The guard looked down on Yvonne as if she were a bug that he would like to squash. "When the Police Inspector Trakas, tells us, we'll tell you."

"And when do you think that will be?" Yvonne clinched her hands into fists.

"After Inspector Trakas questions everyone at the conveyor belt where the body was discovered. You will all remain here until he is ready for you."

Two hours later, satisfied that no one had actually seen the murder, Inspector Trakas allowed the tourists to be on their way. He requested and received a copy of their itinerary in case he had any other questions.

Yvonne took command of the situation. "Attention, everybody, please gather 'round, so that we can regroup. I know we've gotten off to a rocky start, but this has nothing to do with us. We need to move on and find our tour bus so we can see first hand the beauty of this ancient city."

Janice looked at Rosanna, her face white and drained. "How can she be so smiley—and enthusiastic at a time like this? I just can't blot out the memory of that poor man. His dead eyes were horrifying."

Rosanna spoke to Janice as if she were a small child. "Don't be so dramatic, Janice, dear. Yvonne is right, we must move on and forget what we saw if we are to enjoy this trip." She turned toward Bill and rolled her eyes heavenward.

"I'm not sure we should continue with the tour—it seems like a bad omen to me." Nicholas shrugged as if he had a chill running down his spine.

"Don't be such a wimp. Just think of it as an adventure. Where's your gumption?" Rosanna turned toward Bill for support.

"Yeah, Nicholas, Rosanna's right. This has nothing to do with us anyway. Let's continue on and have our usual good time."

The tourists followed Yvonne in her search for the tour bus-operator. Her mind raced as she struggled to maintain her composure. *Why was that man killed? I can't believe it happened just as we arrived in Athens. What if Nicholas is right—is this a sign of things to come?* Yvonne sighed as she realized she couldn't follow her own advice to move on.

Exiting the airport, she greeted a young man with a bored expression, shifting a sign from one hand to the other that said Pinkerton Travel Group. "Hello, my name is Yvonne Suarez. I'm in charge of the Pinkerton Travel Group for this tour. Are you our bus driver?"

"Yes, Madam, I am Ari, short for Aristotle, and I'll be your driver and tour guide while you are traveling around our wonderful country of Greece. Please have your group follow me." Ari's demeanor brightened considerably when he found himself ready to perform.

"The sights are looking up," said Cynthia, admiring their Greek guide's lean and muscular behind.

"Ditto," said Mark.

Everyone boarded the small air-conditioned tour bus and Ari started his spiel, "I'd like to welcome you to Athens, the birthplace of Democracy. I know you Americans think that you have the best democracy, but I want to remind you that we Greeks were the first to explore and perfect the democratic society." He paused for effect, "You will forgive me for starting our tour by philosophizing, but that is what we are best known for, after all."

Most in the group gave a chuckle as they realized that Ari was kidding with them.

"I understand that you had an unfortunate incident upon arrival which has set us behind schedule a couple of hours. I would like to apologize for the bad start and say that murders in Athens are very rare. So, sit back and relax while I show you the wonders of our Athenian culture.

"The city of Athens and the surrounding suburbs are built around the Acropolis. If you look out the window you can see it rising in the distance off to your left. The Parthenon sits on the highest spot and it was here that democracy was born."

"Look, Richard! These ancient streets are so narrow it's a wonder the bus fits on the road at all. Everything is crowded and jammed together and small as if from another time. I love all the white, doesn't it seem so exotic?" Evelyn, seated in the first row behind the driver, barely took a breath as she quizzed her husband for his opinion.

"Yes dear, it does." Richard looked at his wife and smiled.

"Athens is a bustling city. The sprawling suburbs bring in millions of Athenians for work or shopping each day. Because the streets are small from the days of horse and wagon travel, the government allows only half of any family's cars to be in town on a particular day. For example, people with even numbers on their license tags can come into town on even-numbered days, and those with odd numbers can come on odd-numbered days. In order to get around the rules, some families will have two cars, one with odd numbers and one with even numbers. So you see, in a democracy there are always—ways to get around the rules." Ari led the group past Constitution Square, the House of Parliament, the Memorial to the Unknown Soldier and the National Library. Then he drove twelve miles north of Athens to the affluent area of Ekali with Ralph Lauren designer shops and chic continental restaurants before heading to the luxury hotel, Life Gallery Athens, where he deposited the group of weary travelers.

Yvonne gave instructions. "Once we are checked in, I suggest a light lunch and then you're free to rest or walk around town on your own. We're scheduled to meet in the lobby at seven for our ride to the Petrino restaurant located in the Glyfada district, the heart of Athens, for dinner."

David smiled boyishly. "Yvonne, would you allow me to buy you lunch and then escort you on a stroll around this charming town?"

Her stomach seized up with anxiety. "David, I'm sorry, that's not possible. I have some reservation confirmations to follow up for the rest of the trip ... Oh, have you had a chance to meet Beverly Nystrom yet? Let me introduce you."

David gave an uncomfortable grunt.

"Beverly." Yvonne waved for her to come toward them. "I'd like to introduce you to David Ludlow. I think the two of you will have a lot in common. David owns L&L Software and designs banking software. You and he are both world travelers and have travelled to some of the same countries."

"How do you do." Beverly cupped David's extended hand into her two-handed grip.

"Beverly, David was just going for a bite to eat and a stroll around town. Perhaps you could accompany him."

"Why I'd be delighted to travel in such handsome company. That is if David doesn't mind?" Beverly's voice lowered in a syrupy sweet inflection.

"Uh, of course, it would be my pleasure." David's smile appeared frozen in place and his movements were stiff as he grasped the situation.

Boy, he thought, was that ever smooth. I bet Yvonne can sell ice to Eskimos. I can understand her being too busy to go with me, but why fix me up with another date. What is she afraid of? Maybe she's had a bad experience or she's on the rebound. Worse yet, maybe she's got someone else. It was only lunch after all, not a long-term commitment. I'm going to make sure to sidestep her match-making efforts— be on guard against her manipulations the next time I invite her out. Isn't that interesting— I just assumed I'd be asking her out again...

Later that evening as the group assembled in the lobby, they chattered and compared notes about their afternoon activities. Yvonne saw David arrive in the lobby with Beverly on his arm. Well, don't they look too cozy for comfort? Guess I expected this, so I can't complain. At least now I can concentrate on my job. Turning to face the group, she went into her tour guide mode. "Did everyone have a nice afternoon?"

"It was smashing," cooed Beverly as she leaned into David.

Just as I expected, oh well.... Firmly pasting a smile on her face, Yvonne, turned to her other clients. "And what about you, Mr. and Mrs. Armstrong?"

"We had a wonderful time shopping and Bill found a lovely antique shop with some museum quality art. He acquired some new items for our home in Fort Lauderdale." Janice bragged, smiling at her husband.

"Darling, no one wants to hear about our latest shopping quests." Bill clenched his jaw.

"But, darling, you always find the best deals and in the most out-of-the-way shops. I think you have a special talent for it." Janice's voice faltered as her smile faded and she realized that he was giving her a look that could kill. She turned her face to hide the scarlet embarrassment that was darkening her cheeks.

Yvonne observed how effectively Bill bullied Janice into submission. Can't she see how rude he is? Why doesn't she tell him to stop talking to her like that? I suppose she's too much a lady or too scared. Yes, that's probably it. With an effort, Yvonne changed her focus to her other clients. "What about everyone else? Did you all get some rest or entertainment?

"We were happy to have a little rest and settle into our second honeymoon, if you know what I mean," said Todd Johnson as he wrapped his arm around Missy with a satisfied grin. Missy squirmed a bit under the tight grasp, but she also looked pleased.

"Here comes our driver, why not finish our discussions at dinner?" Yvonne turned to greet Ari as he came through the front door. "Good evening Ari. We're ready if you are."

"Good evening ladies and gentlemen! Come with me on this pleasant evening to the Petrino located in a beautiful traditional building in the greenest part of Athens well known for its quality international cuisine, including many favorite Greek dishes. It is also known for the celebrities that frequent it and the excellent service provided by the establishment." Ari bowed formally. "It would be my pleasure to escort such handsome visitors for an evening out in our fine city."

Cynthia Forsythe caught up with Ari and fell into step with him. "Hello, Ari, I was wondering if you could tell me how I should dress for our excursion tomorrow?" She realized this was a totally inane question, but she was determined to get to know him a lot better before the night was over.

"Just dress casual with lightweight clothes and good walking shoes. We are going to walk up the Acropolis to the Parthenon. It will be the thrill of a lifetime, I assure you." He opened the door to the bus, and indicated that she should climb inside. Then he turned and motioned for the others to follow.

It was a ten minute ride traveling down some very small side streets until they arrived at a tall narrow white building. Ari stopped in front of the restaurant and allowed the passengers to disembark before parking the bus further up the street.

Yvonne led the way into the brightly lit foyer. It was decorated in royal blues, greens and amber, looking both cozy and cheerful at the same time. The furniture had modern straight lines and looked solidly built for comfort. To the right was a stairway leading to rooms on the upper floors. To the left was a simple doorway that led to the dining room. It was about half full with an eclectic mix of businessmen, locals and tourists. The lighting was dim. Only candles illuminated the straight-line tables elegantly covered in white tablecloths and chairs. The Murals painted with Greek gods and mythological characters seemed to make even the walls come alive as part of the ambience in the dancing candlelight. In the background, pleasant Greek music played. This is heaven, Yvonne thought.

After everyone was seated, a lull occurred as each person enjoyed the classic atmosphere.

David had managed to position himself between Beverly and Yvonne. "By the way, Yvonne, I would like to be excused tomorrow afternoon to visit my business partner's family. They live here in Athens and I promised to check in and give them his regards."

"That's quite okay. Tomorrow afternoon we are on our own anyway. If you have anything personal to do, it would be a good time to do it." Yvonne realized she'd be disappointed if he couldn't make dinner.

"Oh David, we will miss you." Yvonne could hear the genuine disappointment in Beverly's voice.

"Everyone—there will be a good deal of walking up hill tomorrow. The steps are shallow, but it's about a twenty minute trek. If needed, you'll find places to sit and rest along the way." Yvonne looked David directly in the eye as she spoke, her concern obvious. He smiled, assuring her he'd be fine.

"Thank you for letting us know. My Richard was thinking he might need to decline this particular tour, but it sounds like he might actually enjoy going if he can take his time and not worry about keeping up with others." Evelyn Malcolm looked relieved. She wanted more than anything for Richard to enjoy this trip of a lifetime.

Richard gave her knee a discreet pat under the table.

The Armstrongs and the Fontinellis could be overheard in conversation. "This is a lovely restaurant and town. I quite enjoy being away from the standard tourist traps in Athens. I'm so glad we've had this chance to revisit Greece. I would count it as one of my favorite places on earth," confided Rosanna. "Janice dear, don't you agree?"

Janice, still smarting from the put-down by Bill back at the hotel, lowered her eyes and begrudgingly answered, "Yes, yes I do."

"That's great, dear." Bill ignored his wife's pain. "Do we want to take the trek up to the Parthenon again? After all, we've seen it before."

"Actually, I would like the exercise and it's one of the most spectacular views, not counting the Parthenon itself. But—whatever you want—dear."

"Why not let the guys off the hook? You and I can go alone. What do you say, Janice? Shall we have a break from the hubbies?" Rosanna's voice cajoled her into acquiescence.

The evening continued with light conversation and everyone anticipating the first real tour day to follow. As they arrived back at the hotel and said their goodnights, Yvonne reminded everyone to be ready by eight o'clock to depart for the Acropolis.

"Thanks for making our first meal such a wonderful one. It's one I won't forget soon." David stepped clearly into Yvonne's physical space.

"See you in the morning." Yvonne's eyes locked on his as she took a step back, turned and dashed into the crowded elevator just before it closed, leaving David to ride up with the Armstrongs and Fontinellis.

THE ACROPOLIS

DAY 3

"**I**t's believed that the Acropolis was established as early as the Archaic period, 650-480 BCE." Ari led his group upward toward the Parthenon.

"It's easy to imagine the early Greeks gathering for their cult activities or the politics of the day as this crowd of tourists walk up these well worn steps," added Yvonne.

In the sunlight David could see the irises of her brown eyes outlined with golden rings that shimmered when her eyes widened with enthusiasm.

David thought the warm weather was pleasant, but he felt slow and sluggish trooping up the hill. Beverly Nystrom started alongside David but left him behind as her excitement picked up speed with the climb. He watched Richard Malcolm find a seat on a stone bench under a shady olive tree, and he nodded knowingly to him. Richard appeared to be breathing heavily.

Ari came to a timely halt. "We will make periodic short stops, so that I can explain some historical facts or point out some important buildings in the area. This will allow everyone to catch up or catch their breath."

"Missy, stand over there by the wall. I want to get a picture of you with the city and mountains in the background," said Todd.

Missy walked up two more steps and found a spot where she could stand alone near the wall. Sightseers were gathered along the barrier wall looking at the view of Athens and beyond with awe. She turned away from the sight to face Todd and gave him a huge smile. When

Todd looked through the camera lens, he noticed that the smile did not reach her eyes. "That's great Missy, you look beautiful."

"The entrance to the Acropolis is the Propylea. It extends 150 feet adjoining the temple of Athena Nike. Athens is built around the Acropolis and the pinnacled crag of Mt. Lycabettus that the goddess Athena dropped from the heavens as a bulwark to defend the city.

"The Parthenon sits on the highest part of the Acropolis built between 447 and 437 BCE. Modern democracy began here," Ari said.

When David finally made it to the top of the first area, he tried to imagine the people who once worshiped in these great edifices now inhabited by cats. They certainly needed strong leg muscles. He wondered when the ancient Greeks had time to dream and philosophize. Perhaps, the physical labor necessary to build magnificent buildings allowed time for them to think and plan. Though he considered himself thoughtful and intelligent, he spent little time thinking about moral issues or the politics of the day. Keeping his business afloat took most of his time. Lately he worried that his partner, Demetrius Maverickos, might be embezzling from their company. Was he being paranoid? So far, he couldn't find evidence of anything amiss but the dollars and cents weren't adding up—considering all his hard work. Why wasn't the money flowing in the way he'd predicted? Did he miscalculate the cash flow? When did he first suspect there might be a problem? No wonder he was stressed out. This trip should help alleviate the stress—but here he was—worried his business might fail. He hoped meeting the Demetrius' family might provide some insight into his mysterious partner. He anxiously awaited his break from the tour this afternoon, so he could meet with them face to face.

The Athena Nike was surrounded by scaffolding and in the midst of restoration. The magnificent columns he'd only seen in pictures until now took his breath away. He pointed upward with his camera like hundreds of other tourists and began shooting pictures in a panoramic circle. He spotted Yvonne. How nice to have a trip with her as tour leader. Just the diversion from his regular routine that he needed in his life right now.

"Yvonne, there you are. Do me a favor and stand over by that wall. I prefer to have people I know in my photos when possible. I think it adds interest, don't you?" David pointed toward where he wanted her to stand.

"Sure, David. Perhaps I can call a few of the others in the group. Oh, there's Beverly with Evelyn. Let me get them to join us as well." Yvonne walked down a few steps and headed toward the front of Athena Nike where others stood talking or taking pictures. Yvonne corralled the two ladies for the pose.

David smiled at Yvonne's efforts. Adding the other two women into the mix only makes Yvonne look that much better. "Thanks, Ladies, having three beautiful women in one picture—well, it makes my heart stop." David placed his hand on his heart in a dramatic gesture and the women giggled dutifully.

As they continued making their way to the Parthenon, they heard a commotion at the next level up. A group of onlookers formed. Someone had fallen down the steps. Yvonne saw Ari lifting up a petite female.

Yvonne and David ran up the steps and recognized Janice. Ari propped her against the barrier wall. "Is she okay?" The tremor in Yvonne's voice, betrayed her fear and concern.

"Everyone, stand back. Give Mrs. Armstrong a chance to breathe and recover her senses." Ari turned his attention back to Janice.

Rosanna pointed to the highest level where the Parthenon stood. "She was standing there one minute, and the next thing I knew, she was flying forward down the steps."

Onlookers stared at them from all directions, and Yvonne's mind reeled. Ari was calling for an ambulance from his cell phone.

Rosanna sat down next to Janice and put her arms around her friend. "Janice, dear Janice, please be all right."

Janice, in a fog, looked around. "What happened? It felt like someone pushed me. I turned around to look down the steps for a second, and the next thing I knew I fell hard down the stairs. My head hurts." Janice reached up and felt a lump that was forming on her forehead. As her hand traveled downward, she wiped at her bloody nose. Her body ached as she noticed the burns and scratches from the fall. I must look awful, she thought.

"Sit still and rest, Janice. There's an ambulance on the way. We're going to make sure everything is okay before we proceed. We'll stay right here until help arrives." Yvonne's tone left no room for argument.

"I don't want to be a bother. I'm just clumsy, that's all." Janice put her hands up to cover her face. "Please don't wait on me—finish your tour." Janice spoke the last word faintly. In a flash of memory, she remembered a hand on her back pushing and she shivered.

"Nonsense, I'm not going anywhere until I know you're completely recuperated." Rosanna patted her friend on the shoulder.

Yvonne said, "Ari, go ahead. Lead the others to the Parthenon, the museum and that great look-out at the top with panoramic views for picture-taking. I'll stay here with Janice and Rosanna and wait for the paramedics."

"I'll wait too," said David.

"It's not necessary." Yvonne's patience was wearing thin. She couldn't help but wonder if someone or something had a grudge against her. If so, the goal was to spoil her first efforts as tour leader. Her thinking was irrational, yet something had sent her emotional radar buzzing. "Ay, Dios Mio." She prayed under her breath. "Give me the strength to stave off this negative energy."

Ari led the sightseers to the Parthenon as requested. David ignored Yvonne's dismissal and stayed anyway. The trio guarding Janice waited in silence. The paramedics arrived in fifteen minutes, but the wait seemed interminable. They determined she had a concussion and transported her to the hospital for observation and a check-up by a physician. Rosanna rode in the ambulance with Janice while Yvonne and David looked for Bill and Nicholas. "You'll find them somewhere in the shopping district at the bottom of the Acropolis or at a coffee shop nearby," Rosanna told them before boarding the ambulance.

"Maybe on my next trip to Athens, I'll make it to the top." David walked down the Propylea with Yvonne. He could see the Theatre of Dionysus in the distance and wondered if there would be an opportunity to return and see it in the future.

"David, you shouldn't be exerting yourself like this. Why don't you have a seat on that bench over there and I'll continue on my own to find Bill and Nicholas."

"No thanks, Yvonne. Going downhill is not strenuous. I'm fine."

"Are you sure? I don't want another emergency. One a day is about all I can cope with." She didn't mean to sound insensitive, but David's Johnny-on-the-spot attitude was starting to annoy her.

"Thanks for your concern. Like I said, I'm fine." David's voice held a clip of anger. He wondered if she was normally so thoughtless or if she was that upset. Of course, being in charge of so many people was a huge responsibility. He supposed he should cut her some slack after the events of the last two days.

They reached the bottom of the Acropolis and found a lane that led to the main shopping street where tourists strolled about in large numbers. A few minutes later Yvonne spotted Bill and Nicholas. "There they are." She pointed in the window of a coffee shop. "They're talking to someone. I guess they've made a new friend."

David followed Yvonne into the little café and stood waiting nearby as she told Bill Armstrong about his wife's accident.

"How could this happen? I left her in your care. Aren't you supposed to watch out for those in your care?"

Is he aggravated at the inconvenience, or unconcerned for his wife, wondered Yvonne.

"I'm sorry Bill, but she and Rosanna separated from the rest of the group and it's very crowded along the steps to the top. It would be impossible to know where everyone is at every moment." Yvonne glanced at David. Did he doubt her abilities too? "I would be happy to give you the information, so you and Nicholas can take a cab to the hospital right away."

"Bill, Yvonne was one of the first to reach Janice after her fall, and if she'd not taken charge so quickly, Janice might have gone into shock. Everyone was warned to wear comfortable walking shoes and be extra careful when looking at ancient ruins. It's in all the tour documents. It's unfair of you to blame Yvonne." David's face flushed. The more he thought about the insinuation that Yvonne was somehow responsible for the fall, the angrier he got. He didn't even admit to himself that this was an opportunity to be her rescuer."

"I'm not blaming Yvonne. I just wondered why it happened. Maybe Janice can enlighten me when I see her. I'll take that information now." Bill Armstrong reached out for the paramedic's card that Yvonne held in her hand.

"Mr. Armstrong, allow me to call a cab for you," said the stranger who had been silent during the conversation at the table.

"Thank you, Damian, I'd appreciate it." Bill left the table immediately to wait for the cab outside with Nicholas following in his wake. The Greek man took out his cell phone and punched in some numbers. He remained seated at the table.

Yvonne nodded thank you to Damian while David led her gently by the arm to another table. Yvonne looked out the window at the sun shining on the quaint street lined with olive trees. A rock wall behind the trees stood about five feet high. Behind the wall was the large expanse of concrete and sparse vegetation that led to the entrance of the Acropolis. She hoped the rest of the tour progressed smoothly.

"David. Thanks for your help and the kind words on my behalf. I'm sorry you've missed the best part of the tour."

"You'll have to give me a rain check." He smiled as he teased her.

"We might as well wait here for the group to come down. They should return in about an hour. Unfortunately, that's not enough time for us to go up at a leisurely pace, see the Parthenon, visit the museum and make it back down with the group." Yvonne thanked the waitress who set the coffee in front of them. She took a sip. "The museum is small anyway. It consists of a few large statues and reliefs on the walls." She took another sip of her coffee "Don't worry, David, there'll be other museums and many ancient statues to see before we leave."

"That's okay, really." David covered her hand with his. "Let's relax and enjoy this cup of coffee that everyone else seems to find so delicious. What's next on the agenda? Will it be lunch? I do believe the morning's activities have made me hungry." David hoped the subject change would be a distraction from the morning's incident.

Yvonne thought for a second. "If there's time after our coffee, we'll take a stroll back the way we came. We can browse through some gift shops while we work our way back to the bus where we'll intercept the group as they come down from the Acropolis. Then Ari will take us to a Greek restaurant in the Kolonaki district. It's known for its moussaka and spinach pie. Their Greek salad is good too."

"You seem to know your way around pretty well. How many times have you been to Athens?"

"Only once, actually—it was on my honeymoon. I always wanted to come again, but never had the chance until now."

"I didn't realize that you were married. I didn't notice a ring on your finger." David narrowed his eyes as his heart began to race at the thought that she might be married. "It didn't occur to me since you are traveling alone and all... I guess it stands to reason someone as lovely as you would be taken."

"Whoa, I'm not married any longer. I've been divorced for about seven months."

The look of relief in David's eyes caused Yvonne to smile for the first time since the mishap at the Acropolis.

"I'm just curious, about why you wanted to come back here?"

"I thought it was beautiful the first time I was here. We didn't spend as much time sightseeing as I would have liked—we were busy getting to know each other. And, my ex-husband Gino, well... we spent most of the time on charter boats fishing and doing the things he enjoyed most."

"I'm glad you've had a chance to return." David leaned back in his chair with a teasing expression. "I can see why so many newlyweds enjoy honeymooning here. The people are friendly and there's so much culture, water sports, and spectacular views if they are so inclined or romantic escapes where they can hide away, if not."

After the coffee began to take its effect, the energy between them increased and all too soon their banter came to an end. "Let's walk back to meet the group now." Yvonne picked her tote up from the floor and rose to leave.

"Sounds good to me." David wished he could linger a bit longer.

As the duo strolled along the tree-lined streets, they noted more pedestrians than car traffic. They found typical tourist shops hawking busts of Aristotle, Plato and other Greek philosophers and stores specializing in fine linens embroidered with olive branches, the national symbol of peace. Jewelry stores selling gold jewelry and charms featuring Aphrodite, Poseidon and Apollo were found on almost every street corner.

"If we turn left here and go up one block, we'll be at the bottom of the Propylea near where the buses park. We can wait for the group there." I'm enjoying myself too much, thought Yvonne. I should get back to my duties as tour leader, so I don't get carried away. After all this is not my vacation. Of course helping my clients have fun is part of my job. Maybe it won't hurt to bring some balance to my emotional life. Why can't I be more reserved like my mom?

As they arrived at their destination, the rest of the group was walking down at a leisurely pace. Some carried bags of souvenirs, and all appeared to be more than ready for the comfort that the bus ride to lunch would offer.

"I trust everyone had a wonderful time on their visit to the Acropolis." Yvonne's not-too-subtle attempt at feedback from the group did not fall on deaf ears.

"Yes, it was wonderful." Evelyn beamed, thrilled with the opportunity she'd waited almost a lifetime to fulfill.

Many of the others chimed in with their accolades as well.

"Ari is a first rate tour guide. We learned much about the mythological gods." Cynthia made sure to sit in the first row opposite Ari.

"Yes, Greek bodies are certainly an inspiration for us mere mortals." Mark climbed over Cynthia to sit by the window and wondered if he'd find romance one day. He was jealous it had been so easy for his friend. Ari made an interesting specimen to be sure, and Cynthia found him the day she arrived in Greece.

Yvonne stepped into the first row behind Ari and remained standing so she could address the group. Beverly made it a point to catch up with David and they sat in the second row facing Yvonne. The others filed in leaving spaces where the missing tour members had sat.

"When we arrive at Prytaneum Restaurant, I'll call the hospital to check on Janice," Yvonne informed the members. "After lunch we'll return to the hotel and you'll have the afternoon on your own. We'll meet in the lobby at 6:45 and remain in the hotel for dinner in their gourmet dining room. Tomorrow we'll have a full day. Our first stop is the National Archaeological Museum, and later we'll take a driving tour to the Temple of Zeus and Hadrian's Arch."

Located in Kolonaki on Milioni Street, an upscale downtown pedestrian area, the travelers found a charming neoclassical house. The house had been renovated to accommodate a popular bar-restaurant with a lively atmosphere, and it soon became a favorite landmark and meeting place for locals and tourists alike. The chef was a Greek-Italian who skillfully offered authentic Greek dishes as well as light Italian and Spanish fare. Desiring a quiet atmosphere, the group found a seating area in the upper level where they could watch the passersby and those dining in the outdoor café.

Yvonne excused herself as soon as all were seated so she could call the hospital. After three phone transfers, she found the appropriate nurses' station and learned that they had released Janice into her husband's care. Apparently, the foursome had returned to the comfort of their hotel.

Returning to the table, Yvonne found everyone immersed in the menus. She heard "oohs" and "aahs" over the choices available. She overheard Beverly follow David's lead to order a Greek salad and a glass of Kee-ma, homemade wine. Greek music played in the background. A smug smile formed on Yvonne's face as she surveyed the table, pleased with herself. Things were finally going as planned.

After lunch Ari returned all but one tour member to their hotel.

David took a cab from the restaurant to Athens's busy shopping district. The cab driver had no problem finding the Maverickos Antique Jewelry store. It was located in one of the busiest shopping areas, Monastiraki. On this crowded street, one could find everything from first-class junk to quality copper and brass, fine art, coins, jewelry and antiques.

David entered the store and noted the efficient use of space. The aisles were narrow, but wide enough to allow two people to stand back and admire the multitude of jewelry displayed in artistically crowded cases. This family had obviously been accumulating fine things for many lifetimes.

"May I help you, sir?" asked a dark-haired young man in a white dress shirt and black slacks.

"Yes. I'd like to speak with Mr. or Mrs. Maverickos."

"May I tell them what it's about?"

"Yes, you may. I'm David Ludlow. I'm here to offer my best wishes from their son and my partner, Demetrius."

"Oh, Mr. Ludlow, it's very nice to meet you. I'm George, Demetrius' brother." He relaxed his demeanor just a bit. "Wait just a moment while I tell my parents that you are here."

As David waited he watched a few other browsers looking with awe at the different pieces in the cases. In the far corner a man who looked like an older, stockier version of Demetrius was talking to another man about a pocket watch. The conversation seemed serious but friendly. Surveying the rest of the room, he saw George leading a woman from a back room.

"Mr. Ludlow, this is my mother, Alexis Maverickos." George deferred to a salt and pepper-haired woman of strong presence in size and stature.

"Mrs. Maverickos, it's nice to meet you." David, a little unsure of protocol in Greece, offered her his hand to shake.

"Mr. Ludlow, please—call me Alexis." She took David's hand in a limp feminine response that did not coordinate with her voice and size.

"Please—call me David." He smiled. "I bring greetings from your son Demetrius. He says to tell you that he misses your moussaka and dolmades, not to mention his family and country."

"Thank you so much, Mr. Ludlow—I mean David. How long are you here in Athens? Won't you join us for dinner this evening?" She smiled graciously. "My husband would so enjoy talking with you about your business and our son. I'm afraid Loukas is very busy at the moment working with a customer. I'm sure he would wish you to come back later."

"How gracious of you. I'd love to join you for dinner." David could see where Demetrius got his gift of salesmanship. He assumed this woman would not take no for an answer in most circumstances. In addition to the fact that she was amply built, she had a commanding voice and a cold stare that made him feel she could see right through to the bottoms of his feet. A cold chill crept up his spine. He remembered seeing the same look from Demetrius during past heated discussions. David regained his composure. "What time would you like me to return, Alexis?"

"How about eight this evening? That will give us time for cocktails and a visit before dinner is served. Our home is in Ekali, are you familiar with it?"

"Yes, in fact our group is staying at the Life Gallery Athens hotel in Elkali."

"You are staying in one of the nicest places, indeed." Alexis gave David a smile of approval. "Until tonight then. George, give David directions." She turned and walked to her office in the back of the store.

On his own, David took his time getting back to the hotel. In another antique jewelry store further up the street, he spotted a wonderful small golden statue of the goddess Hera. He had seen a similar one in the Maverickos Antique Jewelry shop, but that one was priced beyond his means. This one must be a gold-plated reproduction. The statue of Hera and all she represented reminded him of Yvonne with her golden skin and lovely brown-gold eyes. It brought to mind a poem he'd read recently:

Golden-throned Hera, among immortals the queen.

Chief among them in beauty, the glorious lady

All the blessed in high Olympus revere,

Honor even as Zeus, the lord of the thunder.

He reminded himself, though Hera was conceived for her nurturing aspects, she could turn deadly when jealous or defending her loved ones against the threat of loss or danger.

Yvonne opened her eyes and glanced at the clock next to the bed. She had dozed off while reading her latest mystery novel. Never without a book, she particularly enjoyed mysteries to challenge her mind.

She tried to outwit the author and quite often guessed 'who-done-it,' before she finished the book.

It was 5:45 pm. She had one hour to get ready before meeting the group in the lobby. A few minutes later stepping out of the shower, she heard the phone ring. Yvonne grabbed a towel from the bar just outside the shower-stall, hastily wrapped it around her and trotted, dripping, to the phone by the bed.

"Hello," she said with a lift to the second syllable.

"Hello, Yvonne. I'm calling to let you know I won't be able to make dinner this evening. I've been invited to dinner at my partner's home, a short distance from this hotel, as it happens." David's voice held a hint of regret. "I just wanted you to know that I'd made it back safely today, and the reason I won't be at dinner tonight. I knew you'd be concerned if one of your 'group' didn't show up as expected." He felt a need to express his concern with all the unfortunate incidents that had happened since starting the tour.

"Thank you. I do appreciate your thoughtfulness. Although I'm sure you'll be missed tonight, I hope you have a very pleasant evening at your friend's family home. Well—I guess we'll see you tomorrow morning then. We're scheduled to meet at seven in the lobby. The bus leaves promptly at 7:15 and breakfast is on your own. Just a reminder, the dining room is open at six—see you then."

As she hung up the phone, she heard him say, "Have a good evening." She pushed away the thought that she might actually miss him and returned to the bathroom to continue dressing for dinner.

Dinner was pleasant enough. Everyone welcomed Janice back to the group. The bumps, bruises and scratches were in full color, but she appeared to be braving the evening with grace and dignity. Bill, Rosanna and Nicholas wrapped themselves in a protective cocoon around her, so that no one was able to discuss much about the fall or even offer sympathy. She seemed fragile in comparison to the others seated at the table.

David arrived at the home of The Maverickos at eight o'clock. It was a traditional Greek villa with a colorful landscape of bougainvillea, lush ferns and elephant ear philodendrons. Mrs. Maverickos met him at the door and ushered him inside. She led him through an atrium walkway filled with tropical plants and small trees. A miniature sparkling stream flowed to a water fountain designed to soothe the senses. The stream followed along a walkway that led to the living area of the house.

"Just a bit further, David. Loukas and George are in the television room watching CNN and taking their evening cocktails. It's the first door on your left." She gestured with her hand to show him the way. "I will be in to visit after I check on dinner."

David entered the television room and found it filled with cigar smoke. Once he had enjoyed the smell of cigars, but in recent years he found that it turned his stomach. He reasoned it took getting used to all over again. "Good evening Mr. Maverickos—George," Turning to the elder first, then the son, he gave a smile and nod to each. In the background he caught a glimpse of the television program they had been watching upon his arrival. A picture of a small gold statue of Hera flashed across the screen. He lost his train of thought as his attention remained riveted on the television. Too quickly, the image disappeared as the newscaster made the announcement: "Police have not yet captured the thief or thieves who stole the dagger and statue from the National Archaeological Museum two days ago."

"Mr. Ludlow, you look ill. Are you all right? Please sit down." Loukas pointed at a worn leather chair. "George, help Mr. Ludlow to his chair."

"Thank you, it's not necessary. I'm fine." David took a seat. "I was surprised when I saw the news—you see—I purchased a similar statue today. Of course mine was just a reproduction. Is there more than one statue like the one that was stolen?"

"No, the one in the museum was priceless. Imitations exist, of course, but only one dates back to 450 BCE." Loukas took a sip of his drink. "I have a very good imitation of the statue in my store. It happens to be solid gold, and is quite expensive, but still would not bring the price of the original."

"And, what would that be," asked David.

"It's hard to say, a lot depends on how many were bidding for it. It's not technically on the market. Someone has already paid a dear price for anonymity if they helped to orchestrate the theft. I'd say the statue could bring anywhere from fifty thousand to five hundred thousand dollars. It is difficult to put a price on antiquity."

"That much—amazing," David shook his head with wonder at the thought of such a small object being so valuable.

"Ah, Alexis, there you are. Come. Join us for a cocktail. It's time for Mr. Ludlow to give us the latest news on our son." Loukas brought a glass of white wine to Alexis.

"Please, Mr. Maverickos, call me David"

"Fine—David, how is Demetrius? Is he doing a good job with your company?"

"Why yes, he's been responsible for bringing us some very important clients. I've often wondered where he got his sales skills, but seeing you in action today at the jewelry store, I can see that he probably inherited his talent from you."

"Demetrius, he could always sell, as they say, 'ice to Eskimos.'" Loukas chuckled at his cliché. "Selling comes so easily to him. He used his charm to wiggle out of all kinds of scrapes as a kid. I sometimes worried that one day his grandiose schemes would get him in trouble and his charm would not get him out of it, but that never happened. He has since grown up to be a very responsible man in spite of himself, a man that we can be proud of. Isn't that right Mama?" Loukas addressed Alexis for confirmation and she nodded her head in agreement.

"Enough bragging about our long lost son, Papa. It's time to eat."

"David, would you care for another drink to carry in to dinner?"

"No thank you, Alexis." David caught a glimpse of a dark look on George's face. Was it their mention of Demetrius he wondered? Alexis rose from her seat and indicated that they should follow her. "What is that wonderful smell?"

"Oh, it's nothing special, just some moussaka and dolmades. Be sure to tell Demetrius that his mama still makes the best, not only for him but for his partner too."

"That's very kind of you. He will be very envious when I tell him." David wondered if he wasn't being paranoid about Demetrius. How could he be embezzling from the company when he had such kind and thoughtful parents? He had seen Demetrius do some of the fast talking that Loukas had mentioned, especially, when it came time to pay bills. He knew expenses were high with the development of their new software, but it should have been offset by all the new customers. The books weren't balancing. David was so busy with the development that he hardly had time to watch over Demetrius. When it came to the accounting and bookkeeping, David despised doing the tedious work and was grateful when Demetrius took on the responsibility. Demetrius wasn't any better at keeping finances under control; in fact, things seemed to be getting worse since he took over. Something wasn't right, and David couldn't quite put his finger on what might be wrong.

"You're not eating, David. Is everything all right? Don't you like my moussaka?" Alexis tried not to sound hurt.

"It's not that. I think it's excellent. I just found myself thinking about work. I guess I'm not used to having so much free time to relax and enjoy myself. Truly—everything is wonderful."

"George, Demetrius tells me you are studying to become an accountant. Where do you attend school?"

"Athens University of Economics and Business. I completed my studies and graduated recently. I hope that my accounting degree will be an important asset to our family business."

"I wish we could afford to hire an in-house accountant. I know your brother would probably be the first to agree we need help in that area." David took a bite of the moussaka. "But, alas, you are here, and we are on the other side of the ocean. Any chance you will want to follow your brother's lead and move to the United States?"

"He has agreed to stay here close to us, David. We've already lost one son to your country. I'm not willing to lose another." Alexis' tone left no room for argument. She reached for her wine glass and took a sip.

"Yes, Mama," agreed George.

"Oh well, it doesn't hurt to ask." David was secretly glad he wouldn't have to consider hiring another Maverickos family member.

The rest of the dinner conversation was a bit stilted as they tried to find common areas of conversation. Loukas talked about his business and the increasing tourist trade in Greece. "The government is cleaning and renovating in anticipation of the Olympics coming next year in 2004." He felt, as did many citizens, that the renovations would not be completed in time. David was skeptical as well, having seen some of the unfinished projects from the bus as they passed by in their sightseeing.

As the evening came to an end, David declined an offer to stay and have after dinner drinks and a cigar, citing as his excuse, a very early morning tour.

ATHENS

DAY 4

The curator stood at the doorway. He'd been waiting for ten minutes. It was 8:40 am when the tourists arrived at the ionic stone columns bracing the entrance to the building. The curator enjoyed the smaller groups because he could interact with each person while answering questions and the tour stayed on track. Small exclusive groups, such as Pinkerton Travel, paid a premium for his services. The price offered them a private tour of the museum before opening to the general public and larger tour groups.

"Welcome, Ladies and Gentleman to the National Archaeological Museum of Athens. I hope that your visit will be interesting and give you pleasure for years to come. My name is Dr. Daedalus. You may recognize my family name derived from the story by Ovid about the architect Daedalus who designed the Labyrinth for the Minotaur in Crete."

"Perhaps you could remind us about that story," said Yvonne.

"Good idea. My memory of mythology is next to nil. I could certainly use a refresher course." David stepped up near Dr. Daedalus and the others followed his lead.

"The story I will tell is the one that relates to Daedalus himself. You may remember that he was banished to the Labyrinth with his son because he revealed the secret for escape to Ariadne who helped Theseus to escape."

"If Daedalus knew how to escape, why would he be banished there?" asked Mark.

"Ah! Good question. King Minos blocked the exits so even Daedalus, the designer, couldn't find a way out. Daedalus realized the entrance and exits of the Labyrinth were guarded, but he also knew that above or below was unguarded. He invented wings and glued them on his shoulders and the shoulders of his son, Icarus. They flew up and away from Crete; however, his son, allowing the power of flight to go to his head, flew too high—his father had warned him not to. The heat of the sun melted the glue that attached the wings, and his son fell into the ocean to his demise, leaving Daedalus to mourn the loss of his son. Never fear, my American friends, the museum will be much easier to navigate."

Dr. Daedalus led the group through the center of a large classically Greek white room with round columns, high ceilings and green marble floors. All eyes were drawn upward as the curator continued. "Above you can see a typical relief of Apollo reclining. This leads us into the first room of statues."

Missy tentatively entered the room taking hold of Todd's hand. She noticed guards standing at attention at every doorway. "Why are there so many security guards about?"

"Don't let the guards distract you. We recently increased security due to the theft that took place a few days ago. It happened in the middle of the night when the museum was closed. I assure you, we are perfectly safe. The extra guards are just a precaution."

"I heard there was a murder as well," said Nicholas. "It was on CNN. They said the police had no leads." His eyes narrowed reflecting skepticism. "I'm not sure the police would share their leads—if they had any—with the media anyway."

"Yes, that is true, but I am sure the police will find the culprit soon." Trying not to appear nervous, Daedalus sucked in his ample stomach and lifted his shoulders in concert with the corners of his mouth. "Follow me. I will now show you the magnificent statues and artifacts housed in the most important museum in Greece." He hoped his attempt to repair the damage the news had caused had worked.

"In this room you will find artifacts from the prehistoric era. That would include the Neolithic, Cycladic, Mycenaean and Minoan eras. Along the right wall, you will see the largest marble statue of a Cycladic figurine." He pointed to a figure of a woman with the characteristic folded arms of the period. "She was found on Amorgos and is dated from 2800—2300 BCE. Another statue from the same period is the "harp player" from Keros; its three-dimensional figure is representative of male idols that were musicians." Daedalus relaxed into his position as curator.

The tour continued for the next hour. Dr. Daedalus was knowledgeable and humorous in his commentary. The small group was halfway through the tour when the museum opened to the general public.

Yvonne studied the group and their responses to Dr. Daedalus' repertoire. She felt that all were enthralled with him and enjoyed his one on one attention. Yvonne was proud that they were being led by the man in charge and not a hireling. Her confidence in her abilities as tour leader grew and the self-doubts slowly dissipated. She daydreamed about satisfied tour members marveling as the beauty of Greece unfolded on the rest of the tour. After another hour, they were taken to an open courtyard for a breath of fresh air and a restroom break.

In his excitement, Mark grabbed Cynthia by the arm. "Don't you just love that statue of Apollo? His body was such perfection."

"Mark, simmer down. It's probably an exaggerated version of a Greek physique. You know—like when they enhance images in a magazine." Cynthia patted him on the shoulder.

"Spoil sport." Mark flounced over to a bench and sat down.

As they gathered in the courtyard waiting to return to the museum, Yvonne spied the curator coming through a side entrance. Yvonne stood up to address her group. "Let's stand over here by this large planter of bougainvillea with this lovely Ionic column in the background. Dr. Daedalus, I wonder—would you mind taking a picture of our group?"

"I'd be delighted."

Yvonne arranged the group on the two steps that led back up to the main level. She placed David, Mark, Bill, Nicholas and Richard in the back row and Beverly, Cynthia, Janice, Rosanna, Evelyn and herself on the lower step. She saw that she had paired Beverly with David as usual and groaned inwardly at her twinge of discomfort, seeing the two of them together. Dr. Daedalus snapped two or three pictures to be sure that at least one would turn out well with all members smiling. Next, Yvonne insisted that he take her place in the group, so that she could get a picture of their esteemed curator too.

"Now let's return to the tour." Dr. Daedalus led them to the room that held artifacts from the Byzantine era. As they made their way through, they came upon the display case that had been robbed. Police tape greeted them.

"Can you tell us about the items that were stolen?" asked David, his curiosity piqued, since his purchase of the Greek goddess.

"Yes—if you wish. Two items were taken: a priceless bronze dagger from 16th century BCE—a picture of it is in our museum souvenir book that you may purchase in the gift shop—and a small but valuable gold statue of Hera from the Roman era." The curator took a breath and continued, "The Hera statue is one of a kind. You have probably seen reproductions of it in the local gift shops. Hera was a popular mythological goddess. She was worshipped for her nurturing powers and feared for her feminine traits of jealousy and revenge." The curator stopped, and looked in turn, at each woman as he continued to address the group. "In the Roman era Hera was known as Juno. Religious cults worshipped Hera in many societies, one as recently as 450 BCE when Amazon priestesses fought for matriarchy in her name." He turned and directed his gaze at each member one by one stopping at Janice. He took note of Janice because she looked frightened. As this thought registered with him, she fainted. Others turned to see why he had stopped talking and watched Bill kneel down beside his wife sprawled on the marble floor.

Yvonne stepped forward and knelt on the other side of her. "Janice, are you okay?"

"Of course she's not okay," snapped Bill. "Nicholas, help me carry her to the courtyard where we can set her down on a bench." He picked her up in a cradling fashion while Nicholas tagged behind looking helpless.

Rosanna fell in behind the men carrying Janice. "This has all been too much for her. She should have stayed in the hotel today until she regained her strength."

David reached toward Yvonne, taking hold of her arm to assist her in getting up. They followed along with Rosanna and the others feeling concerned and helpless.

"Mr. Armstrong, if you would allow me, I will call an ambulance. Perhaps she should be transported to the hospital." Dr. Daedalus turned to walk away.

"Wait just a moment," Bill commanded. "Janice—Janice, dear, wake up—Janice, are you okay?" He gave her a slight shake of the shoulders and she began to respond.

"Wha—what happened? Where am I?" Janice studied her surroundings and remembered fainting. "Oh—I—felt so light-headed. I'm sorry. Did I faint? Please—forgive me for disrupting your tour again." Her eyes pleaded, but it was clear to all she was still disoriented.

"Janice, no need to apologize. We're the ones who are sorry. This is too much exertion for you after your fall yesterday." Yvonne gave a reassuring smile. "Rosanna is right. You should have relaxed at the hotel today. We can call for a cab right now. You can return to the hotel and rest. We're leaving Athens tomorrow and there may not be time to relax then. Or, maybe—you should go to the hospital to be sure you haven't developed complications from yesterday's fall?"

"No!" Janice snapped her head up and then fell back again as she became woozy. "I'll be all right. I just need to lay down for a bit."

"That's right. She needs rest. She'll be fine." Bill took control. "Let's call that cab, so we can get her back to the hotel."

"Bill, why don't you stay here and finish the tour. I'll get more rest if I'm alone." Janice pleaded with her eyes.

He felt uncomfortable as if he'd been rejected. "Fine, suit yourself." He exhaled like a deflated balloon.

"I won't hear of it," said Rosanna. "It could be dangerous. You could faint again on your way to the hotel. I will see she makes it back to the hotel safely. After she's tucked into bed, I'll pamper myself with a spa treatment and enjoy the rest of the day on my own. Nicholas, you keep Bill company and the two of you enjoy the tour."

"Are you sure you'll be okay? I'd be more than happy to come back with you," said Nicholas.

"That's not necessary. Bill can use your support more than I can just now. Don't worry, darling, I'll be fine." Rosanna dismissed Nicholas with the wave of a hand as she turned to help Janice.

Dr. Daedalus radioed for a wheelchair kept for such instances. Rosanna pushed Janice in the wheelchair to the front portico to wait for the cab.

After they departed, Dr. Daedalus ushered the group through the rest of the museum tour. Yvonne found it difficult to pay attention to his narrative. Thoughts raced through her mind. *What's going on? I can't get over the feeling that the fates are conspiring to sabotage me and my efforts to lead an enjoyable tour.*

Listen to me, thinking about my own problems. Poor Janice, she must be feeling awful. What made her faint? Of course, she's still recuperating from her fall yesterday, but I get the feeling there's more to it. Something's amiss in that marriage. She seemed afraid to be alone with her own husband.

One by one the members of the group descended from the museum to the street where Ari was waiting with his bus. The group climbed aboard while Yvonne explained to Ari that they were once again short by two members.

In the tight quarters of the tour bus, Beverly inched herself closer to David until her thigh touched against his. Her closeness disturbed him. *Would I feel the same way if Yvonne was sitting next to me? Of course, Yvonne would keep an appropriate distance,* he thought. *I suppose Beverly's attractive in a clinical sort of way, but Yvonne's warmth outshines Beverly in every way.*

"David, darling, I was thinking that when we arrive in Santorini, you and I could skip the guided tour and do one on our own. What do you think?"

Unconsciously, David moved away from Beverly. "I appreciate the offer, but never having been to Santorini before, I think we'll gain more knowledge by staying with the tour group. Don't you agree?"

Beverly's cold blue eyes showed none of the disappointment she felt. She was an expert at hiding her feelings when minimized by others. "You are right, of course. It would be much better if we stayed with the tour." She then lowered her voice in a sexy conspiratorial tone that caused David to continue moving to the very edge of his seat. "I thought an unplanned adventure might be nice too."

Yvonne looked around the bus. The sun beating in the windows dueled with the noisy air conditioner blasting out cool air. Evelyn was writing in her journal. Richard's head bent backward against the seat and lolled side to side with the rocking of the bus. Cynthia and Mark pointed out the window at the Athenian shops, amazed at seeing fast food restaurants like McDonalds and stores like Ralph Lauren set into the unusual Athens city landscape. Missy, seated by the window, watched the world go by. Todd held Missy's hand content to watch her sightsee. Bill and Nicholas each stared straight ahead with scowls on their faces. Were they missing their mates? Yvonne wondered. David looked strained and uncomfortable, sitting ramrod straight next to Beverly who stared out the window deep in her own thoughts. Heaven help me, thought Yvonne, I wonder what's going to happen next?

Hadrian's Arch, an impressive monument, overlooked one of Athens busiest streets at the entrance of the Plaka district. "Okay everyone, get your cameras. This is a good spot for photos," said Ari.

"This will be a good opportunity to stretch our legs and walk off some of that fabulous Greek food we had for lunch." Cynthia reached in the overhead compartment for her camera. First off the bus as usual, she stood chatting with Ari while the others disembarked.

Leading them down the path to get a more centered view, Ari recited some history. "The arch was built by Athenians in 131 CE to honor their Roman benefactor Hadrian. It was located at the end of the ancient city and the beginning of the new Roman section. The inscription found on the side of the Arch that faces the Acropolis states, 'This is Athens, the ancient city of Theseus.' The inscription on the other side facing the new section states, 'This is the city of Hadrian and not Theseus.' You can imagine just how well the inhabitants of the day got along with such a division as this. Some revered Hadrian and felt that he was good for Athens; others, of course, preferred the old ways. Similar conflicts have happened in most cultures around the world many times through their respective histories."

The group digested this information while they spread out to inspect the Arch and pictures were snapped by those with cameras.

After the allotted time allowed for sightseeing and picture taking, the group reassembled where Ari waited to continue the tour. "Follow me across Amalias Street to the Temple of Olympian Zeus. You can see it just up ahead."

Making her way toward the next ancient ruin, Beverly kept her distance from David. She reached in her belly pack for a tissue and blotted moisture from her forehead and above her lip. She hated the way she sweated in warm weather.

Okay David, she thought, go ahead and play hard to get. Two can play that game. You're no different than the attorneys in the office who think they're better than me. I'll show them someday and then you will all show me the respect I deserve.

After all, my research and hard work produces the evidence that wins the important cases, but do I even get a pat on the back? No. Those cocky young attorneys take all the credit for my efforts and they rake in the big fees. All I get is enough money to pay for my apartment, some clothes and one decent vacation a year—hardly seems worth the trouble considering how much I do. One of these days I'm going to save enough money to get my law degree. We'll see who gets the big fees and the respect.

Beverly smiled and nodded agreeably as Evelyn commented on the beauty of the structures. Poised, she lifted her camera and clicked a photo of Yvonne standing in front of the ancient temple. For Pete's sake, she doesn't sweat at all in this weather.

David saw that Beverly was miffed by his rejection of her attempts to get him alone. For some odd reason, he felt sorry for her. He concentrated on being genuinely interested in the sights and stood well away from Yvonne by tagging along with Richard and Evelyn Malcolm.

After the group finished snapping photos from all angles including landmarks and their fellow travelers, they returned to the bus in a more enthusiastic frame of mind.

Yvonne waited for everyone to be seated. "From here, we'll return to the hotel. This last evening in Athens, you are on your own. The hotel concierge will provide you with many wonderful restaurants to choose from. One in particular that may interest you is the roof-top restaurant in the Atheneum Intercontinental Hotel. It has a panoramic view of Athens. The Acropolis seen by night is a wondrous sight and a nice way to spend your last evening in this ancient historic city. For those of you who like a bit more excitement, check-out one of the local ouzeries before or after dinner. You will be amazed at the number of varieties of ouzo offered to the Greek population."

The chatter on the bus had an air of excitement as the last day in Athens was winding down and the prospects of a new adventure tomorrow seeped into their discussions. Evelyn Malcolm began noting things in her journal. It had a map of the Mediterranean Sea that included the Greek Islands on the cover. She tried to capture all she had seen and heard that morning while the others settled down for the drive back to the hotel.

Yvonne, found her way to the empty seat next to David. "Have you enjoyed your day so far?"

"Yes, very much. By the way, are you planning to dine at the roof-top restaurant this evening?"

"Yes, I am. Would you like to join me? Others might wish to join us. I can make the reservations."

David's heart beat a bit faster as he leaned toward her. "Wouldn't you prefer to have a quiet evening with just a friend? After all you've been babysitting this group for a few days and could probably use a break."

"That sounds very tempting, but I wouldn't want to offend anyone."

"How would that offend anyone? Chances are most everyone is looking for an opportunity to spend some time on their own anyway. Isn't that what you told them tonight was for?"

"That's true—well—okay, but if anyone asks to join us, I will have to include them."

"Good. What time would be good for you? How about finding one of those ouzeries you mentioned before we go to dinner?"

Yvonne thought for a second. "Sure, why not. It will be fun. I know of one that has musicians who play and sing every night. It's where all the locals hang out. I'll make dinner reservations for nine o'clock. That will give us time to enjoy a drink and local color first."

"Great. I'll order a cab for seven. May I stop by your room about five minutes prior to escort you to our cab?"

"That would be nice." He's as polite in person as he is on the phone. I like that about him. I'm not used to anyone being so concerned about my wishes, but I think I could get used to it.

After the bus returned them to the hotel, Yvonne encountered Rosanna coming back to her room from the spa. With a towel wrapped around her hair and a clingy champagne-colored robe wrapped around her body, her skin shone with the oils from a full body massage. Yvonne caught a faint smell of olive oil, the Greek's secret cure for everything, with a hint of lavender. "Have you had a nice afternoon, Rosanna?"

"Delightful. Thank you,"

"Have you seen Janice? I thought I might check on her. Do you think that would be okay?"

"She's probably still sleeping, poor dear. I gave her half a sedative to help her relax. I thought it would be best since she has a tendency to overdo on most occasions. Bill is with her now, so I'm sure if there's a problem we would be informed right away."

"Well, I guess I'll check in later then. See you in the morning at seven if not before."

Yvonne watched as Rosanna rushed down the hall to her room and wondered at the sudden change in her relaxed demeanor.

David arrived at 6:55. When Yvonne answered his knock, the light behind her emitted a soft glow. She appeared luminous, wearing a simple black sheath that hinted at the cleavage and curves of her slim body. Instead of the standard string of pearls, she had on a small elegant gold cross with one small diamond in the center. For earrings, diamond studs. Her hair was swept up around the sides, but left down in the back giving the impression of a well-groomed school girl. He found it irresistibly sexy and wondered if he'd be able to bring it all down around her face before the night was over.

"Good evening, David. You look especially nice this evening." She watched as he stared at her. I don't believe I've ever seen him speechless before. He's kind of cute when he's groping for something nice to say. Very sexy indeed and thanks to you, Mom. You've always said 'less is more.' I guess you were right.

Yvonne's scrutiny caught David off guard. He found his voice. "Yvonne, you take my breath away. I'll have to stay very close to you tonight, lest someone should want to steal you away from me."

"Why thank you, David. I'm sure you have no need to worry about that. Shall we go?"

At the Platia Iroon in the Psiri district, tables were spread across the square and simply overflowed from the crowded interior of the restaurant. Although the food was excellent, the ouzo selection and the music attracted most patrons in the early evening hours. Yvonne and David found a table for two on the edge of the outer café area. "It looks like we got here just in time. All the tables are full," said David.

"I believe that it's always crowded from spring through the summer. I hear that even in the winter the locals spend hours jammed inside listening to music on the weekends."

The couple ordered their drinks and listened to the loud musicians who seemed to pour their heart and souls into the air as the sunset cooled things down. They heard everything from Greek rembetika music to rock and roll to hard rock. It was difficult to talk, but they each smiled and drank and just reveled in the festive atmosphere.

Yvonne and David arrived at the restaurant in a warm glow created by the ouzo and merriment they had enjoyed. They passed through the European style dining room with well-lit crystal chandeliers and windows that offered a view to the roof top garden dining area and the city lights below. On their way through they waved at Evelyn and Richard seated by themselves; Todd and Missy also at a table for two; and Mark, Cynthia and Beverly seated together nearby. David had a twinge of guilt when he waved at the last table, but it appeared to him that Beverly was having a good time laughing as if she was enthralled with Mark and Cynthia's company.

When the time came to be seated in the rooftop café, they were given a quiet table in a corner overlooking the Parthenon.

"What a magnificent view!" David waved his arm indicating the panoramic spectacle. The Acropolis glowed in golden light. Hadrian's Arch as well as the Temple of Olympian Zeus could all be seen in different directions.

"You must have pulled a few strings to get us this great table," said David.

"It's my habit to always ask for a view when requesting hotel rooms or dinner reservations. If I mention that I'm a travel agent I usually get VIP treatment since they know if I'm happy, I'll be more likely to refer future business to them." Yvonne blushed as she realized she was patting herself on the back.

David smiled at her sincere embarrassment.

They both chose the sword-fish steaks fixed in the Mediterranean style with tomatoes, garlic, onion and kalamata olives, served with a potato and artichoke casserole and a terrific melitzanna salahta made with eggplant. To go with this, David ordered a fine French Chablis.

The evening turned out to be a most pleasant experience for Yvonne. David had an easy way about him, and she found herself being drawn to him. He was interested in her life and seemed surprised to hear that she had a six-year old daughter at home.

"The one regret that I had in my marriage was that we did not have any children, but I suppose, in the long run, it was for the best."

"I know what you mean." Yvonne gave David a rueful smile. "And yet, I feel very fortunate—the one good thing that came from my disastrous marriage was my beautiful daughter, Christy. It's not easy—raising a child alone—but I'd be lost without her." She had seen the disappointment in his eyes when he spoke about having no children and thought that this was someone who would make a good father.

Goodness! Now I'm really scaring myself. It would be nice to find someone who could be a good father to Christy, but really, I'm just having a nice evening with a charming man who happens to be a client, that's all.

Yvonne felt a chill even though the breezes were warm as goosebumps crawled up her bare arms. She crossed her arms over her chest and rubbed them with her hands. David stood, pulled off his jacket and wrapped it around her without saying a word. Should she offer to pay her share of the meal? After all, she invited him, but she knew instinctively that David would be insulted if she offered to pay. "David.

Thanks so much for a delightful evening. The dinner, the view and the company were all great." She bestowed her biggest and brightest smile on him.

"You are even more beautiful when you smile. I hope I continue to have the chance to see that smile many more times in the future." Reluctant to leave, he asked, "Shall we go downstairs and hail a cab?"

Yvonne rose up from the seat as David pulled out her chair. He put his arm around her shoulders and escorted her from the restaurant to the elevator. Other members of the group were nowhere to be seen.

When David stopped to speak to the valet attendant, Yvonne walked out from under the portico that sheltered the cars for disembarking passengers. Along the bottom wall were rows three deep of colorful iris and tulips. The scent was pungent and she breathed deeply wishing to remember the moment. David came up behind her as she bent over to have a closer look. "It should only be just a few minutes until a taxi arrives. What are you admiring?"

"I was just trying to see the exact shade of purple. In the dark they seem almost black, yet iridescent."

A distant scraping noise caused David to look up. A large pot of flowers came tumbling down toward Yvonne. He shoved her hard to move her out of the way, knocking her down and shielding her with his own body as the planter slammed into the sidewalk with such impact that it broke apart sending pottery, dirt and flowers all over his shoes and pants. As he tried to lift himself up he felt pain in both elbows where he'd tried to fall without putting all his weight on Yvonne.

"Yvonne. Are you okay?" Panic was evident in his voice.

"I think so...wha—what about you? Can you lift yourself off me?"

As David stood up, the valet ran forward to help them.

The hotel manager had been called and came running to their assistance. "My goodness, what could have caused such a thing to happen?"

"You'd better send someone up to the roof right now to see exactly what did happen," commanded David.

60

"Yes sir. I will do so right away. Why don't you and the lady come inside and sit down. I will bring you some brandy to help settle your nerves.

"Please, come with me. Mr.—what is your name?"

"Ludlow, David Ludlow, and this is Ms. Yvonne Suarez.

TRAVELING TO OLYMPIA

DAY 5

The shrill ring of the phone jarred her awake. She glanced at the clock and couldn't believe that it was six already and time for the wakeup call. The confusion from the night before replayed in her mind. After the hotel manager and security officer realized the pot of flowers could not have fallen without being pushed, they insisted on calling the police. Police Inspector Trakas questioned Yvonne and David relentlessly. "Do you have any enemies? Why are you traveling in Athens? What about the others in your group? Could any of them be holding a grudge?"

By the time they'd finished with her, she wondered if she'd made someone angry without knowing about it. They'd have to be more than angry to try and kill her though. Throughout the course of the night she wondered if David might be the target. What did she really know about him? All these questions and more kept her from falling asleep. The last time she looked at the clock it was after three. When she finally dozed off, she slept fitfully.

Yvonne dragged herself out of bed and into a hot shower, hoping this would revive her enough to get her through the day. She remembered that she needed to pack. They'd be checking out of the hotel to travel to Olympia. She'd intended to pack last night before going to bed. Now, she thought, I'll have to skip breakfast, and I won't be good for anything without at least tea and toast in my stomach.

Stuffing clothes into her suitcase, it hit her like the pot of flowers. Something strange is going on and I'm going to figure it out.

She added up the bad incidents in her head. Enough. I'm going to take back control of my tour and see that everyone gets the safe enjoyment they planned for. I'll start by steering clear of David. That way our attraction to each other won't distract me from my duties, and I'll be better able to keep a clear head and watchful eye on my fellow travelers. Maybe I can figure out what's happening. With this new resolve, Yvonne hung the strap to her carryon over her shoulder and pulled her suitcase through the doorway leaving the hotel room door to close on its own as she walked to the elevator.

When she arrived in the lobby, most of her clients were either in line to check out or lounging on one of the hotel couches waiting to depart. David, sitting with Richard and Evelyn Malcolm, looked weary but brightened and rose from the chair when he saw Yvonne.

Here he comes. Now stay cool, Yvonne chastised herself.

"Good morning, David. Are you doing okay?"

"Yes, I'm fine," he lied. "How are you holding up?"

"I'm fine too. Excuse me. I need to check out." Yvonne turned her back on David.

"Yvonne, what's wrong? Are you upset with me?" His voice was scratchy as he stifled a yawn.

"No. Of course not, why would I be? Didn't you save my life?"

"I suppose if you look at it like that. I just reacted to move us both out of harm's way." He moved next to her in line so he could see her face. "Have you thought of anyone who might wish to harm you?"

Yvonne clenched her jaw. "No. I can't imagine anyone who cares enough to dislike me that much. What about you? Maybe it was meant for you?"

"Oh, you think I could be disliked that much?" David stared at Yvonne. The look of hurt and rejection on his face made her uncomfortable.

David softened his tone. "I expect you're right. It's as likely as thinking you might be the target. I only wish I knew why it might be either of us."

Yvonne turned toward the check out counter. David stepped close enough to lean his upper arm against her shoulder. He lowered his voice. "Yvonne, don't shut me out. Not now. We need to stick together to find out what's happening and why."

She kept her voice low while creating a small space between them. "David, I think we need to keep our distance and get on with the tour. I can't afford to have any more problems with the tour or I'll have mutiny from my clients. Please, you must understand, it's important for me to stay in control."

Before David could respond to her last remark, they were interrupted by Inspector Trakas. "Good Morning, Ms. Suarez, Mr. Ludlow. I'd like a few words with you before you leave for—let me see—your next stop is Olympia, is it not?" He waved a copy of their itinerary in the air.

"Inspector Trakas, we answered your questions last night. I don't know what more you could want from us." Yvonne stepped out of line.

"I would like to question anyone else from your group who was present at the restaurant. We don't take attempted murder lightly here in Athens."

"Of course you don't, Inspector. Are we sure it was attempted murder? I can't think of any reason why anyone on our tour would wish me harm. Besides, everyone else from our group was gone when we left the restaurant."

"I agree with Ms. Suarez," said David. "It must be a crazy coincidence. Harassing the tour members will only serve to cause Ms. Suarez undue embarrassment and will inconvenience everyone."

"It has come to my attention that you were present at the airport when the attendant was found murdered, and—well, it's quite a coincidence? So, if you don't mind, Mr. Ludlow, I will be the one to decide who we will question and why."

Stunned, Yvonne could not disagree with Inspector Trakas. It was indeed a coincidence hard to ignore.

David stepped between Yvonne and the detective. "Inspector, you can't believe that it's anything but a coincidence. We'd just arrived from a long Trans-Atlantic flight. We couldn't possibly have anything to do with the dead man." He balled his hands into fists. He could feel the sweat on his palms. He rubbed his palms together in an attempt to dry them and finally shoved them into his pockets. He was fast losing restraint. He willed himself to calm down while he waited for Trakas to respond.

"I repeat, Mr. Ludlow, after I question the other members of your group, I will determine if it was a coincidence or not." Inspector Trakas stroked his black handle-bar mustache and straightened his back like a general about to walk out on the battlefield.

Yvonne, sensing David might lose control, switched gears. "Inspector Trakas, why not allow me to check out of the hotel. I'll gather everyone together so you can question them. In the meantime, you could arrange for a private conference room here at the hotel. You're not planning to disrupt our travel arrangements by taking us down to your police station, are you?"

Bill, Janice, Nicholas and Rosanna strolled in from the hotel dining room and stepped in line to check out.

Yvonne watched the inspector's expression. He seemed to be mulling over her request. In the long run she thought he would agree in order to gain their cooperation.

"All right, Ms. Suarez, I will arrange for a room to be used here before you leave. You must realize, however, that you may still experience a substantial delay in your tour."

Yvonne gave a rueful smile. "Thank you for your consideration. I know that you'll do your best to keep us no longer than is reasonable. I'm also sure you'll see that we have no possible connection to the incidents that have happened, and you'll be glad to send us on our way."

Yvonne returned to stand in line again. The brightly-lit counter was made of rich teak wood and had space for at least four hotel clerks. Only two helped with check-out now. She waited patiently behind the Fontinellis, and the Armstrongs.

David moved back to the area where the other tour members were talking. He watched and wondered how they'd react to yet another delay and police interrogation. Would this be the beginning of the end of the tour, or would Yvonne be able to keep them on track in spite of the crazy things that had occurred?

Ari arrived in the lobby sharply at eight, ready to drive them to Olympia. Yvonne called everyone together for instructions. "I'm afraid there will be a short delay to our tour. Police Inspector Trakas wishes to speak with everyone at the restaurant last night regarding the mystery of the fallen planter." Grumbling could be heard among the travelers and Bill Armstrong's voice could be heard above all. "Janice and I will be departing soon if this tour doesn't start running smoothly." Janice paled.

Janice reached to take Bill's hand. "Bill, please don't make matters worse. I'm sure there's nothing to worry about. Yvonne is doing a fine job, and so far the tour itself has been delightful." His posture stiffened and she let go of his hand.

"Oh yes, we must overcome this little nuisance," said Evelyn Malcolm. "I've waited years for this opportunity, and I'll be darned if I'm going to leave without seeing everything I've come to see. Don't you agree, Richard?"

"Well, if it's not safe dear—I'm not sure—perhaps we should think about coming back another time?"

"Nonsense, I won't hear of it. I say we all stand behind Yvonne and make this the best tour ever." Evelyn stood up to show her support.

"I agree with Evelyn," said David. "Is there anyone else who's ready to stand loyally with our very capable tour leader?"

"Why, David, darling, It's just like you to be so chivalrous. Yes, I think we should all stick it out." Beverly came over to David and linked her arm with his to show support.

"Why not, I'm game," said Mark. Cynthia, Todd and Missy nodded in agreement.

"We don't want to be party-poopers, do we?" Rosanna followed Beverly's lead and linked her arm through Nicholas'. He looked down to study his shoes.

"Well, I suppose if everyone else is willing to continue, we can too." Bill scowled while Janice smiled anxiously.

David smiled, glad that he'd been able to rally their support for Yvonne. No way did he want this tour to end early.

It took two and a half hours of questioning before Inspector Trakas allowed the tour members to leave. "Ms. Suarez, a friendly warning. I suggest that you keep your group close and watch over them not only for their safety but yours as well. Do I make myself clear?"

"I'm not exactly sure what you are implying, Inspector, but I can assure you I plan to keep very close tabs on my group, so the rest of our tour goes as smoothly as was planned."

"I'm warning you, I don't want to hear of any other incidents concerning you or members of your group while you're in Greece. Understood?"

"Believe me, Inspector, I'm just as anxious to put all this behind us and get on our way."

"Good. Then I wish you all a happy holiday." Inspector Trakas nodded to the group and marched out of the hotel to a black nondescript sedan where a uniformed police officer ushered him into the back seat and drove him away.

Facing the group from the front of the bus, Yvonne read from her itinerary. The others watched a small freighter ship crossing under the bridge far below. The murky water flowing through the narrow passageway of gold colored rock gave off an odor of diesel fuel mixed with dead fish. "We have just crossed the Corinth Canal dug between 1882 and 1893. Though it is obsolete in this era of mega-container ships, a few freighters and tour ships still squeeze through its 23 meter or 75 foot channel." She looked up to see Cynthia holding her nose. "From the town of Corinth known as Korinthos in Greece, we will pick up highway E65, drive through the Peloponnese region and arrive at the mountainside city of Mycenae. Once there we will walk through the Lion Gate to see the giant Cyclopean stones used to build the city walls and visit the Beehive Tombs."

Yvonne was having trouble concentrating on the job at hand. She tried her best to sound upbeat and enthusiastic, but the words seemed to trip coming out of her mouth.

"This all sounds fine, but when can we expect to stop for food? Missy and I are starved." Todd gave Yvonne an impish grin.

"Interrogations make me hungry," said Mark.

"We'll stop for lunch in Tripoli. At that point we'll be about half-way to Olympia. Tripoli is a small town with nothing more than a few neoclassical buildings and some nice restaurants. It will be the perfect place to stop, stretch our legs and grab a quick lunch."

Ari spoke into his microphone. "We're approaching Mycenae which gave its name to one of the most important bronze ages. Excavations there uncovered the gold death mask that prompted self-taught scholar and amateur archaeologist Heinrich Schliemann to boast 'I have seen the face of Agamemnon.' Schliemann believed that Homer's epic writings should be taken literally, and he set out to find the ancient city that was 'rich in gold.' Modern archaeologists talk about his sloppy and inept work, but can't find fault with the fact that he led others to find many treasures that are now located in the National Museum in Athens."

Yvonne looked at each of her fellow travelers and, with the exception of Beverly who was thumbing through a magazine, all seemed interested in Ari's spiel. Evelyn made notes in her journal, and Richard listened attentively.

Ari continued, "After lunch, our drive will take us through the Arcadia Mountains."

Disappointment was evident in Yvonne's eyes as she interjected, "We were to see the statue of Hermes in the museum in Olympia before heading to our hotel, but because of the delay this morning, we will have to eliminate that stop."

"We'll visit a wonderful museum in Delphi tomorrow." Ari gave Yvonne a reassuring smile.

"I thought there'd be more opportunities to meet single men on this tour." Mark pouted. His baby face and mussed-up blond hair made him look young and immature to Cynthia.

"Mark, for Pete's sake, it's not a gay tour after all. We talked about this. We're supposed to be here for fun and relaxation. Remember—an escape—with no expectations of romance."

"I know, but we are in Greece. Wouldn't you expect romance somewhere along the way, no matter what we said?"

"Be patient, Mark. We have yet to get to the islands. I'll bet Santorini has all kinds of available men. Let's break away from the tour and go sun ourselves on those wonderful black sand beaches we've read about. You never know—someone cool may turn up. How does that sound?" Cynthia looked to see if he'd replaced his pout with a smile.

Mark shrugged. "Okay, I'll be patient. I guess this isn't so bad. It's relaxing and the scenery's pretty nice." Mark gazed at the mountains in the distance.

"Look, Richard, the sky is so blue and the landscape so green and lush. I don't know when I've seen the sun shining so brightly." Evelyn poked him in the arm to prevent him from snoozing. "You'd think I'd be used to bright sunshine coming from Florida, but it's different. The colors are more—oh I don't know—more colorful. Don't you agree? Richard?"

"Mm. I see what you mean." Richard's eyelids drooped. He tried to stay awake but the movement of the bus seemed to mesmerize him. He dozed on and off until they arrived at their next stop.

Bill chatted with Nicholas and Rosanna. They commented on the scenery and delighted in the fact that they had not seen this part of Greece before.

Janice tried to nap, but the chatter prevented it. She felt wrung out, worried about something she was too scared to name. Had she imagined someone pushing her down the steps at the Acropolis? The helpless feeling of falling down the steps replayed over and over in her mind. Soon everyone would think she was losing it. Why did she even care? No one else did. Bill all but ignored her, and Rosanna just humored her—treated her like a child. She needed to pull herself together. Maybe one of the sleeping pills Rosanna gave her would help. She would take one at bedtime. Maybe then she'd avoid the nightmares of falling endlessly down the Acropolis steps that had been keeping her awake. Determined to rest now and get a good night's sleep later, she closed her eyes and listened to the chatter.

David watched the traffic on the Autobahn. He noticed a plain looking black sedan keeping pace with the bus. It would drive alongside and pass, only to later fall back and follow from behind. The tinted windows prevented him from seeing the driver or how many people were in the car. Were they being followed? Maybe the police were keeping tabs on the group. Should he tell Yvonne? He thought about it and decided not to worry her for now. After all, he thought, it may turn out to be a false alarm.

"Are you okay, David? You seem distracted." Beverly placed her hand tenderly on David's upper arm.

"I'm fine." He smiled. "My mind is just wandering back home to the work that's piling up in the office and things I can't do anything about anyway. Thanks for pulling me back to the present."

"My pleasure. Ah—speaking of the present, I just saw a sign for Mykínes. That's the turn off for Mycenae, so we should be stopping soon. If you don't mind, I'd like to have a picture of us by the Lion's Gate.

David's good manners squashed his desire to grimace. "That would be very nice."

Arriving at Mycenae, the tourists found a fortified palace in ruins on a ravine-flanked ridge meant to be easily defendable, not a town as they imagined. In fact, little remained of the palace that was above waist-height, and most artifacts from the site had been moved to the National Museum. Missy found a secret stairway that descended to a siege-proof cistern located in the northeast corner. She, Todd, Mark and Cynthia were the only ones game enough to take the stairs down into the dank smelling room and then up again. Out of breath but invigorated, they agreed that the exercise made up for all the sitting on the bus.

Ari led the group toward the tombs. "According to legend, Mycenae was the capital of Agamemnon, the Achaean King who conquered Troy. It is also considered to be the main site of the Late Bronze Age in Greece, and many artifacts discovered here prove that to be true."

Evelyn followed Richard into a tomb through a rectangular doorway made of heavy stone bricks built into the side of a small grassy hill that formed entry walls leading into the tomb. Above the doorway was a brick opening in the shape of a large triangle. She wondered if it was meant to let in light. Would the light be for the benefit of the living who buried their relatives or the dead who resided in the tombs? "Imagine, Richard. Here we are visiting the actual burial tomb of Clytemnestra. The stories about its construction, refers to it as a 'beehive.' I feel claustrophobic. Don't you?" Evelyn hurried to catch up with Richard who was moving deeper inside. She'd read about the similarities to Egyptian tombs—the dead buried with gold and silver cups, jewelry and other valuable belongings. She marveled at the wall paintings depicting the dead engaged in chariot races and living the highlife in their afterlife. I guess that's one way to gain immortality, she thought. I don't suppose anyone will remember me after I'm dead. She decided to keep this thought to herself. Richard had been thinking too much about his own mortality lately, ever since his heart trouble the previous year. Was he having similar thoughts as he studied the tomb?

David scanned the crowd of tourists as they made their way around the site, trying to see if anyone looked familiar or out of place. He made a mental note to check for the black sedan when they went back to the bus.

"Yvonne, would you mind taking a picture of David and me?" Beverly handed her camera to Yvonne and showed her which button to press.

Yvonne looked through the lens while backing up to include the whole massive stone gate including the large peaked triangle point centered above the opening. She wondered about the significance of the triangles in the architecture. She'd have to remember to ask Ari about it.

David followed Beverly on the cobblestone road to stand in the center of the opening of the Lion's Gate. He stood a small distance away from her, but Beverly stepped in to close the gap and gingerly placed her arm around his waist. Yvonne saw David's forced smile. She admitted, they made a handsome couple. Beverly glowed. Yvonne's heart sank. She chastised herself. She had no claim on him now. Deep down Yvonne knew that David had no serious interest in Beverly, yet she hated thinking that he might change his mind about Beverly, if she continued to push him away.

David stood next to Beverly but his thoughts were focused on Yvonne. She looked great in slacks and the fitted tee shirt he glimpsed under her navy blazer. He thought she looked professional, yet sexy.

He wondered what Beverly would think if she knew what was on his mind. He wondered why he cared. I feel like a fly caught in a spider web, he thought. I've made sure to be nothing more than civil to her, so why does she want to glue herself to my side?

In the small gift shop located just outside the exit, the younger members of the group were buying trail mix to snack on while warm diet Coke was popular among the rest of the travelers. Refreshed and back on the bus they headed to the next stop.

As promised, the small taverna in Tripoli offered a delightful lunch selection including Greek salad, cheese or lamb sandwiches and a variety of wines and beer.

Beverly stuck close to David during their lunch break. Afterward, the group browsed through a few touristy shops on the street. They offered the same trinkets seen in Athens.

Back on the bus everyone was quiet and subdued. The women gazed at the mountainside scenery. The men dozed, except David who wondered if he'd been premature worrying about the black sedan. The last time he saw it was before Tripoli and he didn't see it parked anywhere nearby when they stopped.

Ari interrupted the quiet. "We're taking the scenic route from this point. We'll be driving along the forested Mount Menalo in the Arcadian Mountains." He steered the small bus up the steep mountain road. After driving for half an hour, the bus jerked hard to the left toward the on-coming traffic. They were on the cliff-side of the mountain. Amid a few startled screams at being tossed sideways, the passengers righted themselves and Ari pulled the wheel back under control; an incessant thumping accompanied by vibrations made it clear one of the tires had a serious problem. Ari searched for a pull off. He strained to hold the bus in control as it continued to pull to the left. He could feel the rim of the wheel hitting the road directly. Not a good sign, he thought.

"We're going to die!" Beverly screamed.

"Everyone stay calm! We'll be fine as long as everyone stays seated." Ari held fast to the steering wheel.

"Please tell me this isn't happening," said Yvonne under her breath. "What next?"

The travelers held on expecting to crash any moment, their eyes wide with fright. Ari rounded a curve and the bus wobbled off the edge of the road. The women screamed and Beverly raved again, "Oh no! We're all going to die!"

"No we're not! Not if I have anything to do with it." Ari shouted above the noise as he regained control of the bus. After what seemed like an eternity, a pull off with a scenic lookout came into view. Ari began to brake. This caused more thumping but allowed him to bump along onto the safety of the lookout.

David pried Beverly's fingers off his arm. Once the bus stopped, he went to the front and followed Ari off to see what had happened.

"Let's all take a deep breath. Everyone get off the bus. The lookout is here, so let's take advantage of the scenery. We can take pictures." Yvonne's smile was weak, her legs wobbly and the exhaustion caused by last night's events weighed on her.

One by one they exited the bus with the smell of burning rubber assaulting their noses. Everyone gathered around Ari and David as they studied the left front mangled tire. David could not determine if it had been deliberately slashed. After driving on it for so long only a few gummy shreds from the tire clung to the rim.

"Everyone, go relax and enjoy the view while I change the tire." Ari opened the hatch at the back of the bus and pulled out a spare tire, a tire iron and a jack.

David watched while Yvonne gathered the others and led them toward the barricaded cliff edge. He turned toward Ari. "Can I help with this?"

"Thank you, it's not necessary. I'm very good at maintenance of my bus, Mr. Ludlow. You should help Yvonne calm the others while I do this."

"Okay, but give a yell if you need anything." David joined the others facing gorgeous views of Levidi and Vytina, popular ski resorts in the winter. In the spring, the picturesque and quaint towns awaited summer tourists. All were deep in thought. He wondered if they had seen their lives flash before their eyes—he certainly had. He switched his focus to Yvonne. "May I speak with you privately for a moment?"

"Sure, David, is there another problem?"

"I'm not sure. There might be." David steered her away from the group. As soon as they were out of earshot, he continued, "I think the tire might have been tampered with."

"What? How could that possibly be? We were all on the bus. Who would do such a thing? No. We've left Athens, and we're on a lovely tour. There's absolutely no reason why anyone would damage our tires." Yvonne spat her words at him.

God, she's beautiful even when she's scared and angry. "I hate upsetting you." His features softened. "Believe me, I was hesitant to tell you, but I thought you should know."

"Know what?" Her voice pitched higher than normal.

"After we left Athens and before we got to Tripoli, I saw a black sedan tailing us. At first I wasn't sure, but it stayed with us until we left Tripoli. After that, I didn't see it again. I'm afraid that the person in the sedan may have tampered with the tire."

"How can you be sure the car was actually following us?"

"I watched it speed up and slow down to keep pace with us. After we stopped in Mycenae, it showed up again. If it wasn't following us, it would have been long gone. Don't you think?"

"I'm not sure what to think. I don't know what to do. How can I protect my group?"

Her confusion tore at David's emotions. He wanted more than anything to answer her questions. "Somehow we'll figure it out, but we must stick together."

"Why must we stick together? Why can't I just handle this on my own? I need to take control of the situation. Can't you see that?"

"What I see is that you need a friend, someone who is willing to help, someone who cares." The tenderness in his eyes was undeniable.

His kindness opened the floodgates to Yvonne's tears. She tried to steady her voice. "I'm not used to having a man offer that kind of help. I'm—I'm afraid that I'll become too dependent on it—on you."

"Would depending on a friend be such a bad thing?"

Beverly walked up and stared at them. "The tire is fixed and Ari wants us to get back on. Yvonne, are you all right? Have you been crying? David what did you say to this poor girl." Beverly place an arm around Yvonne's shoulders steering her away from David.

Yvonne looked at David, reached in her pocket and retrieved a tissue. She dabbed at the corners of her eyes as she proceeded toward the bus. She pulled free of Beverly, allowing her to remain behind to board with David.

It was dusk when the weary travelers arrived in Pyrgos. They had temporarily bypassed Olympia to stay at the Pyrgos Mantania, a superb inn offering picturesque forest walks and river kayaking. The rooms were clean and charming with modern walnut furniture. In a separate stone building was a well-regarded restaurant and bar. After checking in and enjoying a brief rest period, they met in the bar for cocktails while waiting to be called for dinner.

Yvonne had trouble concentrating on the group conversation. She thought about her talk with David. She couldn't believe that anyone would actually follow them, much less, slash their tire.

"I wonder what kind of delays we can expect tomorrow." Bill's voice reverberated off of the stone walls.

"Bite your tongue Bill. Be careful what you expect, you may just get it," said Rosanna.

"She's right, Bill. Don't start looking for problems. Besides, what more could go wrong?" Evelyn declared. I think tomorrow is going to be a perfectly wonderful day." She smiled and thanked the gods that she wasn't married to such a negative and boorish man.

OLYMPIA

DAY 6

Yvonne strolled with David, Evelyn and Richard to the edge of the stadium. Still frazzled from the mishaps of the previous day, she tried to focus—to say something interesting about the ruins—instead she read from the notes on her itinerary. "Olympia radiates a calmness that belies its exciting history. Beginning in 776 BCE, the Olympic Games were held every four years for over a thousand years." To her own ears she sounded enthusiastic—upbeat. She took a breath. "The games themselves would become the hallmark of Greek culture as men competed to showcase their superior strengths and expertise as warriors." She looked up from her notes. Her companions were listening to her. Encouraged, she continued. "Winners would commission poets of the day to write a ballad that linked them to famous forefathers and mythological gods gaining 'undying glory' for themselves and their future heirs."

"It's amazing how fame can be passed down through the centuries—all because of a poet who made their deeds immortal." Evelyn gazed at Richard, looking through him to an imagined history. "I wonder if the heroes of today will become gods to some future century?"

Richard walked up to the massive stone archway that was the entrance to the Olympic stadium. He studied the slabs of stone that had enclosed the Olympic torch when it was lit for each Olympic Game. He looked at the flatness of the stadium. "No grandstand," he remarked, "just these grassy banks surrounding it. It's disappointing. I wonder about the imaginations of the people who wrote the ballads.

They make this place and the games seem so much bigger than they are in real life."

"Go ahead, Yvonne. Continue. We're enjoying the narrative." David enjoyed listening to Yvonne's voice. It soothed him. Like a sedative, it washed away the troubles of the past few days. He looked to Evelyn for confirmation.

Evelyn smiled and nodded her agreement.

Yvonne's spirit's rose. She grinned and added more emphasis to her words. "At first the Greeks competed as individuals coming from all over Greece. Later as popularity of the games grew, the City-State religious leaders and politicians who wished to gain fame and notoriety for their cities sent their own athletes, solidifying the competitive nature that the Greeks cultivated.

"During the eighth century the Panhellenic truce prohibited states from warring with each other during the Games. Those who broke the truce received painful punishment and stiff fines." Yvonne folded her itinerary and tucked it into her belly-pack. Now, if only our small group can get along as well as the Greek Olympians, she thought, the rest of our trip will go smoothly. Yvonne headed across the grassy plain in the direction of the ruins at the Temple of Hera. Richard and Evelyn smiled, watching David follow Yvonne at a comfortable distance.

Ari arrived at the edge of the ancient stadium with a small group that included the younger travelers. "You will notice that the large clay rectangle that measures 600 Olympic feet in length is one of three stadiums. They were built one on top of the other in different shapes and sizes. The original one facing the Temple of Zeus honored him. The Heraia Games for women held in one of the stadiums honored the goddess Hera.

"I'm impressed," said Cynthia. "I guess the ancient Greeks were rather enlightened. Imagine—allowing women to compete that many years ago and in honor of a female god, no less."

Ari continued, "The first Games began early in the sixth century BCE as an annual foot race of young women in competition for the position of the priestess for the goddess Hera. A second race was instituted for a consort for the priestess who would participate in the religious traditions at the temple. By the time of the Classical Greek culture in the fifth and fourth centuries BCE, the games were restricted to male participants and women weren't allowed to even view the games. So I'm afraid that the men weren't always that enlightened."

"It reminds me of a baseball field." Mark turned away from the stadium, drawn toward the Temple of Zeus, its white columns blazing in the sunlight. Missy and Todd followed.

Cynthia and Ari walked in the opposite direction to the church ruins. Ari stopped at the entrance, reluctant to enter. "Aren't you coming inside with me? You could show me around, answer questions, you know..."

"Okay, though it's not very large. There won't be much to see."

Cynthia stepped through an opening for a door. Ari was right, nothing but plain stone walls. She looked at the massive stones lying in disarray and the ceiling open to the sky. She spotted a corner somewhat closed off with a decorative lattice look to the stone walls that provided a small amount of privacy. Cynthia walked inside and Ari stepped in close behind her. She caught his musky scent and was overtaken by an impulse. Cynthia stepped sideways out of view of the doorway, turned and with a single graceful movement grabbed his hands, pulling him close so that they were nose to nose.

Ari blinked with confusion and then smiled. He tilted his head and leaned in to meet her soft lips. Her breath was fresh with a slight taste of mint, clean and pleasant. He liked the way she wrapped her arms around his neck, and he hugged her close. Their kiss escalated from tentative to passionate.

"Um... Excuse me." Yvonne had stepped into the church ruins looking for a quiet respite. Her cheeks turned red as the heat of the moment registered with her. Another problem to deal with.

Startled, Ari took Cynthia by the shoulders and moved her to arms length. He looked sheepishly at Yvonne. "I'm sorry. That was inappropriate. Please forgive me."

"Why? Aren't tour guides allowed to have fun too?" Cynthia's eyes twinkled.

Ignoring Cynthia's comment, Yvonne looked into his eyes, "You're right, Ari. It was not only inappropriate, it was unprofessional. I expect you won't let it happen again."

"Hello—Cynthia. Are you in there?" Mark's voice could be heard from outside the ruins.

Ari's guilty look and Cynthia's Chesire Cat grin said it all as they descended the steps to greet Mark. "Come on girl-friend, we have to talk." He pulled Cynthia by the arm and headed in the direction of the Palaestra training center. Ari glanced back at Yvonne and bounded off in the direction of the Temple of Zeus ruins shaking his head as he went.

"What's going on?" asked Mark. "Are you finding love on this tour after all?"

"I don't know what came over me. I suppose I am finding—at least a very strong attraction, but my timing seems to be off." Cynthia pouted.

"Now we're getting somewhere." Mark delighted in his friend's discomfort, secretly wishing he was in the same predicament.

Yvonne sat on a stack of stones and thought about what she should do. *I can't be everywhere at all times. How will I know if something dangerous is about to happen? I can't even keep on top of relationships blossoming among my clients. Maybe I should take David up on his offer of "help." He could be another pair of eyes and ears. Then again, maybe he's part of the problem. He's always close at hand when trouble is brewing.*

Yvonne shivered but enjoyed the coolness of the ancient stones and the peace offered by the old ruins. *It's quiet here. Nice having time to think,* she mused. *Ari and Cynthia, that's interesting. I suppose it's just one of those summer romance things. I hope it doesn't complicate the tour. Of course, I could take my own advice. I've been letting my own feelings for David distract me from my duties. Ay Dios Mio! I've got to stay in control of my emotions, keep a level head. That's the only way I can be sure to keep the tour on course and get everyone home safely. Mom always says that I inherited my Dad's hot Latin blood. She's right. Why else would I have jumped into marriage with a man who enjoyed hurting me? The passion of the lovemaking fulfilled me, but I was never enough for him. His power came from belittling me. With him, life would always be unpredictable and dangerous. No, from now on...*

"There you are. May we talk for a moment?"

Yvonne jumped and blushed, feeling like a child caught stealing from the cookie jar. Pushing thoughts of Gino from her mind, she replied too cheerfully, "Oh, hi, David."

"Sorry, I startled you."

"I was just day dreaming."

David held back. He hoped she'd been daydreaming about him. "I need to discuss something with you. Not to alarm you further, but I think it would be a good idea if you didn't go off by yourself, at least until we find out what's happening to cause these suspicious accidents."

"What could be the harm in this charming little church sanctuary? After all, isn't that what it was designed for? I'm not certain I'm in danger anyway."

"Really? Let's think about it. First the dead man at the airport when we arrived in Greece; then Janice fell or was pushed down the steps at the Acropolis; next a heavy potted plant fell from the sky aimed directly at your head; and finally, yesterday a tire blew out on our bus while riding on a mountain road with steep cliffs."

"I still can't see how any of this is related, and the falling planter missed me." She crossed her arms protectively over her stomach. It took effort to quell the spasm she felt deep in the pit of it, recalling how David knocked her to the ground landing on top of her with his warm hard body.

"I've upset you. That's the last thing I wanted. Come on, let's go enjoy this beautiful day." He extended his hand for her to take. He would stay close to her one way or another.

She allowed him to take her hand and help her up. They were still holding hands when they stepped out into the sunlight and came face to face with Beverly. A look of hurt and anger flashed in Beverly's eyes. Yvonne instantly let go of David's hand.

"Beverly—hi—uh—David was just rescuing me. I mean—reminding me that I should return to my duties as tour operator. I—uh—hope you haven't been feeling neglected." Yvonne bit her lip, realizing she had just made matters worse.

"Why, how efficient you are, Yvonne." Beverly's smile was wooden. "I have no need of your services. I've just come to explore this lovely building. David dear, how gallant of you to be rescuing damsels in distress again. What would this tour do without you? Excuse me." She swept past them into the sanctuary.

"Boy, if that didn't feel like an ice storm blowing through."

"David, don't you see? This is exactly why we must keep our distance."

"No, Yvonne. I don't see any such thing. Beverly has no claim on me, and I'm free to go wherever and do whatever I please. With whom I please. And what I please is to stay close to you during this tour until we find out what's going on. So get used to it!" David waited and watched for Yvonne's reaction to his command.

Yvonne suppressed a smile. She was beginning to like this man and his firm but kind manner. She felt special knowing he cared. She wondered what Christy would think of him. *Is it too soon to be thinking of bringing him home to meet Christy? Ay Dios! I haven't talked to Christy for two nights. I need to call home tonight. I never realized how difficult working fulltime would be. Coordinating schedules, confirming reservations, watching out for everyone, and participating in the tours—it doesn't leave much time to check on my family back home. Get a grip. You can do this.*

Yvonne turned her thoughts back to the present. "Okay, David. I suppose it wouldn't hurt to have you on my side. Maybe between us we can figure out what, if anything is going on."

Her facial expressions had undergone several phases. In the end, her trusting smile warmed David's heart. He resolved again to make sure she was safe. "Good. Now let's go check on everyone."

"David, don't forget, this is my tour and I will continue to be the leader."

"Of course." He feigned submission.

"What's with Janice? Why is she so timid and scared of her own shadow?" David asked Yvonne while they strolled a discreet distance from the others.

"I don't know for sure. I think she has been verbally abused, if not physically. I'm concerned about her, but I don't know how to broach the subject. I wouldn't want to put her in jeopardy, and what can she do to change her circumstances while on tour anyway?"

"I get the feeling there's more to it than that. Remember, she was fine and chipper at the beginning of the tour. Something happened along the way to scare her." David stared at a single tall Doric column, still standing at Hera's temple. In his mind he saw Janice crumpled on the steps of the Acropolis.

"She changed after she fell. I'm sure of it. Do you think she was pushed?"

"My thoughts exactly, and that might explain why she's become timid and tentative about everything." David grabbed Yvonne by the arm to prevent her from bumping into the waist-high rectangular stone while they maneuvered around the ruins of the Temple of Zeus.

Yvonne straightened her posture, pulling away from David. "Yes, I agree. But, who do you think pushed her? Her husband wasn't even with her when she fell. He and Nicholas were in town having coffee at that little coffee-shop, and I can't believe that Rosanna would have had anything to do with it. She dotes on Janice, very protective of her."

"Let's keep a closer watch on her anyway. Something may turn up." David and Yvonne were joined by Ari and some of the others viewing the Temple of Zeus.

Ari arranged couples in front of the columns for picture taking.

"Ari, while you're at it, how about a picture of the whole group?" David stood next to Yvonne in the picture.

Yvonne pointed to a man wearing dress slacks and a white shirt holding a jacket over his shoulder reading a plaque about the temple. "Ari, why not ask that man over there if he will take our picture? Then we can have you in it too."

"Sure, why not." Ari approached the man standing alone and asked him to take the group picture.

The man spoke English with a Greek accent. "Uh... I'm not very good at that kind of thing, but... sure okay." The man stepped nearer the group, quickly aimed the camera and shot the picture. "Uh... I hope it turns out all right." He handed the camera back to Ari and walked away.

David watched the man. He seemed familiar. Maybe he'd seen him at another tourist stop. David continued watching the man move with determined steps toward the church ruins.

"That's peculiar," said Yvonne.

"What?"

"Did you notice the way he was dressed? Not your typical tourist, is he?"

"That's exactly what I was thinking. He might be the person who's been following us. We should follow him and see where he goes."

"Are you sure? I don't want the rest of the group to get suspicious."

"Quick, before we lose him." David nudged Yvonne and they walked in the direction the stranger had gone. "He must have ducked behind one of these ruins. Try to hurry without being obvious. I don't want to lose him."

"Look! There he goes. He's heading back to the car park." They followed the path leading to the cars walking faster, getting close enough to see the mysterious man get into his car.

"That's the black Mercedes that followed us earlier. Look! There's a rental tag on the car. I bet he thought we would recognize him. That's why he left so abruptly." David shook his fist at the back of the car as it sped out of the driveway and onto the highway in the direction of Olympia and their Amalia Hotel only one and half kilometers from the archaeological site.

Where will he turn up next? I'll be glad David's nearby the rest of the day, thought Yvonne.

All from the Pinkerton group met for dinner in the hotel dining room. Yvonne glanced around the room and to her relief did not see the strange man from the ruins. Her group was divided among two tables seating seven at each. Yvonne and David were with Ari, Janice, Bill, Rosanna and Nicholas. Separating Ari from Cynthia seemed like a good idea. The Malcolm's sat with the younger members and Beverly. They enjoyed themselves with quiet conversation. Yvonne noticed Cynthia sneak a look at Ari. Turning her attention back to her own table, she said, "Janice, I hope you're feeling better today. Did you enjoy Olympia?"

Janice glanced at Bill then mumbled her dull answer, "I'm feeling fine—and found Olympia fascinating. Thank you." Janice made no further eye contact with anyone and stared at her plate of half-eaten food. An uneasy feeling came over Yvonne watching Janice's reaction to her simple question.

"Yes, we all had a fine day." Bill lifted a glass of red wine to his tablemates.

DELPHI

DAY 7

The scowl on Yvonne's face bothered David. "Cheer up Yvonne. We're bound to have a cloudy day once in a while. Look, Janice is so enthralled with Ari and what he's saying about Delphi that she's actually smiling." David took a handkerchief from his shorts pocket and wiped the sweat from his brow.

"Yes, but Delphi has the most spectacular mountain views, and it's hard to appreciate it through this cloudy haze. I wish it would break down and rain. It would be messy but a relief from this muggy weather." She twisted her umbrella, impatient, expecting to use it soon. "I suppose I can't expect to control the weather." Yvonne sighed and turned her attention back to Ari.

"Delphi is the most popular archaeological site on the mainland. From here you can see that the city was built on terraces in the side of these steep cliffs. It makes me feel as if we might slip into the Plistos Gorge at any moment." Ari pretended to slide downward startling everyone. "Now that I have your attention," he chuckled. "Legend has it that after being set free by Zeus, two eagles, one flying from the east and one from the west, assembled in Delphi. From then on it was considered to be the center of the planet, known as Omphalos, meaning literally, naval of the universe."

Ari walked carefully along the path that led to the Athenian Treasury. "The Treasury was first used as a temple and later as a store house. As with many of the ruins in Greece, we are not sure exactly when the Treasury was built. Most believe it was the late 6th or early 5th century."

Sandy-colored ruins tucked into the side of the mountain displayed the sophisticated stone masonry and marble work of the period. Ari pointed to the large cracks in the Doric columns and explained how the French had pieced them together during their excavations from 1904 to 1906, using inscriptions that covered their surface as guides. The sound from several cameras clicking gave Ari pause at the appropriate interval in his spiel.

The air was heavy and the sky dark with clouds. The dampness heightened the smell of aged ruins and mingled with nearby vegetation making Yvonne's nose twitch. "How discouraging," she whispered to David. "Delphi is known for having drier than average seasons, but no, not today. Today the lousy weather is going to spoil it for everyone." She grimaced. "I'm sorry, David. This pessimistic attitude is not like me, but every day something has gone wrong, and it's beginning to take a toll on my spirits."

David reminded Yvonne that it was spring after all and rain was to be expected when Evelyn cut in. "I had no idea so many temples were named in honor of Apollo and Athena. If that's not enough, there are sanctuaries named for them as well." She jotted notes in her diary. "I imagine that they were as important in their day as Christ and the Saints are in ours."

"That's an astute observation," said Ari. "During the eighth century BCE, the oracles of Delphi were high priestesses consulted on everything from advice on where to start new communities to the best days to go to war. They mediated border disputes between the city-states and set government policies while remaining neutral and in control of Greece. The last known recorded response of Oracles in Delphi ended in 393 CE."

"Once again, it sounds like women were held in high esteem in ancient Greece. It's too bad they're not revered in the same manner today." Beverly's caustic remark forced a moment of awkward silence.

"Beverly, darling, speak for yourself. I've certainly had no problem being revered by the men I've known." Rosanna winked at Nicholas and Bill.

"Look at the delicate yellow and pink wild flowers popping out all over the cracks of these ancient ruins. That's one of the reasons

I wanted to tour Greece in the springtime." Evelyn bent down and picked several flowers, offering up her small bouquet for all to see. "Oh my goodness! I shouldn't have done that. I don't know what came over me." Evelyn remembered that they had been cautioned while visiting tourist sites not to pick flowers or disturb the ruins in anyway. Embarrassed, she dropped the flowers and clutched the small tote that stored her journal, camera and other items to her chest.

Evelyn recovered from her faux pas when she looked at her husband. "Richard, dear, sit down. This climbing is taking its toll on you." Richard's chest heaved as he tried to catch his breath. Sweat oozed from his pores and his legs felt rubbery. He lowered himself to a hard stone bleacher shaded by the circling theatre. He gazed out at the distant mountain peaks rising above the clouds that were covering the view of the valley below.

"Evelyn, please—stop hovering. I'm okay—really—I just needed a moment to rest."

Ari paused. Concerned for Richard, he waited until Richard began breathing normally before he guided the rest of the group to the Delphi theatre. "You may also note that many of our Greek Orthodox Churches are named for Jesus Christ and his disciples. Later today we'll travel along the coast and the foothills of Mt. Parnassus to the Monastery of Osio Loukas named for a 10th century follower of Luke the Physician."

Ari waved his arm indicating that everyone should sit while he gave the history of the theatre. "This theatre-stadium was originally built in the 4th century BCE but completely restored during the Roman era. You can see how large it is. There's enough room to seat 5,000 people."

Taking a seat next to Cynthia, Mark exclaimed, "Can't you just hear the crowds cheering and booing as they must have done during the chariot races all those many centuries ago?"

"I sure can, Sugar." Cynthia smiled and leaned sideways bumping her shoulder against his.

Yvonne seated herself a row above the others. From this vantage point she watched the interactions of her fellow travelers. She caught snippets of conversations blowing upward on a light breeze.

Stepping in front of Janice, Bill Armstrong escorted Rosanna and Beverly to a seat. He sat down and made himself comfortable between the two ladies, leaving Janice and Nicholas to fend for themselves. "Ever the charming gentleman," said Nicholas. He placed his arm protectively around Janice and stepped up to the next level where they both sat facing Ari.

Yvonne watched Janice hold her chin up, hiding her hurt feelings. She glared at Bill, though he was oblivious. Ay, Dios Mio. I'd like to wring his bloody neck.

Ari stood up to face his audience and continued reciting his well rehearsed script. "Performances of centuries past were part of religious ceremonies...."

Yvonne noticed tension between Todd and Missy. She turned her attention to what she was afraid might be a quarrel between the honeymooners. It must be this gloomy weather, she thought.

"Missy, Sweetheart, move a little closer. The others will think you're mad at me." Todd tugged on Missy's arm.

"I am mad at you. If I'd known this second honeymoon was going to be your attempt to get me pregnant, I never would have agreed to it. I've told you—I'm not ready to have children, not when my career is just taking off."

"But, Darling, we're in our 30's. If we wait much longer, we'll be too old to handle children. When they're in their teens and need us most, we'll be pushing 50."

"Why must we keep going on about this? Maybe we're not meant to be parents." Missy clenched her jaws and tried to focus on what Ari was saying.

"You can't mean that. We agreed when we reached our 30's, we'd start our family. I can't believe you're reneging on our promise to each other." Todd pulled his arm from around Missy.

"Todd, for Pete's sake, I didn't anticipate my career would take this long to get off the ground. I've worked too hard and I won't give it up." Missy inched further away from him.

"Well, maybe I'll give mine up. You can bring home the paycheck and I'll stay home to take care of the kids."

"Now who's being silly? Come on Todd. Let's give it a few more years. We'll be more financially set, and neither one of us will have to give up our careers."

"We'll see about that." Todd moved closer to Missy.

"Todd, I'm warning you. If you keep after me about this, I will leave this tour and return home without you." Missy stared him straight in the eye.

Todd stared back, but his nerve quickly faded at the thought of losing her. He would have to find another way to approach her with his desire to have children. He wondered how many of the others had heard their argument. That would be humiliating. As he looked around the others seemed to be listening to Ari drone on about the early Greeks. His great plan to have a second honeymoon had so far been a bust. Maybe he could help recapture some romance, then Missy would lighten up and think twice about having a child. He moved closer and put his arm around her shoulder again. He felt her stiffen at his touch, but she didn't pull away.

Yvonne pretended to be absorbed with Ari's presentation. Silently she worried that this latest discord between Missy and Todd meant that everything was falling apart again.

As promised, they arrived in the afternoon at the Greek Monastery of Osios Loukas.

"It's amazing that these mosaics withstood an earthquake in 1659 and are still in such beautiful condition today." David was pointing at a wall where the group gathered in the narthex of the main church. "Just look at this intricate work depicting the Resurrection and Washing of the Apostles Feet."

"I agree with David. That it is still here after all these years..." Evelyn looked around at the group. She encouraged any and all positive comments, eager to love everything about her trip, she wanted everyone to feel the same excitement in these ancient sacred places as she did.

After exploring the interior of the church, they all wandered the grounds leisurely. Evelyn breathed deeply and aimed her camera lens at the spectacular view of the valley and Mt. Elikonas seen from the rear of the church. She turned in a slow circle and absorbed the spirituality of the magnificent architecture sweeping from the valley below to the blue skies above. Her heart soared along with the birds seen in the distance. She had finally fulfilled her life's dream to travel to this ancient country of Greek gods and Christian saints. "What more could I ask?" I must remember to thank Richard with an extra hug for making all this possible. She walked back inside the church for one more look at the mosaics.

Outside Yvonne held up her unopened umbrella, the signal for all to return with her to the bus. After everyone was seated on the bus, she explained, "We'll have a relaxing two-hour ride back to Athens— back in time for supper. Tomorrow we'll have our first Greek island cruise to Andros Island. Once we arrive on the island, we'll be on our own to shop or soak up some sun."

"Spoken like a true travel agent," said Beverly.

"It sounds like heaven to me," countered Mark. "I think we're ready for some relaxation and fun. It's time to give our brains a break. Don't you agree, Cynthia?"

"Sure is, Sugar. It'll be nice to have some time to ourselves and to do our own thing." She glanced at Ari and wondered if he might catch her underlying meaning. She meant to have him to her herself on a secluded beach hide-away.

Yvonne shivered. She wondered if the storm clouds would follow them all the way to Athens. In answer to her thoughts, the sky darkened and large rain drops began pelting the bus. She made a mental note to call home from the hotel since this would be their last night on the mainland.

ANDROS ISLAND

DAY 8

"**C**ynthia, darlin'. Would you look at the size of Port Piraeus? I've never seen so many cruise ships and tankers all in one spot." Mark gave Cynthia a friendly jab on the arm and quickly counted five cruise ships and at least ten other tankers, ferries and tug boats.

"I feel so small beside these enormous ships." Cynthia's adventurous spirit was evident in her voice.

Though it had rained heavily during the night, the dampness burned off quickly in the morning sun. The drive to the port of Piraeus, the heart of the Greek ferry network, uplifted the spirits of the travelers. A sparkling new day was ahead of them.

Evelyn was busy recording everything she saw in her journal. She noted several other tour buses lined up at the pier.

While the group waited for their small bus to drive aboard the high speed ferry, the squawking of seagulls and the smell of saltwater and engine oil seeped in through the windows. The montage of sights, sounds and smells would leave a lasting impression on their senses.

Once the bus was parked on board the ferry, Yvonne placed her light-weight tote with the umbrella over her shoulder and grasped her clipboard with the attached pen in both hands as if it were a sacred treasure or a security blanket. The group went to the top passenger deck to join others traveling to Andros Island and beyond.

Yvonne and David spied a seat for two passengers. As Yvonne sat down, David pointed to a stocky Greek dressed in gray slacks and a white short-sleeved shirt. "Yvonne, look. Do you see that man over there?"

"Yes, his name is Damian, or something like that. Remember, we saw him with Bill and Nicholas in the coffee shop across the street from the Acropolis." Yvonne smiled at the man. He responded to their stares with a cursory nod. Then he turned and walked in the opposite direction. The ferry jerked away from the dock, hitting the waves head on. In his effort to keep from falling sideways, the Greek held on to the wall railings and disappeared around the corner that led to the aft section of the boat as quickly as his stout frame would allow.

"That was odd," said David.

"It looked as if he was avoiding us."

"Maybe we weren't supposed to see him." David frowned.

"I wonder. Do you think he's here to see Bill and Nicholas?" Yvonne turned from the sea spray that was lightly misting her face and took a deep breath of the fresh salty air and spoke in a loud voice. "Could he be connected to some of the strange things that have happened? But if so—why in the world would he be? It doesn't make sense."

"Maybe we should talk to Bill about him." David squinted to minimize the ocean spray that was hitting him in the face. "Yvonne, let's move to a quieter spot. All this shouting back and forth, I'm afraid our voices will carry over the noise of the engines and the sloshing seawater. We don't want anyone overhearing what we have to say."

Yvonne rose with David from the fiberglass bench that lined the perimeter of the ferry. Their empty seats vanished as the passengers on the crowded bench spread out. "Okay, let's find Bill and Janice. I'll bet they're with Rosanna and Nicholas, as usual."

Working their way through the crowd toward the front of the ferry, David bumped into another familiar face. "George, what a surprise."

"Mr. Ludlow—David—how nice to see you again." George Mavrickos turned to smile at Yvonne.

"Yvonne, please allow me to introduce George Mavrickos. He is the brother of my business partner, Demetrius. George this is Yvonne Suarez our travel agent and tour leader."

"How do you do, Miss Suarez. It's a pleasure to meet you." George threw David an approving glance.

"It's a pleasure to meet you as well. Are you traveling to Andros Island too?" Yvonne inquired.

"Why, yes, I am."

"To what do we owe this pleasant coincidence?" asked David.

"Our family owns several jewelry and antique shops on various islands. I visit them on a regular basis to check on management and the finances."

"How nice that you have the opportunity to visit all these wonderful islands, even on business!" Yvonne grabbed David's arm as a swell rocked the ferry.

George continued with his story as if he had told it many times. "For many years our store in Athens was the only store we owned. It was passed down from father to son and so on. About fifteen years ago, my father decided to expand his business by purchasing small stores in the busiest sections of the more affluent islands. He knew that I would be going to college and wanted to insure my loyalty to the family business. It has proven to be a very good idea and a lucrative one as well."

"And what about your brother, David's partner, didn't he wish to be part of the family business?" Yvonne's eyes were wide with curiosity.

George looked at her quizzically.

"I'm sorry, that was none of my business—I shouldn't have asked that." Yvonne, embarrassed by her bluntness, glanced at David apologetically.

"Well...," said George. "Demetrius was the rebellious one as you Americans would say. He never wanted to follow along with what our father wanted. He always wanted to travel and see the world." George reached for a railing to steady himself as the boat lunged. David steadied Yvonne by grasping her shoulders protectively.

George continued talking about his brother. "Demetrius left home at an early age and traveled to North America. He roamed around there for a while and eventually moved to Miami where he worked in a popular Greek Restaurant—I can't recall the name. He finally decided to settle down and worked his way through the University of Miami earning a bachelor's degree in business administration. He couldn't hide from his upbringing forever. I think that our father's harping on the importance of a college education stayed with him. He grew up hearing that a good education was important and the only way to succeed in life."

"And that he has." David wondered if his concerns about Demetrius were misplaced. He had to give him credit for going out on his own to succeed rather than use his parents' support. "It was nice to see you, George. Perhaps we'll get a chance to stop into your store while we're on the island." Making their goodbyes, David steered Yvonne past George, and they continued working their way through the ship looking for Bill.

They found him forward in the bar. It was a small space furnished with metal tables and benches that were bolted to the floor. The windows on each side of the ship allowed sunlight and ocean breezes into the area. Bill and Nicholas were deep in discussion with their beer bottles half empty. Janice and Rosanna were sipping water and looking bored.

"Hi!" Yvonne's cheery voice surprised the foursome.

They each looked up speechless. "Do you mind if we join you for a few minutes?" David slid onto the end of the bench next to Bill.

Yvonne followed suit, sitting next to Janice. "How are you feeling, Janice?"

"Much better, thanks."

Yvonne turned her attention to Bill. "By the way, we ran into that friend of yours from Athens—you know—Damian. The man you and Nicholas were having coffee with the day Janice fell at the Acropolis. He's here on the ship."

"He acted rather strange when he saw us. He took off running the other way. Would you have any idea why he'd act so weird?" David watched Bill's face closely as he asked the question.

"How would I know? He's not exactly a friend of mine. Anyway, he's just someone that I've done business with in the past when I've visited Athens."

"Really? What kind of business is that?" asked David.

"It's—really—none of your business, but since you've asked so nicely I'll tell you." His sarcastic remark lost its impact when the boat heaved to one side as everyone grabbed for their drinks. When they were settled again, Bill continued. "He's an agent for an art dealer."

"It was funny the way he turned and ran the other way when he saw us. You're sure you have no idea why he'd do that?"

"That's what I said! How much longer before we dock in Andros anyway? Come on, Janice, let's get out of here." The look he gave his wife warned against an argument. The foursome got up and left the table before Yvonne had a chance to answer his question.

"Correct me if I'm wrong, but didn't it seem like we hit a nerve?" asked Yvonne.

"Either that or they just aren't into getting the third-degree from amateurs like us."

Ari entered the bar, saw Yvonne and approached her table. "We'll be docking at Gavrio in about fifteen minutes. Are we still on for a short tour of the island before checking in to the hotel?"

"Absolutely. We'll be in early enough, and once we're acclimated to the island, we'll know better where to explore when we're on our own. Thanks, Ari." Yvonne returned her tote to her arm, picked her clipboard up from her lap and hugged it to her chest. "I'll gather everyone as soon as we dock and we'll meet you at the bus."

David smiled inwardly when he recognized that Yvonne was armed and ready to continue as leader of the tour.

Beverly strolled on her own through Andros Island's Archaeological Museum. It held the prized statue of Hermes of Ándrhos, a 2nd century copy of Praxiteles' statue. Tired and overwhelmed from viewing so many ancient Greek artifacts, she changed course and headed to the Modern Art Museum. She'd read about it in the travel brochure she picked up in port. The story particularly interested her because it told about the wealthy Goulandris shipping family and how they'd donated the money to create the new museum. Wealth meant power to Beverly. She imagined a future when she could support such a cause and have it named after her. The Goulandris family had filled the museum with original works from modern day Greek and European artists. Not only did they wish to help support this unspoiled area, but they also wanted to provide culture for the island where they made their home on weekends. With a boat ride of less than three hours, it was the ideal island for many rich Athenians who would appreciate such culture.

After investigating the whimsical sculpture garden, she entered the museum and discovered, to her surprise, that she was not the only member of the group who had ventured there. Catching up to Bill, Rosanna, and Nicholas seemed like the friendly thing to do.

"What is it that you're admiring?" Turning abruptly to see who had interrupted their study, they each looked at Beverly as if she had three heads. "I'm sorry. Am I interrupting something?"

"No, of course not." A seductive smile formed on Rosanna's face, reminding Beverly of a cross between Mona Lisa and Sophia Loren. "We were caught up in the beauty of this small but powerful painting. It's by that new Italian artist who is so popular on the continent, Vincent Tedeschi." Rosanna stepped aside so that Beverly could move in closer to get a better view.

"I love the intense color contrasts, but I'm not sure what it's supposed to mean."

"Well you know art," said Bill. "It probably means whatever you want it to. I like the bold patterns and bright colors. Something like that would look great in my art collection at home."

"Unfortunately, Bill, these aren't for sale, so you'll have to find a print or a similar style from an unknown artist." Rosanna patted his arm.

"Everything's for sale at the right price." Bill chuckled and winked at Beverly.

Unusually charming for him, thought Beverly.

"Do you collect art too?" asked Nicholas.

"Me? No. I'm too busy earning a living to have the time for such luxuries." Beverly gave them a little wave and wandered away to admire the art on her own.

Yvonne watched the reddish glow cast by the island's dusty soil merge with the blue sky. Seated in lotus position on the balcony of her room at the Paradisos Hotel, her mind drifted to home.

Meditation is bound to settle my nerves. It's always helped in the past, but I can't help worrying, what's going on with Christy? When we talked on the phone this morning she was chatty until I asked if she'd heard from her dad. I pray that Gino hasn't pestered them to take her anywhere. I still have sole custody and until he finishes anger management and can prove that his temper is under control the courts won't allow him take her. Though, they did say he could have supervised visits, but only with me as the supervisor. I'm sure Mom and Dad realize—under no circumstances is she to go with Gino. You never know—he can be very convincing and charming when it serves his purpose. I've got to stop worrying like this. I'll remind them the next time I call. I sure miss Christy more than I thought I would. I hope she's having a good time with Nana and Papa. Yvonne held a picture of Christy smiling in her minds eye, then focused on her yoga breathing and the scene before her, blotting out all thoughts of home.

A cool moist breeze carried the smell of the ocean just a few hundred yards away. Breathing in the salt air, she thought. Taking some time for myself is important. That's what the therapist told me, and she's right. Why do I feel so guilty for leaving Christy? I have no choice—it's my job after all. I do have a good support system. She couldn't be in better hands. This time alone will help me. I know it will. I'll stay in control of this tour and my life.

Yvonne performed a few of her favorite yoga poses and her focus improved. She finished by meditating on the ocean waves, breathing in and out with the motion as they hit the beach and receded. Feeling centered and strong, she was unaware of the look of longing on David's face as he watched her from his balcony a few rooms away.

Urgent knocking on her door drew Yvonne from her trance. Slowly, she pulled herself out of her cross-legged position. She straightened her legs, shook them to bring the blood circulating back to her feet and ankles, stood up in one easy movement and went to answer the door.

"Who is it?"

"Yvonne, it's me. Janice."

Unlatching the lock and opening the door, Yvonne ushered her in. "What's wrong? You look awful. Has something happened?"

"I think they're trying to kill me!"

"Janice, please calm down. Who? Who's trying to kill you?"

"Bill—my husband and Rosanna—and—and Nicholas. They're all in it together."

"In it together? In what together?" asked Yvonne.

"I don't know, but something is very wrong and they're trying to kill me." Janice's face was distorted with fear.

"Here, sit down in this chair. Take a deep breath and tell me what's happened. Why do you think they're trying to kill you?" Yvonne crossed over to the mini-bar, poured a glass of water and handed it to Janice.

Her eyes were red and rimmed with dark circles. Her hands shook as she took a sip and tried to get control of her nerves. "They wanted to go to the Modern Museum on the main square. They'd heard that Tedeschi, a popular artist, was displaying some of his valuable art. I thought it would be good to visit the museum. I thought it might help restore some good feelings toward my husband and our friends. Things haven't been right since my fall at the Acropolis. Instead they urged me to stay in the hotel. I tried to argue that I was fine, but Bill insisted that I needed rest. Rosanna reminded me about fainting at the museum in Athens and said she'd give me one of her tranquilizers so I could sleep. I don't like them. The tranquilizers make me feel like a zombie, but eventually Bill and Rosanna wore me down, and I took one. They waited until I fell asleep—at least I think so, it's all foggy now—and then they left." Janice took a short breath and another sip of water. "I woke when I felt a chilly wind blowing in from the window, and the room started to darken. I was about to turn on my other side with my back to the window so I could go back to sleep when I noticed this horrible dark mass moving across the bedspread toward my ankle. It was the most horrible looking spider I've ever seen." Janice's chin trembled and she fought back tears. "I screamed and rolled out of bed as fast as I could, but it felt like I moved in slow motion."

"Were you hurt? Did it bite you?" Yvonne looked closely at Janice for any tell-tale signs of a spider bite.

"The maid in the hall heard me. She knocked on the door. When I let her in, she saw the spider and hit it with her broom. She said it was a poisonous spider native to these Cycladic islands. She'd never seen one in the hotel before and couldn't believe it was there since she carefully cleaned away all spider webs and insects. Don't you see? Bill planted it there to bite me while I slept."

"Why do you think he would do such a thing?"

"That's just it. I don't know. There's some sort of secret that they're keeping. I don't know what it is."

A loud knock on the door interrupted Yvonne's next question. "Yvonne, it's me. Bill Armstrong. Have you seen my wife? She's not in our room." Yvonne opened the door.

"There's no need to bang on the door, Bill. Janice and I are just having a visit. It seems you left her to go sightseeing, and she was lonesome." Yvonne looked him in the eye and watched as he flinched at her words. "We're not quite finished with our visit. She'll head back to your room in a short while." Smiling, she closed the door in his face with distinct satisfaction.

"He's going to be angry with me. There's no telling what he'll do next." Janice fidgeted in her chair.

"Do you have any proof that he placed the spider in your room? Where would he have gotten it and when?

"I don't know. He has friends and connections everywhere. He could have had help. Do you remember the day that I fell at the Acropolis?"

"Yes?"

"I felt a hand placed right in the center of my back. Just as I was going to turn to see who it was, someone pushed me. The next thing I knew, I was falling head over heels down the steps. It scared me so badly I can't think straight. Why would anyone do such a thing? I talked myself into believing it was an accident because the truth is too scary."

Janice sat up straighter in the chair and leaned closer to Yvonne who was sitting on the edge of the bed. "Over the years, Bill has occasionally been thoughtless toward me, but lately he's been worse. It's as if he can't stand the sight of me, and I don't understand why." Janice tried to fight back the tears, but they rolled down her cheeks anyway. "I'm afraid to be around him, but I'm even more afraid to let him know." She sobbed.

Yvonne dampened a washcloth from the bathroom and handed it to her. Janice held the cool cloth over her face. Yvonne remained quiet and after a few minutes, Janice handed the cloth back to Yvonne. "I feel better now." Her eyes were still red and puffy, but she smiled. "I'm so sorry to have troubled you with this. I'm embarrassed I've come running to you like a cry-baby." Janice sniffled once.

"Don't be silly. You have good reason to be scared. Believe me. I know what it's like to live with someone who is abusive. You know—this almost sounds like he's trying to gaslight you."

"Gaslight? You mean like in that old movie where Charles Boyer plays a man who does things to make his wife think she's crazy?"

"Yes, that's exactly what I mean. You know, the way Bill tries to make it seem like you are ill and need rest, all the while feeding you pills so that you won't be up to par mentally as he pretends to be the doting husband. Also, how is anyone going to prove that someone actually placed a spider in your hotel room? That's the kind of thing most people would brush off or say that you imagined. No one would believe that your own husband would do such a thing.

"I don't understand why he's doing all these mean things." Janice cleared her throat, still congested from crying. "I better go back to our room or he'll get even more frustrated and angry with me." She stood on shaky legs.

"You should stay with me. I'd be more than happy to share my room with you. After all, he may try something again."

"How would that look? I'd hate to think what he might do if I embarrassed him like that. No, I'll have to brave it out until we get home to Ft. Lauderdale, then—then I'm going to leave him."

I hope you can make it that far, thought Yvonne as she searched Janice's eyes for strength. "Don't let anyone convince you to take more sleeping pills. You'll need to have all your faculties about you to protect yourself from any other incidents. Please remember, I'm here if you need help." Yvonne gave Janice a hug before seeing her out.

Yvonne dialed the phone. "David. Hi. We need to talk. Can you meet me out front for a walk along the beach—now?"

"What's the hurry? Is everything okay?"

"It's about Janice. Please, just meet me. I'll fill you in then."

"Okay. I'll be right there."

David waited on the porch. He noticed she'd put on clean white shorts, a red knit top and shoes. Her hair was in a ponytail. He was reminded of a cheer-leader entering the field before a game, and he wondered how he'd ever keep up with her nonstop energy. "Which direction would you like to go?"

"Let's walk away from town. We'll be less likely to encounter anyone we know." Yvonne headed across the street and onto the red sand beach.

David grasped her by the arm. "It will be difficult to talk if we walk so fast."

"Okay." Yvonne shrugged, took a breath to relax and slowed her pace. "I'm worried about Janice. She thinks her husband and her friends are trying to kill her."

"Whew—what makes her think that?"

"There have been some incidents starting with the fall at the Acropolis. She thinks she was pushed. Today Bill, Rosanna and Nicholas insisted she stay at the hotel while they went to the new museum. They coerced her into taking a sedative and while she slept a poisonous spider crawled in bed with her. Janice thinks Bill left it there to creep up and bite her.

"I know it's far-fetched, but I think she has cause for concern. We've witnessed him verbally abusing her, and I get a feeling there's something going on with his friendship with Rosanna and Nicholas that doesn't quite add up."

"What do you propose we do about it?" asked David.

"That's a good question. Janice wants to leave it alone until she gets home to Fort Lauderdale. Then she plans to leave him. But, I don't know—that might be too late? Any suggestions?" Yvonne gave him an earnest look.

Being needed by her gave him a good feeling. He wanted to be there for her. Though he wasn't sure exactly why he felt that way. Maybe he had some sort of rescue complex or needed to be a hero. Maybe he missed the idea of having someone in his life to share the good times and the bad. Whatever it was, he'd better slow his pace or he'd blow it with her.

"What do we know so far?" David's brow wrinkled. "We know that Bill wasn't around when she fell, but Rosanna was. We know that no one was present while she slept; yet, they kept her drugged while they spent their time strolling around a museum waiting for her to be bitten by a spider."

"Put that way, it sounds crazy." Yvonne kicked sand with the tip of her shoe in frustration.

"We'll keep a closer eye on Janice to make sure she has no more accidents." David found a large rock to lean against. He could see sail boats drifting slowly in the distance. It had a calming effect on him.

Yvonne leaned on the rock next to David. She stared at the horizon. After a minute of silence, David looked at Yvonne's profile and gathered his nerve. He took hold of her shoulders and drew her to him. Yvonne gave in to the moment. It felt good being wrapped in his arms, safe, secure, just what she needed.

His kiss was light and tentative. She relaxed into it and pressed against him. His kiss hardened. She kissed him back. She felt free. He pulled her in tighter. His hands moved down her spine and settled on her hips. The musky taste of him mingled with the smell of fresh salt air. Out of breath, she pushed him away, afraid she was losing herself. She opened her eyes and saw lust mixed with worry and confusion on his face. "I think we should head back to the inn," mumbled Yvonne.

"Now? But why?"

"I can't—I can't lose control of myself like this, not while I'm supposed to be in charge of this tour. I'm sorry David. I should have stopped you before..." Yvonne turned and started walking back to the inn, her shoes sinking into the sand, slowing her every step.

Except for the Armstrongs and the Fontinellis, all members of the group gathered in the dining room. "I do declare, we found a lovely beach between Gavrio and Batsi," Cynthia spoke to all.

"It sure was crowded with hot bods," said Mark.

Cynthia nudged him in the ribs. "Crowded, yes, but I'm not so sure that all the bodies were hot. I surely saw some not so hot.

"Honey, what would you know anyway? You and Ari were totally absorbed in each other. I'm surprised you didn't drown while you were in the water, sucking up each other's air supply the way you did." Mark rolled his eyes, puckered his lips and wiggled his head to give the worst impression possible. Cynthia turned red and lowered her eyes as if concentrating on the moussaka layered artistically on her plate.

"Yes, it was a great day to relax. I'm excited about our tour to the Byzantine monasteries tomorrow." Evelyn placed her napkin in her lap. "I can't believe that I've finally had the opportunity to see so many ancient ruins. It gives me goose-bumps to think we're spending even a small amount of time in such ancient historical places. It brings me back to my high-school days. I always loved the stories in the Odyssey and the Iliad."

"You do realize that those mythological characters weren't real?" asked Ari.

"Well, of course I do, but they wrote about actual places, and we are getting the real history as we go along too, aren't we?" Evelyn lifted her journal in the air and pointed to an open page showing notes taken as they toured. "I'm not going to miss anything or forget anything for a very long time."

"Put your book down, Evelyn, they're just pulling your leg." Richard took a sip of water. He wanted her to enjoy every moment, not worried about what others might think.

David reached for a hearty piece of country bread. "I can certainly understand why the ancient Greeks thought that the gods were spawned in these islands. The spectacular beauty from mountain-top to sea-shore is a magnificent contrast in nature."

Yvonne studied the enormous room with white pillars, white decor and large picture windows that showed off blue skies and green mountains dotted with the white architecture of Greece. It all added to the cheery ambience of the meal. Yvonne surveyed the table. David conversed easily with the group at the table. He seemed relaxed and happy. Why is my stomach tied in knots every time I look at him? I hope he doesn't think that I am leading him on or being a tease. I'm glad it's a small group tonight.

Yvonne noticed Missy and Todd spoke little during the meal. They've certainly cooled off toward each other since their quarrel in Delphi. I wonder where Bill and Janice, and Rosanna and Nicholas are. Perhaps they're eating in town. I hope Janice is okay, but there's not much I can do about it. Beverly's absent too—maybe she wanted a quiet evening alone—whatever. Hopefully things will wrap up early, so I can escape to my room and think. Perhaps it's the wine or the food, but I'm feeling more relaxed than I have all day.

David was last at the table. "How about joining me for a nightcap?"

I should probably say no, but that pure look of pleasure at having me all to himself—how can I resist? Am I being selfish? Why not enjoy the company of an attractive man? Who am I hurting this far from home? Well, I'll figure it out tomorrow—tonight I'll have fun.

ANDROS ISLAND

DAY 9

"**D**avid, quick, wakeup," whispered Yvonne. "You need to get back to your room before people start stirring." She shook his shoulder with a gentle push of her hand.

David awakened with a smile, rolled over and grabbed Yvonne, wrapping his arm and one long leg around her.

Yvonne pushed him gently away.

"Now is that any way to start your morning? Shoving a guy out of bed like he's a rascal caught cheating." David grinned, mischief written all over his face.

"Be serious. Last night was—well... it was—you caught me off guard. I never should have..."

"Never should have what? Been human?" David's grin faded. "I thought you wanted me as much as I wanted you."

Yvonne held her breath. "I'm sorry, David, I did—I mean I do, but this is not the right time. It was the after dinner drink and the romantic night. You can be quite charming, you know." Yvonne got out of bed holding a sheet around her, grabbed her robe and ducked into the bathroom. When she returned to the room from her shower, David was gone.

She felt let down and disappointed, but knew it was for the best. She didn't have time in her life for the complications a man and an affair would bring.

While Ari drove the mini-bus to their first destination, Evelyn Malcolm read aloud to the group from the Insight Guides to the

Greek Islands: "'The Monastery of Zoodhohos Pighi or 'Life-giving Spring' also claims to be on a sacred spot situated in the hills northeast of Batsi. The monastery is looked after by a diminishing group of nuns guarding a library of precious sacred manuscripts.' Wouldn't it be exciting to read those manuscripts?"

Ari kept both hands on the wheel, glanced in the rear view mirror and interrupted Evelyn. "We'll bypass that site for the more spectacular Byzantine monastery Panahrándou, 'wholly immaculate.' It's over a thousand years old and sits above a beautiful green valley town called Massariá. After that we'll have lunch at Andros' most popular beach in Batsi."

Yvonne heard Bill snoring in the back of the minibus. She turned around to take a look at him. That's strange. Rosanna and Nicholas are dozing too in spite of the noise emanating from Bill. It's early. Why are they all so tired? Janice looks rested, and gracias Dios, I don't see any bruises on her.

Yvonne's attention was diverted from Bill when Beverly began talking to David loud enough for all to hear.

"I tell you, David, that modern art museum in Andros is amazing. To see fine art like the Tedeschi oils in such a small museum so far from a major city is quite remarkable."

What's remarkable thought Yvonne is that Beverly can always get David's attention. He's a good listener. I'm sure he's only being polite, but she wants everyone else to hear what a grand time she had wandering around town on her own. Not too subtle about the fact that she doesn't need to be with a man to enjoy herself. I wonder who she thinks she's kidding?

"We've arrived," said Ari. He pulled into a dirt parking lot alongside several other minivans and cars. "From here it will be a three-hour round trip walking tour. Take your time. I want everyone to enjoy themselves without strain." Small clusters of tourists could be seen walking up the forested path toward the monastery.

"Would you look at that?" Todd began taking pictures of the monastery. "It reminds me of what Camelot must have looked like in the distance." He snapped another picture. "Look at the ancient outbuildings and that massive white cathedral. What a brilliant spectacle set against the dark green forest and blue skies." Missy and the others gathered around Todd. Beverly, Bill and Nicholas followed suit and began snapping photos.

Missy whispered to Cynthia. "The silly idealist, it's just like Todd to see Camelot in some old Greek buildings. I must admit, he did get everyone excited. I see now why his boss says he's a super salesman."

Cynthia nodded. "Darlin', I'd settle for an idealist any day of the week. I think he's sweet."

Missy shrugged. "Oh, believe me he is... sometimes too sweet."

Noisy whinnying and a strong smell of manure caught Mark's attention. He walked toward a weathered wood fence enclosing a good size patch of dirt. Six donkeys wore worn leather saddles, ready to carry tourists up the long pathway to the monastery. The sign read 20 US dollars. Mark called out. "Look, Cynthia! They're renting donkeys."

Cynthia and the others strolled over to pet the donkeys' heads stretching over the fence. They stood calmly enjoying the attention.

Ari hailed everyone to start up the path.

"What do you think? Shall we rent one?" Mark pointed to the caretaker who was collecting money from a young couple who had come from the car park.

"No thanks, Sugar. I'd like some exercise. We've done enough sitting on the bus." She headed off to catch up with the others who were starting up the walkway toward the monastery.

"Yeah, sure, you just want to stick close to you-know-who." Reluctantly, Mark turned and followed along with the group.

It was slow going along the path as they encountered ruts and dips. The rocky road was surrounded by landscape overgrown with scruffy shrubs, native olive and fig trees and other tropical vegetation. Pungent smells from wild orange and lemon trees mingled with the hot dry air teasing their noses.

Remnants of vineyards from ancient times mixed in with the vegetation that grew denser as they drew closer to their destination. His senses overwhelmed, Richard commented, "It feels like we're walking back in time through the Garden of Eden." He held on to Evelyn's hand tightly. Though short of breath, he was excited. Her enthusiasm was rubbing off on him.

"Ah... the sweet smell of nature." David smiled and looked behind to see if the hike up the mountain was having the same effect on Yvonne. He caught her watching him. She looked away just as Janice fell in step beside her. Janice looked around nervously. David assumed she was worried Bill was watching.

"Yvonne, I have something to tell you. Can we meet privately later?"

"Of course, we can take a stroll along the beach at Batsi Bay after lunch to digest our food. How does that sound?"

Janice frowned.

"Don't worry. Bring it up very casually that you'd like to take a walk, and I'll ask to join you. I'm sure Bill won't suspect a thing."

"All right, fine. I'll see you later then." Janice withdrew, strolling along in her own world of thoughts.

Yvonne picked up her pace to catch up with David. "Hi there, I have a meeting scheduled with Janice. It seems she has something important to tell me."

"Hmm, I wonder what it is." David didn't query further.

"I guess I'll find out soon enough. Maybe it'll shed some light on what's going on with Bill and the Fontinellis."

"Maybe." David picked up his pace.

He's still mad at me, thought Yvonne. Maybe I should tell him I don't need his help after all. That would give him an easy out.

Yvonne kept up with David. "Have you noticed? We've had no dangerous incidents in the last two days? I hope this means everything's fine, and we've worried for nothing..." Short of breath, the words raced out of her mouth losing steam at the end.

David stopped and looked directly at Yvonne. "I wouldn't get my hopes up." He turned his gaze back to the path. They continued walking in uncomfortable silence until they caught up with the group.

Ari stopped and gave everyone a few minutes to catch their breath. He took the opportunity to observe the group, noting they were particularly quiet. After a few minutes, he waved to all to follow him, and he continued up the path. "In about five more minutes, we'll be at the entrance of Panahrándou."

The brilliance of the stark white monastery awed the sightseers as they moved from the wooded path into the bright sunlight. The contrast between the mountain, the shining sky and the bright edifice caused everyone to squint. Ari was the first to speak. "Once inside you are free to wander and explore at your own pace. Please, remember this is a sacred place of worship. Be quiet and respectful.

In the narthex, the center of the church, Yvonne overheard Todd whispering. "Missy, you can't still be upset with me. I've apologized 'til I'm blue in the face. You can't blame a guy for trying to have a baby with the woman he loves." Todd's blond hair was tousled and his cowlick made him look like an unruly little boy.

"I can if you try to orchestrate it without my consent. Shush." Todd's boyish charm used to be one of Missy's favorite things about him, but now it irritated her. Missy separated from Todd, her concentration on the intricate architecture and beauty within the monastery instead.

Yvonne watched Todd follow after Missy. She could see that he hadn't given up his cause.

"Look. I said it won't happen again. Won't you just pretend it never happened? After all we're supposed to be on our second honeymoon. What will people think if you hardly give me the time of day or much less, simple respect?"

"Let's take this conversation outside and finish it once and for all." Missy looked around and spotted a door with a discreet exit sign on a small stand.

Yvonne watched Missy exit through a side door leading to a courtyard with Todd on her heels. She resisted the urge to follow them. I will not become one of those busy bodies who spy on people. I'm in church after all.

"Respect, you want respect? Then stop acting like a big baby who can't get his way and understand that I have needs too. My needs do not include being pregnant at a time when my career has just begun to take off. It's important to me—to us!" Missy put her hands on her hips.

"How do you think we were able to take a second honeymoon? We can travel more if we aren't tied down with children. Think about it, Todd. We're still young, and we need to do these things before we're saddled with the extra responsibility of raising a family." Missy was red-faced by the time she finished her tirade, and she felt the wind go out of her like a balloon. When she breathed in again, she felt a surge of pity for Todd who might be losing his dream. "Come on," she said. "Hold my hand. We can walk the rest of the way together."

Todd took her hand, a bitter taste caught in the lump in his throat.

When Todd and Missy returned they were holding hands but not speaking, each focusing on a different aspect of the cathedral. Yvonne hoped for their sake and the sake of the tour, they'd begun to resolve their problem.

Later on the outskirts of Batsi Bay, the group dined on local fish and Greek salads. During lunch they chatted little, content to watch the activity on the beach where the young and fit water-sports lovers wind-surfed in the distance.

"Look at the way those colorful sails glide along catching the waves? It's like art coming to life." All heads turned in the direction Evelyn was pointing.

Yvonne surveyed her group. Janice could be beautiful if she didn't worry all the time. What's Beverly whispering in David's ear? He's laughing too hard. If he's trying to make me jealous, it's working. No. He's not that childish. I've got to stop mooning over him like a school girl for Pete's sake."

"I think I'll take a stroll on the beach." Janice spoke to no one in particular.

"Janice, darling, do you think you should? You've had a strenuous morning and I wouldn't want you to overdo." Rosanna placed her hand on Janice's forearm.

"I'm feeling fine. I wish you'd stop worrying so much about me!" Janice jerked her arm from Rosanna's grasp.

Yvonne signaled the waiter for her bill. "I'll walk with you, Janice. That is, if you don't mind the company."

"I'd love the company." Janice got up without excusing herself to Bill and the others. She walked to the beach-side exit of the café and waited for Yvonne to join her.

Cynthia paid her bill. "I'm going to find a spot on the beach to stretch out and soak up some sun." "Anyone else feel like coming with me?" She put on her sunglasses, picked up her tote stuffed with her towel and suntan lotion and rose from her chair.

Mark, Todd and Missy followed Cynthia's lead. Ari glanced at those remaining at the table, hesitated for a moment, then followed the younger group.

"I for one would enjoy staying right here where I can watch the world go by." Evelyn opened her journal and retrieved her pen from her tote bag.

"Good," said Richard. He looked as if he were ready to nod off.

"That suits me." Bill remained where he was and ordered a bottle of wine to share with the remaining tablemates.

"Care for a stroll on the beach?" Beverly was trying to be nonchalant, but David could see she was anxious.

"Sure, why not." He shrugged, stood up and held her chair as she rose. He led her in the same direction that Yvonne and Janice had gone.

Everywhere they looked, people were sunning themselves while children played at the water's edge. The colorful array of blankets and umbrellas made for a fun and festive atmosphere. David smiled thinking about Yvonne in bed last night. She'd surprised him. He'd expected her to take things slowly, but she was impatient at best and totally uninhibited in her lusting. He was sure she'd enjoyed herself. Of course, that's why she's so afraid. I need to make her feel safe—safe enough to be herself with me.

Beverly tightened her grip on David's arm. "David, you seem happy. Are you enjoying our stroll?"

The sound of Beverly's voice brought David back to reality. He almost blushed but held tight to his smile. "It's a beautiful day, isn't it?"

"Janice, what was it you wanted to tell me?" Yvonne stopped and looked around for a dry spot before she sat in the sand and looked skyward at the noisy gulls.

Janice sat down next to her and took a deep breath of salt air. She spoke quietly as she gazed at the receding ocean waves. "My suspicions are confirmed. He is having an affair, and that's probably why he wants me dead." She pulled up her knees and hugged them to her chest.

"Did he admit it to you?"

"No. He didn't have to. I saw him sneak out of our room in the middle of the night. He was gone for two hours from one to three." She took a breath. "Why else would he leave our bed like that? I've been such a fool!" Her eyes welled with tears in spite of her anger.

Yvonne got to her feet. "Let's walk some more." A warm breeze blew salty moist air into their lungs.

Janice stood. "Of course it's Rosanna. Those two are thick as thieves, together all the time, laughing at their own private jokes. I'm such an idiot! Why didn't I see it sooner?" Janice took another breath. "I wonder if Nicholas knows? It all makes sense now. That's why they've been drugging me. Last night I refused to take a sleeping pill so I wasn't sound asleep like I've been other nights."

Janice looked directly at Yvonne. "How long do you think it's been going on—his sneaking around in the middle of the night?"

Yvonne didn't know how to answer Janice. She steered her in another direction. "I'm worried about you. If you confront him, it may get ugly."

"What should I do? Play dumb? I'm certainly good at being dumb, but I'm afraid I'm not meant to make it home. I'm afraid I'm supposed to have some sort of accident while traveling. That way it will be difficult to prove they murdered me."

"Janice, first of all, you've got to stop belittling yourself. You're not dumb. I know I probably shouldn't say this because I'm just your travel agent, but I've been where you are. I've seen first hand how being the victim in an abusive relationship can erode one's self-esteem. Bill is unbelievably thoughtless and inconsiderate towards you. Everyone can see that." Yvonne stopped walking and faced Janice. "You're right to be frightened."

"From now on you've got to be extremely careful about how you react to Bill. I want you to promise me you'll be careful. You know

I'm here for you and will watch Bill's every move. David and I will protect you." Yvonne hesitated. "Please don't be upset, but I've taken David into my confidence about this." Janice's eyes widened. "Don't worry. You can trust him to keep quiet. He suspects there's something fishy going on with Bill's relationship with Rosanna and Nicholas too. He's agreed to help me keep you safe." Yvonne looked behind them and saw David walking with Beverly. Her stomach muscles tightened, and she quickly turned away.

"Just keep your thoughts to yourself and don't let on that you suspect he's cheating on you, not even to Rosanna. Do you think you can handle this?"

"I don't know if I can." Janice hung her head.

"You must. You need to be strong and smart. I know you can do it—and don't forget—you're not alone." Yvonne gave Janice a quick hug. "You should get some rest. You're going to need to keep up your strength both physically and emotionally." Yvonne turned and started ed walking back. Janice followed.

"Yvonne. Thank you. I don't know what I'd do without your help."

"No need to thank me. Everything's going to be fine." Yvonne said a silent prayer that it would be all right.

They passed David and Beverly coming the other way. While Yvonne smiled at the duo, Janice barely nodded at them. Yvonne's eyes locked on David's. She hoped to convey that trouble was brewing.

David couldn't resist the pleading look on Yvonne's face. He was worried about her involvement in Janice and Bill's marital problems. She had enough responsibilities without adding marriage counselor to her list. He would keep an eye on things concerning the Armstrongs and the Fontinellis himself.

When David returned to the hotel, he headed to Yvonne's room. He knocked gently on her door. "Yvonne, it's me, David. May I come in?"

"Hi, David, I was afraid you wouldn't come."

"I hope it's not too late."

"No. I've been waiting. I need to talk to you about Janice—if you're still interested in helping me." She turned and he followed her into the room. Yvonne seated herself in a chair by the side table that doubled as a desk and bar. She motioned toward the only comfortable chair in the room. "Would you like a glass of water? Sorry, it's all I've got."

"Yes. Please." David could see that she was avoiding physical contact with him. He had a nice view of the small balcony and the night sky. He could hear and smell the ocean, but it blended into the darkness, invisible. He sat forward in his chair, shrinking the space between them, ready to listen.

Yvonne poured a small glass of water and handed it to David. "Janice is convinced that Bill is having an affair."

Yvonne filled him in on her earlier discussion with Janice. "What do you think? Any ideas about what she should do?"

"I agree she should keep her thoughts to herself. Let's hope Bill isn't stupid enough to flaunt his affair in her face. This could put a real damper on the tour." David shifted in the chair, leaned back and closed his eyes.

"David, don't worry about the tour. I can see you're tired. Forgive me for dragging you into all this."

"I'm not tired, just thinking. Even if Janice is right and Bill is having an affair, I still think there's more to it. Why not just divorce her? Why bring her here to Greece and plan a murder or accident? There must be some reason why he can't just divorce her and be done with it."

David sat up again. "We need more information. See if you can talk to Janice again. Find out if she's worth a substantial amount of money. Maybe he'll inherit if she dies—or maybe she's seen something or knows something that could cause him legal problems."

"That makes sense. I'll talk to her tomorrow, but we're leaving for Mýkonos in the morning. It's going to be a busy day. It might be difficult to get her alone."

"You'll do whatever needs to be done." David stood up. He looked at the water glass in his hand, took a drink and handed it to Yvonne. Their finger tips touched briefly. Caught off guard by the warmth of his hand and the close proximity of his body, Yvonne jerked away the glass, splashing herself with water. David turned to leave.

"David. Wait. I wish I could tell you why— I can't get involved in an affair. I will explain—just not right now."

"There's no need to explain. I'll be here when you're ready to talk." David looked directly into her eyes.

A warm glow came over Yvonne. Could he see clear to her soul?

He smiled, kissed her on the cheek and wished her sweet dreams.

She stood there staring at the door, for how long she wasn't sure.

In bed she dreamt about a glorious vacation to a sunny resort somewhere in the Caribbean. Christy was there with Mom and Dad, and David was there acting as tour guide. He was showing them mountains and waterfalls and all the sunniest places to see. He only cautioned them from time to time to stay away from the beach where the sharks swim.

MYKONOS ISLAND

DAY 10

"**G**reek authorities are puzzled by the theft of a painting by popular Italian artist, Vincent Tedeschi, stolen from the Modern Art Museum on Andros Island. Museum security discovered the painting missing yesterday when they made their morning security check." David nicked himself with the travel razor when he heard the newscaster reporting the theft on CNN.

"Damn!" He reached for a piece of tissue to stop the bleeding and then turned up the volume on the television. The reporter continued, "The museum thefts have the police baffled and they are talking about bringing in Interpol to help with the recent cases, despite the political dissension between the two organizations." The newscaster went on to talk about the theft at the museum in Athens and the murder that had taken place a few days before. A rift between Greek authorities and Interpol had existed for many years, and it was a sign of desperation that they should be included in this investigation. Many suspected that the theft-ring, if there was one, had come from Western Europe.

David finished dressing and hurried to Yvonne's room.

"Good morning, David. What brings you by so early?" Yvonne peeked out from behind the door grasping her robe closed.

"We need to talk. Have you heard the news this morning?"

"No. I haven't turned the TV on. Why?"

"You better get dressed so I can concentrate on the problem at hand." David looked at her cleavage where the robe had slipped open.

Yvonne blushed and picked up her underclothes and the outfit she had set out for the day and retreated to the bathroom. When she was out of sight, David stepped into the room and closed the door.

A few minutes later Yvonne came out of the bathroom dressed in navy slacks and a white t-shirt with red and navy trim. She seated herself on the desk chair and slipped on her sneakers.

"Okay, David, what's up?"

"The Modern Museum on Andros Island was robbed. It happened night before last."

"Oh—that is—you don't think that has anything to do with us, do you?"

"I'm not sure—it seems a strange coincidence. First, a theft the morning we arrived in Athens, and now this."

"But what makes you think they are connected?"

"The newscaster says the Greek Police think they're connected. They even talked about including Interpol to help with the case."

"I still don't see what that has to do with us." Yvonne ignored the situation as she donned her watch and earrings, then spritzed her wrists and neck with a lightly scented perfume. She followed up by packing the items away in her travel case. When finished she sighed, wishing she could pack away the problems on her tour as well.

David watched her organized movements, thinking she moved with the grace of a ballet dancer. He also thought she was not taking the theft seriously. "Don't you think it's suspicious that the theft occurred the same night that Bill made his midnight disappearance?"

"I was afraid that might be where you were heading. No. I assumed he was having an affair with Rosanna, as Janice said. But now that you mention it—what if they're all in it together? Bill, Rosanna and Nicholas?" David had Yvonne's undivided attention. "That would explain why they left Janice alone at the hotel and visited the museum together."

"That's exactly what I thought." He watched as Yvonne took a seat on the edge of the bed.

"What should we do next? Should we call the police and report it?"

"I think it's too early to call the police. We need to get proof that they are involved, and we'd better be careful not to let them know we suspect them of the thefts. If they are involved, they could be dangerous."

Yvonne hesitated, speaking her thoughts out loud. "Maybe I could ask Janice to search their room and luggage. For what, I'm not sure. When we get to Mýkonos Janice will have little opportunity to do it unless Bill goes out for a tour and leaves her alone again. I'm afraid she'll insist on me doing the search. That's a problem. I have strong misgivings about snooping on my clients or rifling through their belongings, but I have never had to worry about thieves and murderers before either." As she thought through the plan, Yvonne stood and began gathering her luggage, ready to continue with the tour. "It will be harder to search the Fontinellis' room, but with any luck we'll find some evidence of the theft before that become's necessary."

"I don't know, Yvonne, that's risky, don't you think?" David resisted the urge to take hold of her shoulders and pull her close.

"It shouldn't be. The big problem will be having the opportunity. We are going to be pretty busy during our stay there." Yvonne reached for the door handle. "We'd better go to breakfast. Ari will be ready to get us on the bus to the ferry in a short while." She had morphed into the efficient tour leader once again.

Yvonne had ample time to go over the afternoons activities in her mind during the high speed catamaran ride from Andros Island. She watched the gulls fly around looking for fish to fill their bellies and the waves of water rise up, catching the light cast from the sunshine. The turquoise ocean sparkled as she breathed in salty air. Vivid memories to cherish, she thought. The catamaran made one brief stop at Tinos Island and arrived in Mýkonos before noon in time for a sunny half-day city tour led by Ari. The small bus rumbled along narrow white-washed streets crowded with the traffic of locals and tourists. They stopped to admire and photograph the town mascot, a pelican named Pètros perched on his favorite fishing pier. They were treated to scenery featuring several popular nude beaches. For the historically inclined, the inland village of Áno Merá was the site of the Tourliani Monastery renowned for its red domes and ornate marble tower.

On the last leg of the city-tour, Ari gave the group helpful hints to plan their evening. "Yvonne has planned a dinner with Greek music and entertainment for the evening. "One of the best chefs in all of Greece is Chef Yiánnis Argýriou at La Taverne, located in the hotel where we'll be staying." Ari glanced in the rear view mirror at Cynthia. "Mýkonos is known for its colorful nightlife, so after dinner, those of you who have much stamina should visit Chora Town by night. I will be glad to drive you to some of my favorite clubs." He deposited the group at Cavo Tagoo hotel just north of Chora Town by about 550 yards.

Cavo Tagoo was the highpoint of all their hotel stays. Yvonne intentionally booked this lavish hotel set in the side of a hill overlooking the Aegean Sea to offer relaxing luxury, a break from the hectic pace of touring.

During check-in, Yvonne watched the group ooh and aah at the spacious clean lines of the bright white and yellow Myconian décor. This five-star hotel was the one splurge in their tour package. The architecture of the building enhanced the water elements of the pool and the sea beyond, creating two serene horizons that appeared as one. Both could be seen from large windows in the hotel or the cabanas by the pool. Yvonne thought of Janice and all she'd been through during the tour. She hoped this sunny façade would brighten her spirits.

After dinner, Ari led Cynthia, Mark, Missy and Todd to the night clubs while the others stayed to enjoy the entertainment offered by the hotel. Yvonne watched while Beverly urged David onto the dance floor where other hotel guests were falling into line with the festive Greek dancers. *She's so obvious trying to seduce him with those moves. Poor David, he looks embarrassed, but he's too much the gentleman to leave her up there alone.*

Yvonne shifted her focus to Janice who seemed more relaxed and happy than before. She wondered what had changed. *If she could get her alone, she'd ask her.* Nicholas asked Rosanna to dance, so that left Bill, Janice, Evelyn, Richard and Yvonne as spectators.

"May I have this dance?" Yvonne jumped in surprise when she felt a breath on her ear.

"David, I'm not sure we should, you—know... I don't want to upset Beverly."

"She doesn't have exclusive rights to me. You deserve to have some fun too." He slid his hand down her arm and took her hand with a gentle tug. She allowed him to lead her on to the dance floor.

I'm so easy, she thought. Yvonne felt him relax as they merged into the Greek line dance. He no longer had the strained look on his face that had been so evident when dancing with Beverly.

David collapsed into his chair. "Whew! I haven't had so much exercise in years."

"I hope you aren't overdoing it." She was worried. Would it stress his heart?

He gave her a silly grin. "Yvonne, don't worry, I promise not to drop dead on you."

"Please don't joke about that. That would be awful, but more than that, I'd miss you." She grinned.

"Well now we're getting somewhere." His smug smile caused Yvonne to give him a light kick under the table.

"Beverly, girl, you might want to wipe that look of pure hatred off your face before your jealousy becomes apparent to everyone." Mark watched her from across the table.

"Why, Mark, I'm sure I don't know what you're talking about. I'm having a delightful time." A false smile revealed a perfect set of upper and lower teeth.

"Sure, whatever," Mark grinned. "I guess I'm not the only one striking out on this tour." He whispered under his breath, but Beverly heard enough. Her phony smile disappeared, replaced with a cold stare that sent a chill down Mark's spine.

The next morning the group was transported to the quay-side of the Mýkonos Archaeological Museum and allowed to browse. Afterward, they wandered about the pristine area known as Little Venice, the artists quarter where a row of buildings with balconies built earlier by wealthy sea captains jut out over the sea.

Yvonne bumped into Janice and Bill who were listening to an animated Beverly gush over the amount of art galleries offering original works of art available in Mýkonos. Rosanna and Nicholas strolled casually a few feet behind. They entered one of the galleries and each of them wandered separately looking at whatever caught their individual interest.

Janice found a small bar outside the back of the building and located a table for two not taken that faced the ocean. The island curved at this point giving her a view of the Mýkonos windmills on a nearby hill. Yvonne took the opportunity to sit with her and have a private word.

"Janice, what's changed? You look relaxed and happier than I've seen you since the tour started."

Janice took a deep breath. "It's just that I've made up my mind what I'm going to do, and I feel a great weight lifted off my shoulders."

"Really? What have you decided?"

"As soon as we return to Ft. Lauderdale I'm going to see an attorney and get a divorce. I will not be Bill's doormat any longer."

"Aren't you worried that Bill will notice your change in attitude?"

"Not really. He doesn't pay any attention to me, much less my feelings, good or bad."

"Janice, I'm rather embarrassed to ask, but is there any chance that you could search through some of Bill's luggage?"

"Bill's luggage? Why?" Janice sat up and moved to the edge of the bench turning to face Yvonne.

"David and I suspect Bill, Rosanna and Nicholas might be involved somehow in the thefts at the art museums."

"Thefts in art museums? What are you talking about?"

"Don't you remember? The one at the Athens National Archaeological Museum the morning we arrived, and now another in the Modern Museum on Andros Island the same night you said Bill left your room those few hours in the middle of the night."

"Do you really think he had something to do with that? I can't believe it—but, if he did, I'll bet Rosanna put him up to it. You don't know how manipulative she can be. I've seen how she can get men to do her bidding. Why that rotten son-of-a-gun! How could he?"

"Hold on, Janice. We don't know for sure, but David and I think something fishy's going on, and that's why we need your help."

"I don't know. Fishy? He's having some sort of a fling or something with Rosanna. At least I'm pretty sure he is."

Yvonne glanced at the door to the gallery to be sure the art lovers weren't exiting. "For one thing, that mysterious man Damian seems to show up at the strangest times. He might be following our group for some reason. Something just doesn't feel right." Yvonne's gaze was intense and questioning.

Janice squirmed under her scrutiny. "You know—there just might be something to it. I've had my own suspicions before—how he always comes up with such wonderful deals art-wise. I know it's his business, but he seems to be pretty lucky when it comes to acquiring really good art. Most of it he sells, of course, but some we've kept. I wonder...?"

"Don't look now, but Bill is heading this way." Yvonne smiled at Janice. "I'm so glad you're feeling better and glad to hear you're enjoying the tour."

"Janice, you keep slipping away. If I didn't know better I'd think you were trying to hide from me." Bill chuckled sounding insincere.

"I saw you were in deep discussion with Beverly and didn't want to intrude. What did she want? Something important, I'm sure. Maybe she's giving up on David and going after you next. But I'm sure Rosanna would object if she had to share you with yet another woman." Bill looked at Janice like she'd lost her mind. He didn't say a word. Janice continued. "I thought I'd chat with Yvonne for a bit and thank her for this lovely tour. It is lovely. Don't you agree?"

"Janice, are you upset about something? You sound funny." Bill looked like he'd swallowed some spoiled seafood and shook his head to clear its confusion.

"Sorry to interrupt, but I need to check on the others. I'll see you later, Janice." Yvonne waved good-bye. She didn't want to be caught in the middle of the Bill and Janice drama. She spotted Evelyn and Richard looking in a gallery window admiring some traditional Greek landscapes. She glanced back at Janice and Bill. Janice was walking away in a determined and dignified manner. No longer the whipped puppy.

"Hi you two." Yvonne peered in the window next to Evelyn.

"Oh, Yvonne, you're just in time. Would you mind taking a picture of Richard and me? There's so much I want to remember, and since I left my journal back in the hotel, I'd like to record this moment with a photo."

"No need to explain. I'd be happy to." Yvonne had them move away from the glass to get rid of a glare and took the photo. She smiled at the happy couple. "I'm glad to see that you're truly enjoying yourselves. I'll see you back at the bus in about fifteen minutes."

Yvonne found Beverly seated on the same bench where she'd found Janice earlier.

"Beverly. Are you okay?" Yvonne refrained from saying she looked ill, but her concern was genuine. Beverly looked peaked as if she was about to throw up. There was sweat on her upper lip.

"Huh?"

"Would you like me to walk you back to the bus to sit down until we're ready to leave Little Venice?"

"No! I mean no thanks. I'll be fine." She gave a weak smile. "I haven't slept well the last couple nights."

"Are you sure I can't persuade you to go sit comfortably back on the bus?" Beverly's eyes widened. Was it fear? Yvonne wondered.

"No, really, I'd rather stay here where there's fresh air."

"If you insist, but please, don't hesitate to ask if there's anything at all I can do."

"There won't be." Beverly lowered her head and stroked the area between her eyes with two fingers as if she were smoothing away a severe headache.

Yvonne left her reluctantly and joined the rest of the group who were seated in an outdoor café sipping coffee and listening to Ari. "Because Mýkonos lacks the trees and lush natural beauty offered by other islands, residents here construct unusual architectural buildings and plant lots of colorful flowers. Their nightlife is famous world-wide for its swanky restaurants, transvestite shows and gay bars. Mýkonos is considered a sexy and exciting town."

That afternoon, Todd, Missy, Cynthia and Ari made a trek to Paradise, the popular straight nude beach. Mark chose to check out the gay nude beach, Super Paradise. When he saw the sparkle of oily tanned and toned bodies, he thought of his pale thin body and got cold feet. He retreated out of sight to a nearby gay bar. It was dark inside in contrast to the bright beach. He sat at a corner table where he thought he could observe life around him unnoticed. A waiter gave him the once over before heading to his table to take his drink order. Mark ordered a beer and pouted, thinking, here I am in the sexiest town in the world for gays, and what do I do? I hide. I'm pathetic. Why don't I just give up? I'll never find a soul mate this way. Shoot, I'll never even find a playmate at this rate.

"My, my, aren't we looking sad, Mister Blue Eyes." The dark complexioned young man gave him a wry smile. "Is this your first time to a nude beach?"

Not wanting to show his lack of sophistication, Mark said, "No. of course not. I've just realized, I've lost my tan from this time last summer and didn't want to spend too much time in the sun. I have the kind of skin that burns easily."

"Oh—I see." The young man started to turn away but hesitated. "In that case, my name is Cosmo, do you mind if I join you?

"What about your customers?" Mark looked around the empty bar.

"I'll return to work when necessary." Cosmo took a seat across from Mark.

David invited Yvonne to go to the shopping district with him, and to his surprise she accepted with no hesitation.

They were strolling down a street lined with shops and crowded with tourists from the cruise ships docked a few blocks away when David took her elbow. "Let's step into this antique store."

"Okay. Are you looking for something in particular?"

"No, but this is my partner's family store. One of those George mentioned that his family owns."

"Oh, I wonder if he's here?" Yvonne looked around and saw the same overstuffed shelves offering knickknacks and jewelry that many of the shops offered. This store, however, was cleaner and the jewelry displayed artistically in locked glass cases. She wondered if that meant better quality. Two women were waiting behind counters on either side of the store. The woman on the far side was older, dressed very business-like with dark hair and eyes. The young woman, dressed in t-shirt and jeans, resembled the older woman.

They must be mother and daughter. Will Christy and I be so different in our manner of dress when Christy grows up? She already knows her own mind, so I guess it's inevitable. Ay, Dios Mio, I really miss her. She's too young. I shouldn't leave her for such long periods. I mustn't do it again, at least not until she's older, more mature, and able to handle the separation. She seems fine when we've talked. Maybe it's me who's having separation anxiety.

Yvonne and David separated while they browsed through the store. After a few minutes, he appeared at her arm. "We can leave now unless there's something you are interested in purchasing."

"No. That's fine. Frankly, I'm overwhelmed by it all. I wouldn't begin to know where to start. I'll need to find souvenirs for Christy and my parents eventually, but so far I haven't seen anything that I know they'd appreciate."

"I'd like some coffee. What about you?"

"Sure, why not?" They found an outdoor café along the main shopping street not far from the ocean. Yvonne inhaled the light scent of salt air. She noticed a sparkle of excitement in David's eyes and wondered what he really had in mind.

They each silently watched the street bustling with tourists and locals dressed in all stages of clothing from business suits to bathing suits.

After David ordered his coffee and Yvonne her tea, David reached into his pants pocket and pulled out a small box. "Here, just a little something to thank you for showing me such a wonderful time."

Yvonne's eyes widened, then narrowed in concern. "What have you done? Really—this isn't necessary. You shouldn't have." She sounded stern even to her own ears.

"Please." He held up his hand to stop her. "Before you make a judgment why don't you open the box?" His steady gaze held her transfixed.

Yvonne shook her head to break the spell and opened the box. "Ay, Dios Mio! They are beautiful—but where—when—did you get them?"

"Just now—at the antique shop. I thought the golden topaz would set off those beautiful brown eyes of yours."

"David, really, I can't accept these. They're too valuable, and I'm just doing my job showing you around."

"I thought there was more to it than—just doing your job. I thought maybe you'd grown to like me as much as I like you."

Embarrassed, Yvonne said, "David, please don't be angry. I do like you, but I still must keep some respectable distance with my travel clients. How would it look? Me accepting a gift from you when we hardly know each other?"

"I know I want to spend more time with you. I want to give you gifts that make you happy—not sad." He reached across the table and took her hands in his. "Yvonne, don't make a big deal out of this. It was just an impulse buy intended to make your day a little brighter. Don't worry. I'm not pressing you for a commitment or anything. Why not accept them in the spirit with which they were given, and I promise not to tell anyone if you don't."

His blue eyes were sparkling again. Why did she have such a hard time resisting this man? He wasn't particularly handsome, but there was something very appealing, very pleasant about him. "Okay, David, they have surely brightened my day. Thank you." Yvonne blushed and placed the small jewel box in her purse.

Yvonne looked up to see David staring beyond her. Instinctively she turned around to see where he was looking.

They watched as Beverly attempted to cross the street. She had a small shopping bag in one hand, and she looked both ways before crossing. A black sedan approached slowly, then sped up as if following her. When Beverly stepped from the curb she heard the car's engine rev, but it was too late to step back. The car hit her and kept going.

David reacted first and Yvonne followed on his heels. By the time they reached Beverly, a crowd began to gather. They both knelt on the street beside her. "I think she's still breathing." David turned towards the crowd. "Has anyone called the police or an ambulance?" More than one person was speaking into their cell phones.

"Beverly, hang in there. We're here and we won't leave you." Yvonne took hold of her limp hand and saw that her left leg was bent in an awkward angle.

"She's unconscious. That can't be good. Why would anyone do such a thing?" David motioned to the crowd to give Beverly some room and fresh air. Yvonne remained silent at her side, the shock on her face worried David. Within a few minutes the sound of sirens from police cars and emergency vehicles blasted the air.

Yvonne rode in the ambulance with Beverly to the hospital while David and others gave their statements to the police. He told them what he'd seen, but it happened so quickly that he couldn't tell them much. He hadn't seen the license number of the vehicle and could only tell them that it looked like a black sedan similar to a Mercedes Benz.

David arrived at the hospital and met Yvonne in the emergency waiting room. "Is there any word yet on how she's doing?"

"None, I've been waiting for over an hour, you'd think we would have heard by now."

The weariness in her voice touched David, but he stayed at arms length. "Why don't you sit over there? I'll stand guard and grab the doctor when he comes out."

"I can't. I'm too wound up. Why did this have to happen? Is it me? What am I doing wrong? Everything is going wrong. This wasn't supposed to happen, and it didn't seem like an accident. Did it?"

"You can't blame yourself. It wasn't your fault," David put his arms around her and gently walked her to an empty seat near the corner of the small waiting room. "She'll be fine." He couldn't look Yvonne in the eye when he said this for fear she'd see that he was worried about Beverly too.

"What did the police say? Do they think they'll catch the person who did this?"

Before David could answer her, an overworked emergency room doctor came into the waiting room and looked around. Yvonne quickly left her seat to see if he had word about Beverly. "Are you a family member?" The doctor spoke English softly in his native Greek accent.

"No. She hasn't any family here. I'm her travel agent. We are on tour with a small group. We were having a free afternoon for shopping when the accident happened. Is she going to be all right Doctor?" Yvonne held her breath waiting for his answer.

"Yes, I think she will be all right. She is still unconscious, but her vital signs are good. She has suffered a concussion and has a broken leg and arm as well as some broken ribs. She was fortunate when the car hit her it knocked her clear. If it had run over her, she would be dead. She will need to stay in the hospital until she regains consciousness. We will need to keep her for observation after that. I'd say possibly a day or two."

"Doctor, will she be able to travel and continue with the tour when she's released?" asked David.

"She'll need time to rest and recuperate. Her ribs will be sore and she won't be able to move around much for awhile. She'll need help with getting dressed due to her broken limbs." He looked at her chart and then continued. "You may wish to find a private nurse for her until she is better able to travel. Check with the registrar's office. They can help you with arrangements.

"Oh, and one other thing, we received a call from the police. They will be sending someone to question her when she wakes up. They will also be posting a guard outside her door. It seems they think she may still be in danger." The doctor turned and went back the way he'd come before Yvonne could ask any more questions.

"David, I can't leave. Not until I know that she's conscious and we can make arrangements for her care. Beverly purchased travel insurance, so we should be able to arrange for a nurse. Surely they'll pay for a nursing home until she's able to travel. I'm not sure what kind of facilities they have in Mýkonos for situations like this, but I'll find out. For now, I want to know she's going to be okay."

"I'm not leaving either. Look. That must be the police officer who's been assigned to her." David pointed to the uniformed officer walking down the hall past the waiting room. "Let's find out what room they've taken her to, and when she can have visitors."

They followed along behind the police officer who stopped at the nurse's station for directions. Sure enough, he was looking for Beverly's room. "Excuse me. Ma'am," Yvonne tried to get the attention of the amply built nurse who'd just given the room number to the police officer.

The nurse looked up at Yvonne with an inquiring stare. "Yeees," was all she said.

"Would it be possible for Mr. Ludlow and me to wait with Ms. Nystrom in her room? We are anxious to know that she is okay and want to be there when she wakes up."

"I'm afraid that won't be possible. The police say she is to have no visitors without their approval. She is still unconscious. The doctor would not approve."

"Please tell them we'll be in the waiting room. If you need me, I'll be available to help with insurance arrangements or anything else Ms. Nystrom may need." Yvonne smiled, hoping the nurse understood enough English to realize they were no threat to Beverly or her recuperation.

"Yeees. I weel do that," said the nurse.

Yvonne and David returned to the waiting room. "David, should I tell the group this was a deliberate attempt to hurt Beverly, or should I just say she's had an accident? *Ay Dios Mio!*" A scared Beverly sitting on a bench refusing to return to the bus alone flashed in Yvonne's mind.

"What?" asked David.

"She was afraid, and I didn't pick up on it. I could have prevented this. Why didn't I insist she tell me why she was frightened? Now it's too late."

"I can't help if I don't know what you're talking about." An exasperated David grabbed Yvonne's elbow. "Let's go to the cafeteria for a cup of coffee. We need a break from this depressing room. Then you can tell me what's going on." David's tone left no room for argument, so Yvonne followed David as he led the way to the hospital cafeteria. "While we're here, let's have dinner. We're in for a long night and we're going to need our strength." The smells of cabbage and moussaka in the cafeteria warming trays caused his stomach to churn.

"I'm not hungry. This place smells gross." Yvonne sniffed the air in disgust. "I'm tired, David, tired of everything. The accidents, the lack of control over what happens on my tour, and now this, one of my good clients injured and I might have prevented it."

David let her blow off steam without comment. After Yvonne took a few bites of the dry cafeteria food and drank some coffee, color returned to her cheeks.

With as little emotion as possible, she relayed to David the conversation she'd had with Beverly, and how she'd failed to convince her to rest on the bus. "I see now she wanted to be in the open around people. I sensed her fear, but because it was Beverly, I minimized it thinking she was being overly dramatic."

"Damn it, Yvonne, stop blaming yourself for things beyond your control. We need to stay on track with our investigations. Don't you see, this is proof someone is sabotaging our tour. I think Beverly stumbled onto something or someone, and that someone tried to shut her up before she could tell what she knows to the police."

His words stung. "You're right, David. It serves no purpose to second guess everything. I'll tell the others it was an accident. As soon as I can arrange for Beverly's care, I'll find a way to search through Bill Armstrong's belongings when we move on to our next stop. Janice is on board with our efforts to find out what's going on, but she won't do the search. She's afraid he'll catch her at it."

"Before you do, we need to make careful plans. You see how dangerous this is. Don't do anything rash." David reached across the table and took her hand in his. He softened his voice and his eyes. "After all, you have a little girl waiting for her Mom to arrive home safely, in one piece, with souvenirs, hugs and kisses."

His words tugged at her conscience. Disappointing Christy was her biggest fear.

Unaware of Beverly's plight, the younger crowd ventured out to enjoy the Mýkonos night clubs accompanied by Mark's new friend, Cosmo.

The older members of the tour decided to have a quiet dinner and turn in early.

"Where am I?" Beverly strained to open her eyes. Her mouth was cotton dry. Everything looked dull white except for the bed rails as the room came into focus.

"Ms. Nystrom you are in the Mýkonos Town Hospital." The attending nurse pressed a buzzer that rang somewhere outside the room.

Within seconds the doctor wearing faded green scrubs entered with the police officer following close on his heels.

"Welcome back Ms. Nystrom. You gave us quite a scare." The doctor examined her pupils and saw that they were still dilated.

"Wha—What happened?" Her voice croaked the question.

"We were hoping you could tell us," said the police officer. "Do you remember anything?"

"I was shopping for souvenirs. That's all I remember."

"It's not unusual that you would suffer some memory loss due to the trauma of the accident."

"Accident? What accident? I feel like I've been run over by a bus. Is that why?"

"You are going to be sore for awhile. The ribs on your left side are broken, and as you can see, your left arm and leg are in a cast. Your leg is broken in two spots."

"Two spots—my head hurts. You still haven't told me what happened."

"You were hit by a car, and in addition to your other wounds, you have a concussion."

The young police officer took over. "Witnesses say that you looked before you stepped into the street. A car a safe distance away rolled to a stop but suddenly sped up and hit you. Is there any reason some one would want to harm you?"

"No. Why would they?"

"Because, Ms Nystrom, people here don't have the habit of running people down with cars for no reason." The police officer opened his notepad. "Now, will you please tell why you were shopping by yourself instead of being with the rest of your tour group."

Perturbed by the tone of his voice, she tried to sit up but winced at the effort. "I assure you there's no reason why anyone would wish me harm. To answer your question, I travel alone every year." Beverly's eyelids drooped, but she fought to keep them open. "Even though I'm on a tour, I enjoy time on my own and book tours that allow me free afternoons." She fidgeted trying to get comfortable. "Also, others on the tour were going to a nude beach and that really is not my thing—Sir." Beverly closed her eyes and laid her head back on the pillow exhausted from the effort of speaking.

"That's enough questioning for now." The doctor nodded his head from the police officer to the door.

"Beverly, your friends Yvonne and David have been waiting for you to regain consciousness. Do you wish to see them for a few minutes now? Or would you prefer they come back later in the day?"

"I wouldn't mind seeing them for a few minutes if it's all right with you, Doctor."

"As long as you promise not to upset yourself and make it a very short visit. It's after three o'clock in the morning."

"I promise. Doctor, could I please have some water? My throat is very dry." Beverly spoke like a vulnerable child.

"Of course, I will send the nurse with water and ask your friends to come in. A Dr.Levros will be in attendance tomorrow morning, and I will return to check on you late tomorrow afternoon. Goodnight, Ms. Nystrom."

After the nurse helped Beverly drink a small amount of water, Yvonne and David stepped into the room. They each made an effort to conceal their shock when they saw the size of the casts on her arm and leg and the swollen bruise running the length of the left side of her face.

"Beverly, we're so sorry that this has happened to you," said Yvonne.

"Thank you." Beverly, her eyes swollen with tears, looked past Yvonne to David.

"We're here to help in any way we can. Yvonne is going to get in touch with the insurance company first thing in the morning to see what arrangements can be made once they release you from the hospital. The doctor says that you will need time to recuperate from your wounds, and you won't be able to continue the tour with the rest of us."

"I'm sure that will be a relief to the two of you." Her voice was raspy.

"Of course we don't feel that way, Beverly. This is the last thing in the world that we would have wanted." Yvonne resisted the urge to glance at David and squashed the guilt she was feeling. "Earlier in the day, you seemed confused and scared. Was there a problem? Did something happen before this accident to cause you concern?" Yvonne pulled her chair up closer to the bed. "I've known you for a few years now, and I've never seen anything rattle you. Today was different. Won't you please let us help?"

Beverly began to cry but fought back her tears. "No, Yvonne, there's nothing that anyone can do to help me now. Just go ahead and leave. I know you'll work out the best arrangements you can. Promise me you'll keep them secret. Don't tell anyone what has happened or where I am. Promise me that much, Yvonne."

"Of course, if that's what you want. I won't say a word, but perhaps we should see if the police will continue to watch over you. Whoever tried to hurt you may try again."

"No—not if they don't know where to find me, they won't." Beverly turned her head and tried to turn on her right side, but the movement made her wince and she came back to center and closed her eyes dismissing the two visitors.

ANCIENT DELOS

DAY 11

"I've racked my brains for the past several hours trying to figure out how to proceed with the day." Yvonne's eyes were bloodshot from lack of sleep. She and David had decided that three hours sleep was worse than none at all. They left the hospital early in the morning to head back to the hotel. After quick showers in their respective rooms, they met early for breakfast to plan what they would do next.

"We're scheduled to ferry to Delos for the day. We're to be at the port by 8:30." Yvonne bit into a piece of baklava and took a sip of tea. Maybe the sugar and caffeine would help her get through the day.

"I want to watch your back, and I won't take no for an answer. We don't know where the next threat may come from." David nodded at her as he took a sip of the strong Greek coffee steaming in his cup.

"First we handle the medical and insurance inquiries for Beverly. I'll ask Ari to lead the tour on his own, so I can stay here to work out the arrangements for Beverly."

"I'll skip the tour and help with Beverly's arrangements." David lowered his voice but he kept his tone casual. "Why don't I search Bill Armstrong's and the Fontinelli's rooms. They will all be on the trip to Delos. This will be our best chance." He waited for the thought to take hold.

"I appreciate your concern, David, but I don't want you in harm's way either. This is my problem and I can handle it."

"I'm sure you can, but we agreed that it would be better if we stuck together," David's jaw tightened. "How about...I go with you to work out the details of Beverly's recuperation and then... we can go together to search the rooms. One of us can act as look out while the other one searches. It'll be like John Steed and Emma Peel in The Avengers. We'll make an adventure out of it." The twinkle was back in his eye and Yvonne was too tired to argue.

"That's not fair. I love that show." Yvonne could imagine herself as Emma Peel, but David, not so much as John Steed. She grinned. "Okay. You can help, but this has to be handled discreetly. We want to make sure there's no more attempts to hurt Beverly. Remember, I promised her no one would find out where she is."

"I wish we knew who attacked her and why. What is it she knows? Maybe we can get her to tell us today." David wiped some toast crumbs from his mouth and took a last drink of coffee.

"Here comes Evelyn and Richard—the others will be coming down soon. I'll find Ari and speak to him before I tell everyone." Yvonne signed the bill for breakfast and looked around to be sure no one could overhear. "David, perhaps you should wait in your room until I've explained everything to the others. I don't want to make a big deal about us being together today."

"Sure." David gave an encouraging smile, rose and walked back toward his room to wait for her.

Yvonne ticked off each name on her clipboard, accounting for all the members going to Delos. Before allowing them to board the bus she asked them to wait while she gave them some news. "There's no easy way to say this—Beverly's been involved in an accident, she was hit by a car while crossing the street yesterday afternoon and she's in pretty bad shape. She has several broken bones. She lost consciousness for awhile but the doctor says she's going to be fine."

"Oh my gosh! What can we do to help?" Cynthia's distress spurred on other concerned comments.

"I'd like to help too," said Rosanna.

"No—I mean she's not up to visitors and I'm making arrange-ments for her recuperation today." Yvonne switched the subject. "You will all be in good hands with Ari as tour leader today."

"How did such a thing happen? Not another accident?" The fear in Janice's voice was impossible to ignore.

Yvonne spoke calmly. "We don't have details yet. I'm sure the au-thorities are doing what they can to find the person who hit her."

"So, it was a hit-and-run," said Mark. "Another crazy coinci-dence, I'd say."

Yvonne could have kicked herself for letting slip about the hit-and-run.

"It's time to get on the bus. I want all of you to have a great day. Don't worry about anything. I will see that Beverly is well taken care of and I'll give you a full report later. I'll be anxious to hear about your day's activities at dinner this evening." She smiled stiffly at them while Ari helped them board. Satisfied they'd soon be on their way, she headed back to her room as Ari begin his spiel.

"Keep your sweaters on. The ferry ride is only 45 minutes long, but it is in choppy waters and the sea breezes can be very cool.

"Once upon a time the small island of Delos was one of the most important islands in the Greek civilization." Ari gave a hand up to all the ladies who boarded the bus and took his place in front of the steering wheel when everyone was seated. "I will mention a few things on the way to the port because it will be difficult to hear my voice above the roar of the ocean aboard the ferry." He drove the narrow roads with ease. "When we arrive on the island be sure to stay with me at all times. Delos is an archaeological wonder with many ruins, but it is easy to get confused, even lost.

"It was in Delos that the goddess Leto who was pregnant by Zeus bore Apollo. There you will find a sanctuary with three sacred temples to Apollo and temples to Artemis and Zeus. For almost a thousand years, Delos was the religious and political centre of the Aegean." Ari paused for effect. "While admiring the many amazing buildings and statues, be careful not to stray from the beaten path. Some of the less trafficked areas can hide snakes, and they have been known to strike at passing ankles." Ari could hear the group shiver in unison. He chuckled and thought at least they won't be likely to stray now.

Yvonne spent the morning in her room on the telephone making arrangements with the insurance company for payment of Beverly's medical bills and to verify coverage for her release to a nursing home until she was fit to travel.

David took a cab to the hospital and met with Beverly's doctor. The doctor expected to release and transfer Beverly to a nearby facility in the next two days. After phoning Yvonne with this information, he visited Beverly in her room.

"Good morning, Beverly, it's David. The doctor feels you'll make a complete recovery. You're going to be okay."

"I don't feel okay." She pouted like a child and David felt a twinge of guilt. He shook off the feeling. Beverly needed someone to take charge, not to get lost in the drama.

"No one except Yvonne and me know where you are and we'll make sure it stays that way. Do you have any idea who might have done this? Perhaps you saw what the person looked like?" He waited and watched her eyes gloss over, becoming expressionless. "Was it a man, or a woman?" He pushed further.

"I don't know. Don't you understand? I just don't know!" Tears seeped from the corners as she squeezed her eyes shut.

"Don't worry, Beverly. I'm sure they'll find out who did this. In the meantime, you just rest. I'm going to talk to the police guard to make sure you are safe until we can move you."

David stepped out of the room to talk to the uniformed police officer. The officer was under instructions to stay until she left the hospital unless she came under another attack. If that happened they would take her into protective custody. So far, however, the police had learned little. Without more to go on, there wasn't much they could do for her.

David returned to the hotel and found Yvonne pacing in her room. "Thank heaven's you're back. We need to get a move on if we're going to search the Armstrong and Fontinelli rooms before they return."

"How do you expect us to get into the rooms? We're not professional lock pickers, you know."

Yvonne grinned as she reached into her pants pocket and pulled out a key that looked similar to his room key. "Janice gave me her key this morning." Yvonne closed her fist over the key. "Let's go, you can watch out for me, you know—be the lookout, while I'm in their room."

"Okay, but before we go—how should I warn you if someone's coming? I might arouse more suspicion if I'm lurking outside a hotel room. Why don't I come in and help you look?"

"You make a good point. I'd better let you come in with me, but you stand guard inside and let me do the looking. I will be careful to make sure nothing looks disturbed." Yvonne walked around David and opened her room door. She checked down the hall and saw no one before she quickly walked to the Armstrong's room and slipped inside.

Inside the safety of the room, David teased her. "You wound me, Yvonne. Do you think I don't know enough to be careful searching?"

"Shhh," she whispered. "Be quiet. No one's supposed to be in here, remember?"

David grabbed her by the shoulders and kissed her passionately, then let her go. "Shhh, now don't say anything. We wouldn't want to draw attention to ourselves. Shouldn't you be searching for something?"

Flustered, Yvonne regained her composure and gave him the dirtiest look she could muster before she headed for the closet. First she patted down the hanging clothes then she pulled out the suitcase she remembered seeing Bill carry. Placing it on the bed, she opened it and rummaged through sweaters, socks, undershirts and... "Ugh, do you believe it? 'Speedo' underwear, how gross! And, at his age, doesn't he know that boxers are supposed to help your skin breath in the warm weather?"

"And how would you know about that?"

Yvonne blushed. "I better get back to my searching."

The suitcase offered nothing else unexpected. She searched some shopping bags they had accumulated, and everything looked ordinary there as well.

"Let's check under the mattress," suggested David.

"Do you really think they might be sleeping on a priceless piece of artwork?" asked Yvonne.

"No, I guess not. What do you propose we do next?"

"I don't see that we have much choice. We'll have to check out Rosanna and Nicholas' room."

"And how do you expect to get their key? I don't think Janice will be helping with that one." David replaced the suitcase in the closet and inspected the room to be sure all was left as originally found.

"Let's go back to my room and think about it. I'll come up with something." Yvonne's throat hurt from all the whispering.

"Hold it, Yvonne." David put his finger to his lips to shush her and pointed to the door. They could hear heavy breathing just outside the door. After a few seconds, they heard footsteps. Someone retreated down the hall. David opened the room door just as a man's figure disappeared around the corner. "Come on, quick! Let's get back to your room."

The halls were empty as they slipped out the door and headed for Yvonne's room. Once inside her room, they both heaved a sigh of relief. "Who do you think it was? Did you see him?"

"Not clearly, but I think it could have been that guy, Damian. He was about the same height, but I only got a glimpse of half his body as it disappeared around the corner. Damn! Maybe I should have tried to follow him." David slammed his fist on the door jamb then grabbed it protectively with his other hand. "Ow-damn-damn-damn!"

Yvonne cupped his fist in her hands. "No, David, if you follow him, you might be the next casualty and give our suspicions away." She kissed his injured hand, looked into his eyes and leaned into his body. He wrapped his arms around her pulling her tight against him. They kissed again. Yvonne ripped at the buttons on his shirt. David pushed her backward and they fell upon the bed.

Their emotional and physical strength spent, they fell into a deep sleep, unavoidable after having had no sleep the night before.

She was on a ferry, the same one they'd taken that first afternoon to Andros Island. This time, however, the ferry was sinking and her daughter Christy and her parents were aboard. There was only one life raft, not large enough to hold all the passengers. David was trying to save Yvonne, but she wouldn't leave until she found Christy and her parents.

"Yvonne, let me save you," David insisted.

"No. If I can't save my daughter and my parents, I don't want to live. I will save them or I will drown with them."

She heard him calling from the life boat. "Please. Let me save you."

The ferry boat sank deeper in the water. People were screaming. She was screaming. "Christy! Mom! Dad! Where are you?"

Water was flooding around her feet. She couldn't move. It was getting deeper. She looked around wildly for her family. Heavy saltwater pushed her backward. It rose up and pulled her under. The salt water burned her nostrils and throat. She struggled trying to hold her breath. She woke up, heart racing, gulping for air.

She looked at the clock on the bedside table. 6:03 pm. David snored softly beside her. She'd had a nightmare, but daylight was peeking through narrow openings in the curtains. She grabbed the covers around her and replayed in her mind the terror she had felt. She fought to stay awake and stumbled to the bathroom to brush old coffee-flavor and imagined salt water from her mouth. She showered until fully awake, forgetting the dream but not the sinking feeling.

"David. Wake up sleepy head." Yvonne kissed him gently on the forehead.

"Um." He smiled in his sleep and rolled over hugging his pillow.

"No you don't. David, please—wake up. We have to meet the others. It's almost dinner time." Yvonne sat on the bed next to him and shook his shoulders.

"Okay, okay. I'm awake. Don't worry. I wasn't planning to sleep through dinner." He forced his lids to open and saw water glistening on her skin from the shower. She smelled clean and fresh, and he breathed in her vanilla scented body odor. He wanted her again in a way he had wanted no other woman.

"I think you should head back to your room to freshen up while I finish dressing. Please be careful so no one sees you leave my room." Yvonne gave him a light kiss on the lips and left so that he could pull himself together. She returned to the mirror in the bathroom to dry her hair and make-up her face.

David was smarting from Yvonne's last remark but tried to understand why she felt the way she did. He wouldn't have respected her as much if she hadn't been concerned for her reputation.

Ari was waiting in the lobby of the hotel to take the travelers to Chez Maria, one of Mýkonos most famous upscale restaurants. Janice hurried over to Yvonne. "How is Beverly doing?"

"With care, the doctors expect she'll recover completely."

"How long will she be in the hospital? We should go visit her," said Bill.

"Why, Bill, I'm surprised you care." Janice's eyes narrowed in skepticism. "But you were having a nice chat with her the other day."

Yvonne jumped into the conversation. "That's very thoughtful, Bill, but Beverly has asked that no one visit her while she's recuperating. She needs rest, and besides we're leaving for Santorini tomorrow."

Rosanna joined the group and moved to the other side of Bill. "Still, it seems rather rude of us to go on our merry way and not even wish her well while poor Beverly is stuck in the hospital."

Ignoring Rosanna, Yvonne gave Ari the okay to lead the way to their mini-van. "I think it's time we went to dinner."

"It's a beautiful evening, balmy and breezy. What more could anyone ask?" Cynthia beamed at Ari as he escorted her to the table.

Others mumbled their agreement. They would be dining outside under the stars in a café-style restaurant near the ocean. Restaurants all lit up with white holiday lights lined the area. The exciting bustle of nightlife and the festive air made it difficult for Yvonne to believe there had been any problems at all since arriving in Athens. At least tonight I won't have to share David with Beverly. What a selfish thought. Of course, I would give anything if Beverly had not been hit by a car. Oh my, what am I thinking? Yvonne tried to focus her thoughts on the chatter at the table. David made matters worse by bumping his knee against hers under the table and playfully attempting to play footsies. *I need to get things on track. I need to find out what's really going on and why Beverly was hurt. There's no time like the present to figure it out. David knows I'm serious about getting to the bottom of this. I wish he'd stop fooling around.*

Yvonne decided to plunge in head first with some questions to see what if anything she could stir up. "Has anyone heard about what happened on Andros Island the first night we arrived?"

David, surprised, gave her a questioning look but didn't say anything.

Yvonne looked around the table at each person to see if anyone had reacted. Janice squirmed in her seat, but no one else reacted. Finally, Evelyn Malcolm's curiosity got the best of her. "What are you referring to, my dear?"

"I'm referring to the art stolen from the new Modern Art Museum. I thought it was a strange coincidence that something was stolen from the National Archaeological Museum in Athens the day before we arrived and then another robbery while we were on the island. The newscaster said the authorities think the two robberies are related."

"How odd," said Evelyn.

Yvonne turned her attention to Bill. "Didn't you, Rosanna and Nicholas visit that museum the afternoon we arrived?"

"Yes we did. What of it?"

Before Yvonne could respond, Rosanna asked, "What was stolen?"

"A small painting by a new artist who is apparently quite popular. Does it ring a bell with you?"

"Not really. We saw so many beautiful paintings that day."

"Don't you think it was a strange coincidence that two robberies occurred at two of our tour stops?" Yvonne looked Rosanna directly in the eye and for a second she thought she flinched.

"Strange, perhaps. More like coincidence." Rosanna picked up her glass of wine, "Let's make a toast to strange coincidences on our very exciting tour!"

Everyone seemed to sense the tension, watching intently or holding their breaths. An audible sigh was heard as they one by one lifted their glasses. The waiter returned to take their dinner orders, and Yvonne continued observing the Armstrongs and Fontinellis until it was her turn to order. After placing her dinner order, she discussed with everyone the schedule for their trip the following day. When her order of Mediterranean halibut and salad arrived, she shifted her attention back to David and the meal. He cautiously began to make small talk. Yvonne noticed he was no longer fooling around under the table.

After dinner, Ari suggested everyone take a walk along the beach to soak up some moonlight and get some light exercise. They would all meet back in front of the restaurant in an hour. The Armstrongs, Fontinellis, Malcolms and Mark walked toward the shops. The other couples, Missy and Todd, Cynthia and Ari, and David and Yvonne, chose to stroll along the beach. David and Yvonne slowed their pace and fell behind.

"That was quite a performance you gave at dinner." David was trying to decide if he could legitimately put his arm around Yvonne as they walked or should he try to hold her hand.

Yvonne was walking at a good clip when David reached out and took hold of her hand. "I'm sorry. Am I walking too fast again?" Yvonne slowed her pace and pulled her hand away to swing naturally at her side.

"I had to do something. I wanted to see if I could shake things up a bit. I thought maybe someone would lose their cool and give us a clue as to what is going on." Yvonne shrugged, "I probably forced them to be more cautious now."

"I'll admit—they are cool customers. I'm sure you caught them off guard. They might even do something stupid and give themselves away. Maybe they'll do something desperate and some one else will get hurt." David slowed his pace further.

"I couldn't stand it if someone else got hurt because of what I've said. David, I've got to figure this out and fix it. We've got to fix it." Yvonne reached for David's hand again, "I wish we were on our way to Santorini. Maybe with a new day and a new destination, everything will be okay again." She knew that it was too late for everything to be okay again. Not only had they experienced delays and accidents, now they were one person short on the trip.

SANTORINI

DAY 12

"**Can you see it?** From the sky Santorini looks like an exotic sand-art sculpture." Evelyn gazed out her small window.

Ari shouted above the noisy engine. "A volcanic eruption during 1500 BCE sank Minoan ships docked in that deep lagoon formed by the crescent shape of the island. The eruption caused earthquakes and colorful sunsets for years afterward." Ari had taken the jump seat so that he could face the group. He watched as they peered out the windows. "Thera is Santorini's ancient and official name. We, Greeks, however, prefer its medieval name, Santorini, after Saint Irene of Salonica who died here in 304 CE."

"Is this rusty bucket of bolts going to land any time soon?" Bill held tight to the armrests; his white knuckles clenched.

Janice turned away, leaned her head against the vibrating window and stared at Santorini rising up to meet the plane.

Ari smiled. "You'd be surprised how often these planes land without incident."

"You're right, I would," said Bill. "I've read all about the airline—their constant labor and equipment problems. It's a wonder they're still in business. Their planes have suffered for years from a lack of decent maintenance."

Ari had heard this complaint from American tourists many times before. He couldn't resist sarcasm. "Well, travelers aren't willing to pay a 'pretty price,' so they can't get 'pretty planes.'"

Bill made no further comments.

The passengers chattered with relief once the small Dash 8-100 turbo prop jet bumped along to a safe landing. They retrieved their luggage and waited while Ari made arrangements to secure their rented minibus. No one spoke about the past accidents, but everyone wondered what catastrophe would befall them next.

On the short drive to the capital of Santorini, Ari continued his narrative. "Firá, sits on the rim of a cliff. The town's winding cobblestone streets terraced into the cliff are mainly for walking. Many of their cafés offer magnificent views of the ocean."

Yvonne interrupted him. "When I was here on a previous trip, I remember my senses overwhelmed with the mingling of ocean breezes, food smells and the rust and purple colors of the cliff side's lava striations. It will be different from anything you've ever seen before. Make sure to bring your cameras along when we take our walking tour."

Yvonne felt guilty about Beverly. She must be in more pain today than yesterday. Everyone knew that injuries hurt more a day or two after the incident. Her mind skipped around from one thing to another. She couldn't focus on anything pleasant for long.

Searching through Bill's stuff for clues had been a waste of time. How are we ever going to prove he's up to something? Robbery, murder, it's hard to believe. There must be some other plausible explanation. I don't think I can risk snooping on Rosanna and Nicholas. I'll have to think of another way to get at the truth.

"I'm finally here!" Evelyn clutched her carry-on close. "I've dreamed of visiting this island since I was a young girl and read The Moon Spinners by Mary Stewart. It's every bit as beautiful as I hoped it would be."

Richard gave her a hug and was pleased she was realizing her lifelong dream. He knew Evelyn had sacrificed all she had for the sake of her children and their marriage. He worried she'd never get the chance to realize any of her own dreams. As a young man he'd sown his wild oats before settling down to a stable marriage and home life, but he felt responsible for taking away her opportunity to have a career and perhaps a more fulfilling life. He wondered if she regretted giving it all up for life as a housewife to a busy doctor and mother to three rambunctious boys. He'd fallen in love with her when he was a graduate student at Michigan State University. She'd come to register for freshman classes, so proud to be the first female in her family accepted to college. Her dream was to become a psychologist so she could help people with mental disabilities and relationship problems. Coming from a dysfunctional family herself, she'd managed to overcome her own relationship challenges— a father who was an alcoholic and an enabling mother overworked trying to protect the family from his abuses. It was important to Evelyn that she help families struggling to get along. Later, after he'd courted her and they'd fallen in love, he proposed. He asked her to give up her career. At first she resisted but eventually admitted it was just as important to raise a happy family with a wonderful husband as it was to become a psychologist. He realized now he'd been selfish wanting her to stay at home, but that was the way he'd been raised. At the time, he thought it was the best thing for Evelyn and for their marriage and family. It was best for him to be sure. She was always there ready to support him in his career and be a mother to their three sons and now grandmother to five grandchildren. It was about time she indulged herself, and he wanted her to have this trip of a lifetime. He'd always promised her this trip, and, by God, he'd see to it that it she enjoyed every last minute of it.

From their small hotel located on the main cliff side street, the group took a walking tour of the city to orient themselves to the town. "You will note that many of the houses have barrel-vaulted roofs made from stone bricks to protect against earthquakes." Ari pointed to the whitewashed curved arches on top of the houses. Stepping down cliff side, he showed them the many apartments, houses, restaurants, discos, jewelry boutiques and shops that set in cave-like dwellings with the amazing Santorini views. "From here we will take our day trips over the next two days. You are free to wander further down to the seaside or go back and settle into your hotel for a leisurely nap. We will all meet later this evening and take a short driving tour to a wonderful taverna north of here for dinner."

At two in the afternoon the group wandered to a nearby taverna to have a light lunch and Greek spirits. Most of the shops shut down from 2:30 pm until 5:00 pm anyway, so this allowed them to relax and soak up the local atmosphere.

Yvonne marveled at the pleasant personalities of the Greeks. They love nothing more than a good political debate when given the opportunity. They spoke loud enough for nearby tables to hear their passionate discourses. They certainly are a fun loving, family-oriented people. Though I do wonder about the freedoms they allow their children that I would never feel safe in allowing Christy. Bringing their young children out to bars and dinners at 10:00 pm on weeknights while most children in the states would be home and sound asleep. The thought of this reminded her that she missed Christy. I wonder how she's doing. I haven't called home since we left Athens. I should have called by now. I'll do it as soon as I return to my hotel room.

Her reverie was interrupted when she heard David talking about the wine tour they would take tomorrow. Ari was daring Todd, Missy, Cynthia and Mark to try the local wine Retsina with a "volcanic" taste.

"I would like to taste it."

Everyone at the table stopped and stared in awe at the usually meek Janice who sounded strong and determined.

"There will be plenty of time to taste it tomorrow." Bill stared hard at Janice trying to gain control of his wayward wife.

"Janice, you do realize, the additive in the wine is resin and requires a strong palate and an acquired taste?" Concern was written all over David's face. He thought she might be too fragile to handle spirits this strong. After all, she needed to keep her wits about her with all that was going on between she and Bill and her so-called friends.

"Well, I can't acquire a taste for it if I don't try it." Janice ignored Bill and looked David in the eye.

"No, that's right. A small amount won't hurt anyone." Ari waved at their waiter. "Bring a round of Kourtaki retsina for our table please."

Yvonne watched Bill grimace.

The retsina was served in small white wine glasses. The pale yellow color was pleasant to the eye. Yvonne's first impression was that it smelled and tasted like a faint solution of pine cleaner, but the alcohol warmed her insides and she thought she might develop a taste for it after all.

"Janice, what do you think? Is it any good?"

David's tone encouraged her to stand up for herself and to speak her opinions. "Actually, I don't care for it much, but maybe I haven't had enough of it yet—you know—to acquire a taste." She giggled like a school girl causing Bill to frown in disgust.

Yvonne saw his mood darken and took another sip of the wine.

Yvonne's head buzzed just a little bit. She wasn't used to drinking. She made herself comfortable on the bed before placing her long distance call to the states. Her mom answered the phone and assured her that all was well with Christy. "She's had good reports from school and this past weekend we enjoyed a mini-vacation to Disney World. Here, let me put her on and she can tell you yourself." Nancy Suarez handed the phone to her granddaughter.

"Hi, Mommy, I miss you." Christy yawned into the phone.

"I'm sorry, sweetie, I didn't mean to wake you so early, but I miss you too. Are you having a good time with Grandma and Grandpa?"

"Yes, Mommy, we've had lots of fun, and guess what? I got to see Mickey and Minnie and wanted to tell you about it. Are you having a good time too, Mommy? When are you coming home?"

"Slow down, sweetie, I can only answer one question at a time. I can't wait to hear all about your trip to Disney. I'll be home in less than a week, and yes, I'm having a good time too. I'm going to send you a kiss through the phone now. Have a great day today. Give Grandma and Grandpa a kiss from me too. I love you." Yvonne smiled as she set the phone down happy that, at least, all was well at home. It felt unreal—like she was a million miles away after talking to Christy. Soon she'd return to safe and normal, but for now in this exotic land with unusual people she enjoyed the taste of freedom and the satisfaction that solving a mystery would bring. And, solve it—she would.

"We're heading north—along the Caldera Road to Ía near the Ammoúdi Beach. A strong earthquake in 1956 disturbed petrified lava and poured it down on the town. Those who survived, dug their way back into their homes and businesses through the volcanic debris and went on with their lives. The families of this island have survived for centuries through their determination to bounce back after any hardship."

Listening to Ari, Yvonne thought that she could take a lesson from these strong-willed Greek Islanders. I can bounce back too. I've survived worse when I was married to Gino. I can certainly survive my first custom tour. If I'm being tested, I'll prove that I can rise above the brutality. I'll figure this mystery out. I'm a travel agent for God's sake. I should be having fun not fearing for my life."

"The town is said to be one of the most photographed sites in all of Greece due to the intense colors of the petrified lava ranging from dark reds and purples to blacks. All those different colors can be found in various beaches around the island." Ari drove along the winding coast road while continuing his memorized script. "Some of the old cave houses have been converted into luxurious hotels and restaurants, and Ía is growing to be a nice quiet alternative to Fíra town."

Quiet, that's what we need, an evening of quiet. Yvonne took a deep breath and sat back in her seat, closed her eyes for a moment and then focused on Ari again.

"In fact, the Taverna Katina has gained the reputation as the finest taverna on the island. Add to that their beautiful sunsets and you will have an experience that will compare to no other."

After exiting the bus, they walked through small cobblestone streets to arrive at the seaside taverna. Fishing boats bobbed lightly in the sparkling water colored by the black sand beneath.

"Oh my! This is spectacular. The water looks like a sparkling blue-black sapphire." Cynthia placed an approving hand on Ari's shoulder.

"Look at the colors on the other side of the island. It's hard to imagine that this place is real." Mark pointed across the bay. "I wish Cosmo had come with us so that I could share it with him. He's probably seen this place already since he's a native, but he hasn't seen it with me."

"What's that peculiar smell? It's mixed with the ocean smells. What do you think it is?" asked Missy.

"Petrified lava. You'll get faint whiffs of the charred smell even now, centuries later." Ari asked them to wait while he confirmed their reservation with the hostess. She led them to a long table near a bank of windows with the best view of the ocean.

Yvonne noticed Janice barely picking at her dinner, and she hadn't said a word all evening. Bill, Rosanna and Nicholas, on the other hand, were engaged in a lively and humorous conversation. Yvonne and David were seated at the other end of the table. Janice and Bill sat across from Rosanna and Nicholas. Yvonne wished she could hear what they were talking about. She caught Janice's eye and indicated that she should go to the powder room. A few minutes later Janice excused herself. Yvonne pretended to follow her lead and caught up to Janice as she walked through the door.

"Janice, what's wrong? You look upset. Has something happened?"

Janice fought back tears. "Bill threatened me—he's mad at me. He said if I didn't stop making a spectacle of myself, he's going to make me sorry. He'd have no wife of his embarrassing him by being a boisterous know-it-all. He told me that you are a bad influence and that I have to stop hanging around with you." She started to sniffle. "I don't know if I can be strong enough, but who—who does he think he is? Talking to me like that? I told him, 'I'm sure if Rosanna made the same comments, you would think she is charming.' The next thing I knew, I was picking myself up off the floor. He actually knocked me down. Can you believe it?" Her tears could no longer be held back.

"Why that mean bastard! He's nothing but a bully. I was afraid he might do something like this. Janice, you can't stay with him any more. So what if he leaves? That would be fine. You can stay and I will make sure that you are taken care of and that you have a place to stay." Yvonne put her arms around Janice's shoulders.

"No, Yvonne, I can't. I'm really afraid. He's never gone over the edge like this before. I'm afraid of what he might do next."

"That's just the point. Next time you could be seriously hurt."

"No—I'll just have to be more careful while I'm around him until I can get away without fear of him coming after me. It's only a few more days before we fly home. Then, I'll be able to find a way to leave him."

"I really wish you'd reconsider and just tell him to shove off now," said an exasperated Yvonne.

"Janice, darling, what's the matter? Are you okay? We've all been worrying about you." Rosanna had entered the too crowded bathroom and was glaring at Yvonne. "What have you done? Why is Janice crying?" she demanded.

"I haven't done anything and if Janice wants to tell you what's wrong that's up to her!"

"Nothing's wrong. I'm fine. I'm just having a hormonal moment. Please, don't make a big deal about it. I'll be out in a minute. Rosanna, please go and tell Bill that I'm fine." Janice ripped some toilet paper from the nearest stall and blotted the area under her eyes to wipe away any tell-tale tears.

Yvonne held the door open. "Let's all go back to the table together." She smiled at Janice, who encouraged, took a deep breath and put a smile on her face as she followed Yvonne back to the table.

Rosanna took a seat at the table a few minutes later without saying a word to anyone about what had transpired.

Yvonne settled into bed with her latest mystery novel that she hoped would take her mind off Janice and all the other things that had gone wrong on the tour. She debated with herself about whether to think things through or to get a good night sleep. She decided that a good night sleep would help the most. She needed to remain alert for anymore problems that might arise. The fictional mystery might just lull her to sleep.

Instead of making her sleepy, it stimulated her mind. She wondered why she couldn't use methods like the sleuth in her novel to unravel the mystery of the missing art work. Maybe she should question all the members of the tour. Maybe someone had seen something crucial or maybe someone other than Bill could be involved in the thefts. Maybe David was somehow connected to the thefts. What did she really know about him anyway? Why couldn't she ask all the right questions like the heroine in her book? In her mystery novels, circumstances always built up to the last dangerous moment, and the hero or heroine would pull the answers and the truth out of nowhere in the nick of time. The clues would all of a sudden become obvious, although they'd been elusive before.

"Well, this idea of reading to get sleepy isn't helping much," she muttered to herself. Yvonne reached for the light switch as someone knocked on her door.

"Just a minute." She put her robe and slippers on and hurried to the door. She unlatched the chain and turned the handle, thinking it was probably David. The door burst open and she was shoved backwards by Bill Armstrong.

His cold angry stare looked familiar. "Keep away from my wife. She doesn't need someone like you filling her head with crazy ideas!"

"I'm sorry? I don't know what you're talking about, but you'd better get out of my room immediately. How dare you barge in here and threaten me. I've been nothing but friendly toward your wife, and it seems to me with a husband like you, she could use a friend."

Fear surfaced in her as he raised his hand. She watched as he swung it toward her face. She rolled out of the way as it came down. When she looked up again Bill was falling face forward. David was holding him down on the floor with his knee pressed into his back. "If I ever catch you raising a hand or a finger to Yvonne—or Janice—or any woman again. I will kill you! Do you understand me?"

"Let me up. You're hurting me. I wasn't going to hurt anyone. I only wanted to reason with your girlfriend." Bill's tone of voice was whiny and irritating.

David released the pressure on his back, pulled him up, turned him toward the door and shoved him out. "Straighten up your attitude or leave this tour early. It's your choice, but I'd better not see you near Yvonne again. If I do, I will call the police and see that they lock you up!" He closed the door and locked it.

Yvonne was sitting on the edge of the bed with her head down between her legs.

"Are you okay, Yvonne? Did he hurt you?" David's voice was gentle.

"No, I'm okay. I was—I don't know—I was caught off guard. I thought it might be you at the door."

"Please, from now on be sure who it is before unlocking it. You had me scared there for a second. When I saw him raise his hand to hit you, I thought I'd kill him."

David quizzed Yvonne. "What did he want? Why would he attack you like that?"

"He's getting frustrated and feeling like he's losing control of Janice. He shoved her earlier, and now she's too scared to say or do anything until the tour is over. She thinks if she makes it home in one piece she can leave him for good.

"Bill thinks I'm influencing her behavior. Of course I am, but only to protect her. He can't let that happen if he wants to remain in control over her every move. Why, oh why do men do that?" Yvonne asked the world in general as she remembered all too vividly Gino's violent rages when they were married.

"I can't imagine why, unless he is such a small miserable person that he can't stand for anyone else to be happy." David answered.

"I'm worried about Janice. It's really strange, Rosanna's more a friend to Bill than to Janice. You'd think she'd have her back as another woman. I can't figure that whole arrangement out."

"I want you to get into bed." David gently pressed her shoulders until she sat on the bed. He lifted her legs and covered them. "Lie back. I will stay here for awhile in the chair until I know you're asleep."

"You can't spend the night sitting in the chair, David. You need your sleep too, and furthermore I need you to help me be alert to any other problems that might occur." She rose and walked to the door. "I will lock the door behind you. Please go back to your room. I'll be fine."

He pulled himself from the one stuffed chair in the room, walked to the door and gave her a light goodnight kiss. "I'm glad you're okay. I don't know what I'd do if anything had happened to you."

"David, I—thank you for coming when you did. I don't know either—what I would have done." Yvonne kissed him again. She almost asked him to stay but made her resolve to let him go. She double locked the door.

SANTORINI

DAY 13

"**R**etsina, our specialty, was developed accidentally during a past war. The local people didn't want the enemy to take their prized wine, so resin was added. Afterward, the resinated wine was all that was left to drink, and strangely enough it became popular."

The winery tour guide shrugged his shoulders and was about to continue when Bill Armstrong interrupted. "That just shows what people will sink to when given the chance."

The guide ignored Bill's barb and began leading them down the hall from the welcome area. "For those of you who like traditional wines, I'm sure you'll find one to suit your taste. We have many wonderful wines to choose from. After the tour you may pick from dry white wines to robust reds, and you will see how the gods have favored us in our wine-making." He pointed to a painting depicting the goddess Hera smiling down on an ancient vineyard. "Many believe our wine flourishes today because centuries ago sacrifices were made to Hera, the original Mother-Nature, to insure bountiful harvests and excellent wine-making. Follow me and you will see where we store the wines."

The group followed single file along the path that led through the enormous building. First they passed the large vats where the various grapes were fermented to a room that displayed hundreds of casks, all in different stages of aging. The guide pointed out the different types of wines and where the grapes for each were located. He explained the importance of storing the wine in oak and how the best casks came from different locations in Europe. "When we finish here you may wander at your leisure outside to observe the different kinds of grapes still on their vines. We have cross-bred some grapes to give our wines their own distinctive flavors. When you return to our café, we will treat you to a wonderful wine tasting."

"Can't we skip the part where we wander through the grapevines?" asked Bill. "I'd like to get a head start on the tasting."

"Come on Bill, the exercise will do you good." Rosanna pulled him by the arm and headed off toward a row of grapes. Nicholas followed them while Janice turned and looked for another way to go.

As Janice walked by, she overheard Ari talking to Cynthia. "There's always one party-pooper in every group." Cynthia giggled and clung onto Ari's arm as they ducked into a row of grapes.

Janice wandered off by herself. Looking closely at the small green grapes just beginning to form, she wondered if there'd be a problem if she picked one and tasted it. Her anger at being put down by Bill made her feel rebellious. She decided to pull one off the vine and taste it. From now on I will have a backbone. Too bad, the grape is sour. I guess it will have to mature before it will sweeten up, or who knows maybe it will always be sour and that would mean the wine will not be sweet but dry. It's so peaceful here. Maybe I'll keep walking for miles and get so lost in the grape vines that I won't ever be found. Probably no one will miss me anyway.

"Janice, are you doing okay?"

Janice grabbed hold of a vine for support. "Yvonne, I didn't see you standing there."

"I thought this might be a good time to check on you. I was worried that Bill might have hurt you again, especially after last night." Yvonne looked so serious it took Janice by surprise.

"What do you mean especially after last night?"

"Didn't he tell you about coming to see me?" Yvonne saw confusion written on Janice's face. "He tried to warn me to stay away from you, and when I said I thought you needed a friend, especially since you were married to someone like him, he raised a hand to hit me. I know I shouldn't have said that, but I was upset by the way he burst into my room. Fortunately, David was nearby and heard him. He put a stop to it before Bill had a chance to do me harm."

"Oh my God, Yvonne—are—are you sure you're okay?"

"Yes. I'm fine. Don't worry about me. It's you I'm concerned about."

Janice let go of the vine and faced Yvonne. "What next? Now, he's threatening my friends. I can't believe how he's gone off the deep end since we came on this trip. Something's very wrong with him. I wish I knew what it is." Janice clenched her fists, but her voice held hope. "Do you think it has something to do with Rosanna? Do you think he might have guilt feelings about having an affair?"

Yvonne's eyes softened. "I can't answer that. I don't know him well enough, but I agree that he's losing control of his temper, and if you're not careful, you could get hurt. I wish you'd reconsider staying with me, or even leaving the tour early. The situation may worsen by the time you return home, and then it will be harder to leave him."

"You're right. I need to think about how to handle this." Janice turned away and continued to walk deeper into the vineyard.

Yvonne left Janice to ponder her problems and found David chatting with Evelyn and Richard. They were outside the café waiting for the wine tasting to begin. "Are you all enjoying the tour so far?"

They each responded with an enthusiastic, "Yes." Within the next ten minutes, they were joined by the rest of the group. All were accounted for except Janice.

"Where's my wife?" Bill asked to no one in particular. "She's probably lost. I guess I'll have to go find her if we ever want to do this wine tasting." He sighed deeply, the martyr.

"That's okay, Bill. You go ahead and taste the wine. I'll find Janice," said Yvonne.

"She's my wife, and I'll find her." Bill stalked off going in the opposite direction to where Yvonne last saw Janice.

A few minutes later Janice strolled up to the group. Yvonne told her that Bill had just left searching for her. "Oh me, I guess I'd better go get him so that you can start."

"Never mind, Janice, I'll do it. The rest of you go on in." David set off in the direction he had seen Bill go.

They were all settled at small tables for four when David returned with Bill. Janice had saved him a seat next to her, but her attention was on the wine steward explaining about the fruity taste of the red wine being passed around. Bill plunked down with a grunt between Janice and Rosanna. David found an empty seat next to Yvonne.

To cleanse their palates between tastes, cheese and crackers were provided. The cheeses were meant to complement the wines. One by one they each tried the offerings.

"Now this is what I call a good time. Wine, women, and song." Bill raised his glass to the table with one hand and put his arm around Rosanna and hugged her with the other. Rosanna laughed it off and pulled away. Nicholas looked at the group and rolled his eyes.

Yvonne watched Rosanna look around the table to see who was paying attention to Bill's obnoxious behavior. Everyone looked flushed with wine, relaxed and oblivious to the relationship issues between the Armstrongs and the Fontinellis except for Janice, and herself.

Rosanna caught them watching her and smiled, embarrassed.

After the tour ended they boarded the minibus that would take them back to Fira and the hotel. David caught a glimpse of a familiar stocky figure climbing into his black sedan.

For afternoon activity, the younger members of the group decided to visit one of the black sand beaches. Evelyn and Richard elected to go shopping. Bill, Janice, Nicholas, and Rosanna did not join either group. Yvonne remained in her hotel room. She needed to check on Beverly, make stateside calls home and to check on her agency business.

David retired to his room where he opened his laptop computer and answered e-mails. All was quiet on the business front. No word from Demetrius. Worried, he shot off an e-mail to him and shared how much he enjoyed meeting and dining with his parents and brother. Then he inquired about some new accounts and requested a report on what was happening with business in general.

Yvonne and David had planned to meet at the hotel pool at 4 pm for a swim and a strategy session on how to solve the mystery of the frequent accidents and help Janice.

The pool area was empty when David arrived. He commandeered a chaise lounge for each of them and waited for Yvonne.

David stared openly as Yvonne dropped her swim suit cover and towel on the lounge. She grinned and took a model turn. "Do you like it?"

"Oh yeah—very much. Who would have thought a one piece bathing suit could look so sexy."

Yvonne turned and made a shallow dive into the pool. When she surfaced, she swam back toward David. Her hair was slicked back and a look of pure devilish delight was on her face as she splashed him with water.

"Okay, now you've done it. You're going to be sorry you did that." He jumped into the pool beside her and grabbed her to him. He kissed her while pulling them both under water. She squirmed, slipped out of his grasp and shot off toward the other end of the pool. He overtook her in a few strokes. They raced and swam and played like children, both feeling alive and younger than they had in years, but unaware they were being watched from a nearby window.

They warmed quickly in the sunshine. Lounging quietly for awhile, they admired the view of the pool water flowing into the turquoise ocean. The sound of the water calmed their senses. The horizon was dotted with small motor boats and sailing vessels. The backdrop shimmered with colors from sea-foam greens to pale blues and white cotton puff clouds.

Yvonne brought them back to the moment. "This mysterious man who keeps turning up everywhere, I wish we knew who he is and what he wants." Yvonne pulled her sunglasses from her tote bag and put them on, shielding her eyes from the glare of the setting sun.

She reminded David of a woman of intrigue, sitting there with dark glasses on. Feeling like James Bond, he toasted her with his gin and tonic. "Shaken, not stirred," he playfully announced before he returned to Yvonne's serious observation. "The only way we're going to get an answer to that question is to confront him the next time we see him."

"It scares me, but there seems to be no other way." Yvonne reached for David's arm. "Promise me you won't do anything on your own? We'll confront him together. If we do, there will be less chance of him getting the drop on us and less chance that either of us will get hurt."

"Sounds reasonable to me." David lifted Yvonne's hand and kissed her palm. "Promise me you won't pull any stunts on your own either."

"Of course, I wouldn't dream of it." Yvonne pulled her hand away and lifted her glass of ginger ale in a mock cheer, then took a drink.

The sun and spirits had sapped their strength. They returned to their rooms to nap and refresh themselves. The evening was left open for tour participants to be on their own. David and Yvonne took advantage of the opportunity. They agreed to find a small casual café away from the touristy restaurants and enjoy a quiet dinner getting to know each other better.

At 7:00 pm, Yvonne invited David into her room. She placed the local city guide on the bedside table and turned toward him with smiling eyes and a formal bow. "For your personal dining pleasure tonight, I have chosen the restaurant Selene for its quiet ambience and the terrace view of the caldera. The food, all based on local recipes, is touted to be excellent."

David grinned in satisfaction. "It certainly comes in handy having a travel agent as a girlfriend."

"Is that what I am? Your girlfriend?"

"Would you want to be?"

"I'm not sure that I'm ready to be someone's girlfriend."

"Well, do you want to date around? Date others—not just me?" David braced himself for her answer.

"Well, no, I'm not interested in dating anyone else, but that doesn't mean I'm ready to be at one person's beck and call either." Yvonne softened her voice. "When I am ready, I hope that it might be you that I'll be calling my boyfriend. It's just that I'm not ready for a commitment."

"Do you mind if I ask why you're having such an issue about being committed? Do you even know yourself what the reason is?

Yvonne looked exasperated. "Don't you see, David, I must learn to stand on my own two feet. I have a child to support, and I want to set an example for Christy, so that she will never fall prey to a sadistic misogynist like I did."

"Okay, I guess I can understand that. Maybe we can talk more at dinner. I want to understand, and I can be patient as long as I know there's a chance that you might choose to be my best girl some day. Shall we go?"

"Yes, let's go." Yvonne picked up her purse and shawl, allowing David to wrap it around her shoulders during an awkward moment as they both tried to ignore their physical attraction.

Dinner was a subdued affair. David continued their discussion from earlier. "Tell me about your childhood. Was it happy?"

Yvonne smiled tentatively. "Growing up, my parents were very protective of me, especially my father. In the Cuban culture men are raised to be very macho. Protecting his family was his number one priority. Thank heavens for my mother. If it hadn't been for her strong will, I might never have been allowed to date. She helped bring some balance to his chauvinistic attitude, and overtime he began to accept that in America women were not simply belongings to be treasured but independent people with rights. He has mellowed quite a bit over the years." Yvonne chuckled and took a sip of wine. "They had some real rows over my teenage years and me growing into womanhood. In the end my Dad was able to realize that by allowing me some small freedoms, I'd be less likely to run away."

David took her hand. "What about your ex? Gino, isn't it? When did you get involved with him?"

"Well, in spite of my desire to grow up and be independent, I was afraid to be on my own. Partly because I'd been so spoiled and protected and partly because I was in love with being in love. I wanted the security I'd grown up with to continue. All I really wanted was to be a good mother and wife to a nice man. I saw how happy my mother was and she inspired me. When Gino came along, he was more than happy to step into the roll of husband and protector. He made me feel safe and secure and adored." Yvonne pulled away her hand. "For a short while anyway. As soon as the honeymoon was over, Gino's dark side began to take over. He controlled me in small ways, first by choosing what clothes I should wear, then, my hairstyle. It got worse. He began telling me what I should think. I grew to be unsure of my own feelings and self worth. Next, he started alienating my friends, and finally my family. Once he had me all to himself, he began to criticize my every move. He wore away at my self esteem until at one point, I actually thought of killing myself. I felt like a prisoner in my own home."

"I can't understand how you'd let him take over your life like that. What about your mother and father? Didn't they see what was happening?" David took a long drink.

"It happened so gradually, and I was ashamed. I tried to hide the worst of it from them. They complained that I was too busy to make time for them."

"How were you finally able to end the marriage?"

"It wasn't easy. I tried to stand up to him. I told him I would leave him if he didn't treat me with respect and allow me the freedom to see my family and friends. He laughed at me. In the blink of an eye, I was picking myself up off the ground. He punched me so hard that my head was spinning. Shocked and shaken, I stayed in bed for days. He told everyone I had the flu. He apologized and swore he'd never hit me again, but by that time, I feared what he would do if I tried to leave." Yvonne fought back tears. "It happened again, and I knew it was just a matter of time before he'd start treating Christy the same way. I couldn't bear the thought of her being subjected to his dark moods. One day I realized if I wanted to live, I'd have to leave him. I waited until he left for the day, and I packed our bags and moved home." Yvonne watched a frown crease David's forehead. "My father was furious and wanted to have Gino arrested, but I just wanted him out of our lives. I'm not sure how my father did it, but Gino finally backed off and left us alone."

"Thank God, you're okay. I hope I never run into him. It will take all my self control not to punch him in the face." David signaled the waiter for the check.

"I dread to think where I'd be today if it hadn't been for Christy. I might have stayed. I'd still be cowering under his domineering attitude, or perhaps by now I'd be dead." David's angry look roused Yvonne from the past.

David sat speechless thinking about the jerk who'd put her through hell, and how he could get even with him.

"David, it's all behind me now, and I am growing independent and strong. Any man that I allow into my life in the future will have to understand that about me."

"I think I do understand, but forgive me if I want to be in your life as a friend and protector too. In the meantime, your ex-husband better hope that I never run into him in a dark alley. He'd be lucky to pick himself up at all when I finished with him."

Yvonne chuckled. Men, if they weren't trying to dominate women, they were conquering each other all in the name of chivalry. "You know, David, I see a little bit of myself in Janice. I can see that Bill is domineering and has worn away at her self esteem. I also recognize that his abuse toward her is escalating—now he's knocked her down. She says it's the first time but I wonder..."

"We may never know, but I want you to know not all men are bastards. Some respect and appreciate women for the beautiful creatures they are." David took a last drink of his coffee.

"I know. My own father is a gentle man. Though he could seem very stern when he was angry, he has never laid a finger on me or my mother." Yvonne walked with David outside the restaurant to wait while he arranged for a cab. "David, for now the most important thing is to make sure this tour finishes smoothly and that no one else gets hurt in any way."

David took her hand and waited silently for the cab to arrive.

It's funny, thought Yvonne. I feel like a great weight has been lifted from my shoulders. Telling David about Gino scared me at first, but now I realize that I can talk about him and still stay strong. Maybe, just maybe, I can put the past behind me for good.

David escorted Yvonne to her room. "We've made it through a whole day without incident. That's a good sign. Don't you agree?"

"Mm, yes a good sign."

They each jumped at the loud noise. "Oh my God! Was that a gunshot? It sounds nearby." Yvonne pushed David out of her way and headed toward Janice and Bill's room. David followed Yvonne. Others having heard the shot came out of their rooms to see what had happened.

Rosanna opened the door to Yvonne's urgent knocking and let her in. David followed inside and closed the door while others gathered in the hall.

Janice was on her knees next to Bill's prone body. The gun lay on the floor near Bill's head. Blood oozed from the hole in the center of his chest.

"Somebody, please, call an ambulance. Hurry." Yvonne turned toward David with her plea.

David dialed the front desk. "This is David Ludlow calling from the Armstrong's room. We need you to call an ambulance. There's been a horrible accident. Mr. Armstrong's been shot."

Yvonne lifted Janice by the shoulders. "Janice, come sit over here out of the way until we get help for Bill."

"Shouldn't someone be giving him mouth to mouth resuscitation or something?" Rosanna wrung her hands.

"It's too late. He's dead." Nicholas had slipped into the room with other concerned members of the group. He placed his fingers on Bill's neck and found no pulse.

"What happened? Janice, did he threaten you?"

"Yes, he threatened her. That's exactly what happened," said Rosanna.

"Please Rosanna, let Janice answer for herself." Yvonne kneeled next to Janice's chair.

More noise interrupted Yvonne's effort to get answers from Janice. "What has happened here? Has someone been shot? Nothing like this has ever happened in our hotel before." Mr. Zambas, the gaunt-faced hotel owner, entered the room with Mrs. Zambas, close behind.

"We have called for an ambulance and the police. Perhaps everyone except those involved should wait outside or in your rooms until the police determine whether they need your help." David began clearing the room and hallway of bystanders.

Rosanna and Nicholas remained along with Janice, Yvonne, David and the Zambas'.

"Janice, can you tell us what happened?" Yvonne persisted.

Janice sniffled as tears rolled down her cheeks. She spoke softly. "It happened so quickly. Rosanna and Bill were discussing where we should go to dinner—when Bill noticed my suitcase standing near the closet door. I had pulled it out to pack my belongings. I told him that I was going to leave the tour early—tomorrow—and that he would be free to spend all his time with Rosanna or whomever he wished without worrying about me being an embarrassment to him. I said that they could both bring their dirty little secrets out in the open and discuss them freely." Her tone seethed with bitterness. "They both told me I was crazy, and he was not embarrassed by me. I told him that I'd seen enough recently to know something underhanded was going on, and I'd made up my mind to leave. It was too late for him to change it." Janice began to cry. "That's when he went into this mad rage. He pulled his own suitcase out of the closet, opened it, ripped at this hidden compartment and brought out a gun." Janice gulped in air to stop her crying. "He pointed the gun at me and said that I was to unpack my suitcase until it was time to return to Athens and that I'd better keep my mouth shut about my suspicions."

Rosanna spoke, "I told him to calm down and put his gun away and that only seemed to make him angrier."

"Yes. So, I said that I would unpack after he put the gun away. That's when he grabbed me and tried to shove me toward my suitcase to pick it up. When I tried to right myself, I fell backward knocking us both down. He tried to grab me and the gun was between us and I was trying to get off of him when the gun went off. I—I didn't mean to kill him. I never would have done that no matter what. Don't you see? That's why I wanted to leave before something awful like this happened."

The sound of sirens overshadowed Janice's last statement.

The police released Janice, Rosanna and Yvonne after taking their statements, satisfied it had been a case of self defense. They would all be required to present themselves at the local police station in the morning to repeat their statements and file formal reports.

SANTORINI

DAY 14

Yvonne insisted Janice stay with her for the night. Not able to sleep, she imagined that tomorrow's activities would be consumed with helping Janice arrange to ship Bill's body home. They each took turns tossing and turning, and it showed in their weary morning faces when David arrived to escort them to breakfast.

"I'm not the least bit hungry. I should go to my room and pack up Bill's things."

"You needn't go through that alone. Come with us, have some coffee. It will help wake you up. Then I'll help you pack up Bill's belongings for the trip home."

"Thanks, Yvonne, I should do this by myself. I've caused you enough worry and inconvenience already. I want you to know— I feel awful about ruining your tour and everything else that has happened." Janice pulled at the buttons on her light-weight cardigan.

"Nonsense, it wasn't your fault. Bill brought this on himself."

"I know, but he wasn't always so bad. Now that he's gone, for some reason, I want to remember the good times we had together." Janice fought back tears.

David held the door open and ushered them to breakfast. "I'm not sure the police will allow you to pack up his stuff yet. Police tape was taped on the door when I passed the room. They'll probably be here soon to re-examine it for evidence. After we're finished eating, I'll check with the authorities to see when you can return to your room."

"Thank you, David." Janice was relieved to have his help. The longer she could avoid returning to the room where she shot Bill, the better.

One by one, each member of the tour stopped by their breakfast table and offered help and condolences to Janice. She accepted graciously, bravely holding back tears.

Janice picked at her fruit and took only a few sips of coffee.

Yvonne touched Janice's arm with a comforting hand. "Perhaps this was a mistake. I can see all this attention is taking its toll on you. Maybe we should return to my room. We can wait there until David clears it with the police to pack up your room."

Her kindness was more than Janice could bear. She rose from her chair and ran from the dining room desperate to make it back to the room before letting her tears flow.

"I better go after her." Yvonne looked at the half eaten meal on the table, then at David.

"Go ahead, follow her. I'll take care of the bill." David remained at the table taking his time. He knew Yvonne would need some time alone to comfort Janice.

"Many people believe that Santorini is the origin of the lost civilization of Atlantis." Ari guided the remaining small group on their morning excursion and wondered who else might be missing tomorrow. Normally, tourists would be most interested in the legend of Atlantis, one reason the island was so popular. "The archaeological sites on Santorini are visited year round by tourists and curiosity seekers, all trying to relate their findings to the lost civilization. Akrotiri is a Minoan town preserved in volcanic ash. It will be our first stop. Later we'll visit three beaches: one red, one grey, and one white." Ari's forced enthusiasm was apparent to everyone on the bus.

Mark tuned out Ari's litany as he whispered in Cynthia's ear. "Just like the lost civilization of Atlantis, I think there's more than meets the eye to what happened to Bill Armstrong."

"What makes you say that? The guy was a real jerk. I'm surprised she didn't shoot him long before now." Cynthia ignored the scenery and focused on Mark.

Seated behind Mark and Cynthia, Missy poked her head up between them to speak, then grabbed Todd's hand and gave him a grateful look. "I agree with Cynthia. If my husband treated me that way, I wouldn't put up with it for a second."

Out of something bad, comes something good. Todd was relieved to think Missy might have come to an understanding about their future. She really does appreciate me. If only she'd change her mind about having a baby.

Evelyn placed her journal in her tote bag. "It's strange the way Bill, Rosanna and Nicholas were always together, the way they'd shut Janice out of their goings-on. I wondered myself if they were in some sort of weird relationship." She leaned across the aisle to whisper to the others. "I never could figure out why they were on this tour anyway. Apparently, they'd been to Greece twice before, so why do a guided tour? Why not just travel by themselves?"

"Come on, Evelyn, don't you be worrying about this. Remember, we're here for your trip, and I don't want anything to spoil it." Richard patted her shoulder.

"Hmph. It's hard to ignore all the accidents and someone getting shot. Then again, it's rather exciting. Reminds me of Murder on the Orient Express or one of those Agatha Christie novels I used to read all the time. Remember, Richard, how I used to read them when the kids were little. It was the perfect escape from boring housework."

"Yes, dear, I remember, but this is coming a bit too close for comfort. I think we should stay out of it and concentrate on enjoying what's left of our tour." Richard turned his face away and shut his eyes, ending the conversation.

David and Nicholas accompanied Janice, Yvonne and Rosanna to the police station. They were led into a bleak waiting room. Yvonne watched and waited while a man with black hair and a shiny bald spot on the top of his head called each person into his office, one by one.

Janice gave her statement, once again omitting her suspicions about Rosanna and Bill being in a relationship. After all, she thought, how foolish would that make me look? It was all a crazy accident anyway. I still can't believe it happened and that he's no longer here. Talk-

ing about the altercation with Detective Stavros brought Janice to
tears again. "I know things weren't right between us, but I still loved
him. I never would have wanted this to happen."

"Thank you, Mrs. Armstrong. You may go back to the waiting
room. Please ask Mrs. Fontinelli to come and see me now." Detective
Stavros stood up and waited for Rosanna to return.

Rosanna claimed to be confused about the argument between
Janice and Bill but stated that Bill had definitely pulled a gun and
become physical toward Janice in his desire to keep her from leaving
the tour early. She expressed sympathy toward Janice confirming to
the police that Bill had been less than kind to her since they departed
on their trip.

Yvonne told the detective how Bill browbeat Janice in front of
the others and mentioned that Bill had barged into her room, accused her of taking control of his wife and knocked her down. She
explained how David's sudden appearance was the only thing that
stopped him from causing her physical harm.

After finishing with Yvonne, Police Detective Stavros had the
witnesses brought in from the waiting room. After they were seated
he took turns looking directly into the eyes of each person present.
"Well, it seems that Mr. Bill Armstrong was not a nice man, nor was
he a loving husband. I wonder what caused his behavior to worsen
while here in Greece. Most family disputes happen closer to home.
Wouldn't you agree?"

Janice cried. Everyone else remained silent.

Yvonne squirmed in her seat. "Detective Stavros, this has been a
horrible tragedy. I don't think any of us understand what caused it,
least of all Janice. Please, we must help her make arrangements to ship
Bill's body home. Can you help us with that? Will his body be released? Our group is scheduled to fly to Athens tomorrow and home
the next day. Would it be possible for him to fly with us?"

"If the coroner finds that Mrs. Armstrong's story is true, we
will be able to release the body. If he finds any discrepancies in the
story, we would need to do a complete autopsy and an inquest, and
then no one could leave." Stavros answered his ringing phone and
listened to the short call before thanking the person on the other

end of the line. "That was the coroner. His report confirms that everything happened the way that you said it did, so I will be able to release the body tomorrow." He turned his stare to Janice. "Mrs. Armstrong, you have my deepest condolences for your loss. I can see that you are genuinely distressed by what has happened, and I wish you well on your return home."

The small group breathed a collective sigh of relief. Before they were able to depart, Detective Stavros stood. "Ms. Suarez, Mr. Ludlow, I'd like to see you in my office for a few minutes before you leave."

"What? Why?" Yvonne was flustered.

Stavros held the door open for them.

When they were seated, he asked them to wait a few minutes. He left the office and could be seen sending Rosanna, Janice and Nicholas on their way. A few minutes later he reentered the office with another man in tow.

"You!" Yvonne's eyes widened.

David stood up from his chair. "Detective, what is this man doing here? He's been following us and I think he may have something to do with several accidents that have plagued us during the tour. In fact, I believe he was somehow involved with Bill Armstrong."

"Please, Mr. Ludlow, sit down. I will explain."

David backed down into his chair.

"This man, who you know as Damian, is here because he's been following the Fontinellis and the Armstrongs. We believe, but are not yet able to prove, that they are part of an art smuggling ring that operates throughout Europe and America."

"Well, if you believe that, why are you talking to us and not them?"

"We wanted to warn you and Ms. Suarez to be very careful. We are aware that you searched the Armstrong's room and that there have been a number of accidents that have occurred on your tour. We want you to understand, these thieves are very dangerous."

"Surely you can't include Janice Armstrong in your suspicions." Yvonne sat on the edge of her chair.

"No. We don't. In fact, we think that Bill Armstrong may have been an unsuspecting patsy set up by the Fontinellis. They took advantage of his greed and his need to be a big shot to enlist him in their schemes. Now that he has been eliminated by Mrs. Armstrong, they can breathe a bit easier. She has solved one of their problems. There will be one less person with which to share the proceeds of the stolen art."

"If you know all this, why aren't you arresting them?"

"Because we do not have enough solid evidence yet, but we are very close. As I said they are slick and have been watched by the authorities for some time."

"We are taking the two of you into our confidence because we want to make it clear—you are to stay out of our way. Pay attention to your tour so it ends with no one else getting hurt. We will tolerate no interference from you in our investigation. Is that understood?"

"Yes." Yvonne looked at David, and he nodded his agreement.

"Well then, please return to your tour, and act as if nothing unusual is going on. And, if you should notice Damian, please do not bring your attention to him in any way." Detective Stavros ushered them out of the office.

Yvonne leaned close to David so the cab driver couldn't hear what they were discussing. "I never imagined this situation could be so serious. Up until now it's all been conjecture, like playing a game or piecing together a puzzle, but I have Christy to think about, and I can't take any risks that would jeopardize her future."

"Of course you can't."

"David, we need to talk, away from the others."

"Where and when should we meet without causing suspicion?"

"First we need to check on Janice. Make sure she's okay. I think Rosanna's sticking to her like glue for a reason."

"She is and I'm beginning to understand why." David's comment was cut short when the cab made a sharp turn throwing Yvonne sideways into David. Their eyes locked for a moment distracting him.

Yvonne pulled herself back into a straight posture. "Do you think Rosanna fears Janice knows something she shouldn't about their art 'dealings'?"

"They've been pretty good at keeping her in the dark so far." The cab jerked to a quick stop in front of the hotel. After David paid the driver, they went to see Janice.

Rosanna opened Janice's room door. "She's napping, poor thing, she's exhausted."

"Rosanna, would you like me to stay with her for awhile? You could probably use a nap yourself. This can't have been easy for you—and Nicholas is probably missing you." Yvonne stepped into the room.

"Janice is a dear friend. I wouldn't think of leaving her, and Nicholas understands completely. Why don't you and David take a break? After all, you'll need to greet the other members of the tour when they return this afternoon." Rosanna moved so that Yvonne was forced out the door.

"All right, if you're sure it's no trouble. Let me know if you need a break watching her or if she asks for me.

"Well, that didn't go very well." Yvonne brought David back to her room.

"You heard what Stavros said. Keep it cool."

"I know, David, but I'm worried about Janice. She's an innocent victim in all this. Do you suppose it was Rosanna who pushed her down the steps at the Acropolis?"

"Most likely, but I'm not sure that I see the point. Why would she do that?"

"Maybe it was all part of keeping her off balance and more under their control."

"I suppose that makes a weird sort of sense. What about Nicholas? He always seems to be so quiet and such a lap dog where Rosanna's concerned."

"I don't get that either."

"You know, we never did find out what agency Damian worked for, but if he is one of the good guys, who ran down Beverly?"

"Another good question, things aren't adding up neatly. There must be more to all this than we've been told.

"Something else has been bothering me. What about the night the planter was dropped off the roof—aimed at you? What did that

173

have to do with all of this?" David couldn't refrain from pulling Yvonne into his arms.

Yvonne relaxed into him. She felt snug and safe for the moment. "Maybe it was a mistake. Maybe it was meant for someone else." Yvonne pushed herself away from David. "If I remember correctly, Janice wasn't even there that evening, and I can't imagine who else would have been targeted." Yvonne poured each of them a glass of water from the make-shift bar on the small oak table in the corner of the room. "Perhaps they were trying to scare me so that I would end the tour early."

"That doesn't make sense either. If we'd ended early, they wouldn't have been able to travel to Andros Island where the last piece of art went missing."

"I'm getting more and more confused by the minute." Yvonne sat on the bed hard enough to bounce herself up and down causing the whole bed to shake. She laughed nervously at herself, and then tears welled up in her eyes. "Dammit! I hate it when I cry. Sometimes I'm so darn female. I hate it when I lose control. I wanted this tour to be perfect. I wanted everyone to rave about the great time they'd had and be ready to sign up the minute we returned home for another tour I'd plan for next year, but everything that could go wrong, has gone wrong. And not only gone wrong, but one person's been seriously injured and another killed. How much worse can it get?"

Yvonne stood up. "I have to pull myself together. We don't have the luxury of relaxing, not even for a minute. Not until we know what Rosanna and Nicholas are up to, and whether or not Janice is in trouble." Yvonne jumped as the phone on the bedside table rang.

"Hello? Okay. Thanks Inspector. I will let her know. Thanks so much for following up on this. I know she'll appreciate it."

Yvonne let out a deep sigh. "They're going to escort Bill's body to be sure it makes it on the plane back to Athens tomorrow morning, and they're going to follow up to be sure it connects to our flight home. I wonder if Janice is still sleeping. She'd want to know about this.

"David, I'll go talk to Janice, that is, if I can get around the watchdog. Why don't you go relax in your room? We can meet later before going to dinner with the group."

"Whatever you say, but be careful. Arousing Rosanna's suspicion could be dangerous."

"Don't worry. I can take care of myself."

David acquiesced to her need to stay in control. "I'll be waiting in my room to hear how it goes." He kissed her lightly on the lips, resisted the urge to grab her close and departed.

Janice answered the door and invited Yvonne inside.

"How are you feeling?"

"Not so hot. Rosanna insisted I take another sleeping pill, but I held my ground and refused. I didn't think she was ever going to leave me alone, so I pretended to be asleep, and finally she left."

"Have you said anything to her about your suspicions that she was having an affair with Bill?"

"No, I haven't. I probably should, but it all seems so pointless now. Anyway, why make poor Nicholas miserable about the whole thing. He must have been blind to what went on. Don't you think?"

"Yes, I suppose." Yvonne bit her lip in an effort to refrain from rolling her eyes and giving away her true feelings. "Janice, how long have you known Rosanna and Nicholas? I had the impression that you had been best friends for years."

"We only met them about three years ago when we were traveling on our first trip to Italy. Bill had made a lot of money selling land in Florida that he'd inherited from his father. Long ago the land was considered rural—old country land, not good for much except farming, but with the expansion of Fort Lauderdale and the surrounding cities, about anything that wasn't swamp land became valuable." Janice sat back in her chair. Her chin quivered.

"Bill had always wanted to travel, so we planned our first trip to Europe. We were on one of those sightseeing bus tours in Italy, the kind you book from the lobby of your hotel, when we sat across the row from the Fontinellis. This was their first time to Italy too. After chatting, we found that they were also from Fort Lauderdale. From then on we travelled together.

"It hasn't always been easy. They had money to burn, and we had trouble keeping up. Bill wanted to live the rich lifestyle they enjoyed.

I always felt they egged him on to spend money even when it was a strain for us. After a year or so went by, they began to let Bill in on some real estate deals and art acquisitions and other things. Bill had a good head for numbers, but I never did." She shrugged her shoulders and continued. "Thanks to Nicholas and Rosanna, Bill did very well financially. Who would have thought that a building superintendent would do so well? He was very proud of himself." Janice dropped her head as the realization hit her once again that Bill was dead and that she had killed him.

"When did you start to suspect something wasn't right? That maybe they were having an affair?"

"Not until this trip. Right from the beginning, even before my fall at the Acropolis, Bill seemed especially keyed up, very unlike himself. I was afraid to say anything or move the wrong way for fear I'd be criticized. It's funny, but I think maybe he was ashamed of something he'd done. Rather than face it or admit it, he took his self-loathing out on me. I'm not sure what happened, but I felt the change then, and nothing has been right between us since. I can't help but think that Rosanna had something to do with it." Janice clenched her fists.

"Rosanna has always been a controlling person, but I never felt threatened by it until recently. It was like she and Bill were becoming closer—like they had some sort of secret between them. Believe it or not, Bill wasn't always as rude or boorish. He could be grumpy when he was angry or upset, but when he was happy, he couldn't have been a more thoughtful and considerate person. I can't imagine what went so wrong."

Yvonne found it hard to imagine Bill being considerate but gave an understanding look to Janice anyway. "I think you should continue to keep your guard up around the Fontinellis. If something fishy is going on with them, they could be worried you might know something. They may imagine Bill let information slip about their scam."

Yvonne relayed the information to Janice that Inspector Stavros had given her confirming that Bill would be traveling home with them at the end of the tour. "Perhaps you'd want to leave the tour sooner, but since we are scheduled to leave day after tomorrow from

Athens anyway, I think it would be better if you remained with us for some moral support. What do you think?"

Janice hesitated. "You're probably right. I'm not thinking too clearly right now. I could use a level headed friend to help me with the trip back home." She hugged Yvonne and shuffled back to bed. "I won't be up to joining the group for dinner this evening. Don't worry, I'll order room service."

Yvonne went back to her room to think about all that had transpired over the course of their trip. She was determined to find out the real cause of the accidents. She found herself thinking about the weeks that led up to the tour. She'd never imagined her travel plans would have gone so awry. She told herself to think things through logically. Put them in order. See where the clues might be. See what she might have missed, what might have been a simple misstep or misstatement. The dead body moving on the baggage beltway came to mind. How could that murder possibly have been related to all the other accidents? And yet, through some sense of dread, she felt it was. Then she remembered something that became the missing link. She knew exactly why it had happened.

Her first instinct was to find David and discuss it with him. She knocked on his door. He didn't answer. That's strange, she thought. Where could he be? We're to meet up before dinner. Now I'll have to wait until we're at dinner, and we may not have the chance to talk privately. I'll find the proof myself. Janice's life could be at stake.

Returning to her room to dress for dinner she thought about ways to gain entry into the Fontinelli's room. Yvonne kicked off her shoes to relax for a few minutes. A knock on her door pulled her from her reverie. "Who is it?"

"It's me, David."

She opened the door. "David, where have you been? I stopped by your room, and you weren't there?"

"I've been doing a bit of surveillance. I happened to see Rosanna and Nicholas leave the hotel and thought it was rather interesting. I watched Damian follow them, and I followed him." He gave Yvonne a smug smile that was worthy of Sherlock Holmes.

Yvonne pulled him inside and closed the door. "Well, out with it. Where did they go?"

"Now, that's the interesting part. They went to the morgue at the police station. It seems that they needed to take one last look at their good buddy Bill."

"You're kidding. What is that all about?"

"I wasn't able to find out, but I'm pretty sure Damian did. I believe he questioned the coroner because he left a few minutes later. I wasn't about to let Damian know I was following them. The police were adamant that we should stay out of it. I don't want to be the one to further jeopardize your tour or prevent us from leaving on schedule."

"How about asking Rosanna why they went to see the body? Of course we can't count on her to tell us the truth. Why do you think they went?

David shrugged. "To say good-bye? To see what may have been on his person at the time he died? None of it makes any sense. Surely they would know that his effects would have been given to Janice."

David took a seat in the bed-side chair. His expression turned serious. "Why were you looking for me? Did you miss me? Did you want to have some fun before dinner?" His eyes narrowed from serious to sexy giving Yvonne goose bumps.

"David, stop." She ignored the blush that rose to her cheeks. "Do you remember when we first landed in Athens and the body appeared on the luggage belt?"

"How could I forget?" The amused twinkle in David's eyes faded.

"I think I know what happened. Remember when they gathered us for questioning and Bill showed up later? We all assumed that he'd stopped at the men's room. What if he slipped in the back and murdered the baggage handler?"

"What was his motive?"

"It's simple. The handler was passing along to Rosanna, via Bill, the stolen artifacts from the museum. They eliminated him to leave no witnesses. Remember, the police confiscated our luggage by that time and were performing their search. But, Bill retained his small carry on when he supposedly stopped in the restroom. I remember he had it in his possession when he caught up with the group, so I don't believe that it was ever searched." Yvonne was keyed up.

"If that's the case, where do you think the artifacts are now?"

"I'm not sure, but I do remember early on when Janice talked about the great deals that Bill always seemed to find on art and the small antique shop they'd discovered and the way that Bill cut her off mid-sentence as if she'd committed some serious crime. It was the next day that Janice had her mysterious accident at the Acropolis." Yvonne gulped in some air and continued. "I don't think he found a special shop or deal. She may have seen the items and that was his cover story. You may recall, he wouldn't even let her discuss it or describe them."

"If what you're saying is true, then Janice may still be in danger. If she were to remember things the way that you did, she would be a threat to Rosanna and Nicholas." David pulled up a chair for Yvonne. "You'd better sit down while we think this through."

Yvonne hesitated feeling she could think better on her feet. "The first thing we need to do is locate the stolen items. Then we can contact the police and let them handle it from there." Yvonne sounded more confident than she felt.

"Why not tell the police what we know now and let them handle it?" David could see that his question fell on deaf ears.

"What if they don't follow up until Rosanna and Nicholas decide to hurt Janice? It may be too late then. The police will move slowly for caution's sake but that may be dangerous at this point. Don't forget we're returning to Athens tomorrow, so they'll have to act before we leave Athens to fly home."

"Okay then, where do you think we should look for the stolen artifacts?" David was at a loss to answer her.

Yvonne continued with her own idea. "What if we wait until we know that they're occupied with dinner? I'll make an excuse to leave the table, and we can meet at their room, find a way to get inside and search."

"Do you really think they'll have it hidden in their room?"

"If we don't find it in their room or luggage at this point, I'm convinced they have already found a way to hide it from the authorities.

Keep in mind they are professional smugglers." Yvonne pointed her finger at David. "For Janice's sake we must try."

David stood up and took her by the shoulders. "Yvonne, this could be dangerous. Don't forget you have a daughter to think about."

"Don't you think I've been worried about that? That's why it's so important that we know where Rosanna and Nicholas are. That's why I need you to watch my back. But, I can't throw Janice to the wolves either, can I?" The pitch of Yvonne's voice indicated that she was bordering on hysteria.

"Okay. I give up. How do you suggest that I slip away from the table as well, and not seem suspicious? I'd like to prevent comments about your reputation, and if we both disappear at the same time, you know there'll be gossip."

"Good point. I hadn't thought about that. Maybe you should stay in your room, and I'll let them know that you have a stomach upset or something that would prevent you from going to dinner. Then when I leave I'll indicate that I've gone to check up on Janice."

"Fine, that could work. Though, you may have to smuggle some food to me later because I will get hungry."

Yvonne laughed at his boyish appetite. He almost made her feel that everything was normal and progressing as it should be.

I should have realized something would go wrong. Everyone is here except Rosanna and Nicholas. Now what? I'll still have to come up with an excuse to leave the table, so I can let David know that we won't be able to search their room after all.

After listening to their rave reviews about the archaeological sites and the colorful beaches on Santorini, the tone of the travelers settled into subdued conversations between couples and their table neighbors, giving Yvonne the opportunity she needed to excuse herself.

"I'll bet she's off to check up on her new lover. The lucky duck." Mark took a seductive bite of his chocolate mousse.

"Oh? I didn't know that you were interested in David." Cynthia, one eyebrow raised, turned to face Mark head on.

"Don't be silly. I just meant they're lucky to have someone to hook up with. It seems that about everyone's been lucky in love on this trip. Don't you agree?" Mark took another bite of his mousse.

"I have an idea that your mind is on Cosmos back in Mýkonos. Am I right?"

Mark's far away look confirmed her assumption.

"What has taken so long?" David grabbed Yvonne's arm as he closed the door.

"There's a major flaw in our plan." Yvonne pried his fingers open releasing the strong grip he had on her. "Rosanna and Nicholas didn't show up at dinner, so I don't see how we can search their room. The best we can do at this point is stay close to Janice and hopefully prevent them from harming her. If we see Damian at any point, we can let him know what we think happened at the airport. Maybe he can get the proof needed to arrest them."

Yvonne turned to leave and David followed on her heels. "I'm going to see if I can get Janice to come and stay in my room."

"I'm going with you. From now on we're sticking together."

Yvonne could smell his aftershave, and the pit of her stomach lurched followed by a warm glow that traveled to all of her erogenous zones. Ay Dios Mio!

When they reached Janice's room the door was slightly ajar. "Janice. It's me Yvonne—and David. Can we come in?" Silence.

Yvonne pushed the door further and entered the room. As her eyes scanned the room, she saw Janice's body lying face down across the bed. Yvonne's goose bumps were back in full force. Something strange about the way Janice was sprawled out prompted her to look at the bedside table. That's where Yvonne saw the opened prescription bottle on.

"No! This can't be—Janice—wake up, Janice!" Yvonne tried to sit Janice up and began shaking her.

David reached for the phone to call the front desk, "Call an ambulance. There's been an accident in room 208. Please hurry! If you have a doctor in the hotel, send him up right away!"

Janice moaned.

"Thank God. She's alive. I hope they hurry. I can't believe she would do something like this. How could I have missed this? I know she was upset, but I never realized that she felt hopeless."

"Yvonne, don't start blaming yourself. It may have been an accident—or—it may have been a deliberate act made to look like a suicide."

All at once the room came into full focus: the royal blue satin draperies hanging a bit too long jumbled on the floor; the wooden window-sills, thick with numerous coats of white paint, indicating many years of maintenance; the old but sturdy oak furniture with the makeshift bar items set on its scuffed top; the white bedclothes covered by a blue-green geometric designed bedspread, all stamped on her mind so she would never forget the horror she felt this exact moment when she might lose someone she'd grown to care so much about.

Yvonne's focus returned to Janice and the crisis at hand. "Come on Janice. Stay with us—please. Help will be here soon." She could hear sirens approaching. Then, many footsteps running up the hall until the paramedics were in the room with oxygen tanks and stethoscopes. David was holding the door so only the emergency crew was let in. As he was about to close the door, Police Inspector Stavros pushed through the crowd of bystanders and entered the room.

Taking in the scene and seeing that Janice Armstrong was being cared for, he turned to Yvonne and David. "We meet again Ms. Suarez, Mr. Ludlow. Can you tell me what is going on here?"

"We found Janice Armstrong unconscious, an open bottle of sleeping pills on the bedside table." David pointed to it.

Yvonne said, "Inspector Stavros—I don't believe that Janice—uh—Mrs. Armstrong took sleeping pills. She has complained to me about how awful they make her feel."

After the paramedics placed an oxygen mask on Janice, they lifted her onto the stretcher and wheeled her out of the room.

Yvonne turned to follow but was held back by the Inspector.

"Stay right here, Miss Suarez." Inspector Stavros was reading the prescription bottle.

Rosanna hurried into the room. "What has happened? Where is Janice?"

Inspector Stavros ignored her questions. "This prescription bottle has your name on it, Mrs. Fontinelli. Can you tell me why Mrs. Armstrong would have access to your prescription?"

"Please tell me that she didn't try to kill herself with my sleeping pills. I would never forgive myself." Rosanna's tears looked genuine enough, but Stavros was not fazed by them.

"Quite a coincidence don't you think Mrs. Fontinelli. First her husband dies in a shooting accident, and then she accidentally overdoses, and both times you are involved."

"What do you mean involved. Why, I never..."

"Were you or were you not in the room when Bill Armstrong was shot? Were these not your sleeping pills so conveniently loaned to a grieving widow?"

Rosanna wrung her hands. "Well, yes, it is a coincidence, but I was only trying to help my good friend. She said she was having trouble sleeping, and I believed her. I assure you Inspector, Nicholas and I would never do anything to harm Janice or Bill. They were our best friends." Rosanna turned to glare at Yvonne. "In fact, if being close by is reason for suspicion then you should be looking at Yvonne Suarez. Remember, Inspector, even Janice's husband was concerned about her influence on Janice. I'm sure that's what their fight was all about."

"Now you're being ridiculous. Yvonne only cared about helping Janice." David shot Rosanna a look that was meant to shut her up. The accusations in his eyes scared Rosanna and made Yvonne uncomfortable.

"Inspector, can we focus on Janice? Can I go to the hospital? I need to know that we got to her in time and that she will be okay."

"Not now. No one will be allowed to see her until she has recuperated enough to tell me whether she took the pills herself."

Mr. Zambas with Mrs. Zambas close behind entered the room shaking his finger at Yvonne. "Two nights in a row you bring the police to our quiet hotel. It's a good thing you are leaving here first thing tomorrow morning. I am tempted to make you and your group, leave tonight!"

Mrs. Zambas admonished her husband. "Now, Stephan, it is not Ms. Suarez' fault. She has no control over what someone does in the privacy of their own room. We can only pray that Mrs. Armstrong will be all right, poor dear. Don't forget, Stephan, she lost her husband only last night, and she is distraught as any wife would be." Mrs. Zambas looked her husband in the eye. "We are not going to kick these nice people out of the hotel. They must stay as long as they need. We are not the sort of people who throw nice people out onto the streets."

"Mr. Zambas, I assure you we have no reason to evict these perfectly harmless tourists. Isn't that right, Ms Suarez?" Inspector Stavros ushered them out of the room. He called for the crime lab to do a routine check of the room, although it was more for show. He didn't expect to find any surprise fingerprints. He knew who had been in the room and as far as he was concerned any one of them could have played a hand in helping Mrs. Armstrong to overdose. Unless she had been crazy enough to do it to herself and that wouldn't have surprised him either.

Richard Malcolm was clearly distressed when he approached Yvonne. "Are we going to be able to depart from here in the morning as scheduled?"

"I'm not sure yet. I will have to see how Janice is doing first." Yvonne and David threaded their way through the crowd. Yvonne gave assurances to everyone that details about their departure would be forthcoming as soon as she knew them. Yvonne felt disoriented like she'd been walking in a fog for several days and couldn't see clearly. This latest event had taken its toll. She needed to get away from everyone so that she could regain her balance and calm down before she had a melt down in front them.

"I suggest that we all meet in the bar for a drink to await word on Janice. It's early yet, only nine o'clock. Surely we'll hear something by eleven. Don't you think that's a good idea? Todd asked the group in general.

"I think that's the perfect idea." Missy took Todd's arm and they led the others to the bar. The lights were dim. Frank Sinatra sang softly in the background, and the one bartender looked like he'd just won the lottery when the party of ten wandered into his domain. One by one they placed their orders and found seats. From Scotch whiskey to after dinner liqueurs, everyone settled down with a nightcap.

Yvonne let David talk her into going along with the group. She refused to take his advice to order hard liquor. Her ginger ale was flat. That's what I get for going non alcoholic, she thought. She wanted to stay alert in case Janice needed her at the hospital. David drank a Scotch, straight up. Yvonne looked around the cozy bar. Rosanna and Nicholas were absent from the group.

RETURN TO ATHENS

DAY 15

When they arrived at the hospital the next morning, Yvonne and David found Janice confused and unresponsive. She had no memory of taking sleeping pills or shooting Bill. The doctor said the trauma from the overdose could cause some short-term memory loss, lasting a day or two. He guaranteed the drugs were flushed out of Janice's system and it would be safe for her to travel—with assistance—until her memory returned. Yvonne assured him they'd stay with Janice for as long as necessary on the trip home. Yvonne sent David to see to the paperwork for getting Janice checked out of the hospital. Yvonne helped Janice out of the hospital gown and into the clothes she'd worn the evening before. They sat on the hospital bed, Yvonne holding Janice's hand and waited for the official release. It came via a nurse pushing a wheel-chair with David close on her heels. Exiting the hospital they found Ari waiting in the mini-bus to transport them back to the hotel.

Yvonne spoke confidently into the phone. "Inspector Stavros, the doctor says Janice can travel as long as we allow her to rest when we get to Athens." Hearing no comment from the inspector, Yvonne continued, "Once she's home she will see her family doctor. In the meantime, if she remembers anything of importance about the overdose I will call you right away. I'll personally see that she stays with the group and out of harm's way." Yvonne, seated on the edge of the bed, played with the twisted phone cord waiting for his response.

"I have no grounds on which to keep her, but I must caution you to keep a close eye on her. She may still be in danger."

"We will. I promise."

"Nevertheless, be on your guard, especially around the Fontinellis."

Yvonne hung up the phone. Janice was sitting on the balcony outside Yvonne's room staring at the ocean. The sunshine will be good for her, thought Yvonne. She finished packing her suitcase and carry-on, then left Janice to pick up a key from the front desk. She entered Janice and Bill's room. Where to start? She found Bill's suitcase already packed. It gave her a chill to remember his bloody body lying on the floor a few feet away. Poor Janice, when would she be able to face disposal of his personal items? She packed up Janice's belongings and rang for the porter.

Janice was greeted with sympathetic smiles when she boarded the bus, but the group maintained an awkward silence during the drive so that she could rest. They arrived at the small airport with minutes to spare before airport check-in.

After liftoff, the plane bumped and lurched upward until it gained altitude. Evelyn looked out the tiny window and spoke in a wistful tone. "Santorini is the most beautiful Greek Island. I will miss it."

"And I will be glad when we're back in our own home, safe and sound." Richard took hold of Evelyn's hand.

As the crescent-shaped island shrank from everyone's view, the passengers confronted a range of emotions from fond memories, depression, and curiosity about what could happen next.

They landed without incident in Athens. Yvonne accompanied a fearful and anxious Janice to the Olympia Airlines Customer Service office to check Bill's body through to Fort Lauderdale. During the flight, Janice remembered the incidents leading up to Bill's death, exhausted from the effort of holding back tears, she accepted Yvonne's help without question. The final flight home would be early the next morning. The tour had one free afternoon remaining in Athens, and Yvonne prayed it would be quiet and without incident.

After checking into the Intercontinental Athenaeum hotel where the massive pot of flowers had been pushed off its platform, Yvonne felt uneasy. As a travel guide she knew that this hotel in the heart of Athens' shopping and dining district was the best choice for a last night.

Yvonne had requested and received an early check-in for the group. She unpacked her overnight toiletries and was about to check on Janice who was booked into the room next to hers, when someone knocked on her door. Surprised, she left the latch on and opened the door just a crack. She caught a glimpse of a familiar mustache attached to the face of Inspector Trakas. "What brings you here, Inspector?"

"Your tour group caused more trouble on the Islands, I hear. You were warned—there were to be no more suspicious accidents."

"But, Inspector— how was I to know..."

Inspector Trakas put his hand up to block her excuses. "Inspector Stavros has informed me of your escapades in Santorini and his suspicions about your clients, the Fontinellis. Furthermore, he has warned me that you and Mr. Ludlow are to be watched closely to prevent you from interfering with our investigation."

"I have done nothing but try to insure my clients a safe trip." Yvonne's face flushed hot and her voice grew louder.

"Listen to me, Ms. Suarez—you are to stop playing detective. Do you understand me?" Inspector Trakas put his face right up in Yvonne's.

Overwhelmed by the smell of tobacco, Yvonne took a step back into her room. "Okay, Inspector. You win. I will not play detective." Yvonne closed the door in his face. She took a deep breath and cursed, "Soy cansado de ser intimidado por hombres estúpidos!"

Another knock on the door interrupted Yvonne's angry outburst. She yanked the door open without thinking. "What? Oh, it's you, Janice. Sorry. I..."

"May I come in?" Janice lowered her eyes in an apologetic gesture.

"Of course—I was just coming to see how you were doing." Yvonne backed out of the way allowing Janice to enter.

"How are you? Is there anything you'd like to do this afternoon?"

"Not really. That's why I'm here." Janice hesitated. "I don't want you babysitting me. This is the last day before we leave and you should be out enjoying yourself—you and David."

"Janice, it's no problem. I promised the doctor I'd watch out for you the rest of the trip, and that's what I plan to do."

"Please, Yvonne. I've caused you and the others enough trouble. I insist. I will stay in my room and rest." Janice lifted her chin, determined to have her way.

Yvonne's mind raced. Should she tell Janice about their concerns for her safety or let her have peace of mind. She wished David were here so she could ask his advice. He had a stabilizing effect and right now she felt unsure of herself. She decided it would be best to be honest with Janice. "We're worried about you. Not just your health, but we think the Fontinellis may try to harm you. We believe they think you may know more about their exploits than you actually do."

"I can't believe they'd actually hurt me. We've been friends for god sake." The frustration in Janice's voice tore at Yvonne's resolve. "No. I'm not going to let you spoil the day." Janice was adamant.

"I have an idea." She picked up the phone and called David's room. He answered on the second ring. "David, would you mind coming to my room? Janice is here and I'd like to ask your advice about something."

"Sure. Give me two minutes and I'll be right there." David finished stuffing his dirty clothes in a bag and jammed it into his reorganized suitcase. Checked for his room key, put it in his pocket and went to Yvonne's room.

"Come in" Yvonne opened the door on the first knock.

"Here's the thing. Janice refuses to let us stay with her this afternoon. She feels she's keeping us from our last day in Athens. To make matters worse, I had a visit from Inspector Trakas who gave me a tongue lashing about our "escapades" in the islands. He accused me of playing detective and forbid me from interfering in their investigation of the Fontinellis—as if I would do such a thing." Yvonne paused a moment and took a breath. "Anyway, if Janice will agree to stay and rest in my room with the door locked and promise to answer to no one. You and I could go for the afternoon to shop for souvenirs and the police who are watching will see that we are no threat to their investigation. We could be back in time for dinner and Janice will be safe because no one will know she is not in her own room." Yvonne looked at Janice who promised to do as suggested, then David.

"I don't know, Yvonne. Are you sure we should leave her? What if Janice remembers something?" David turned his skeptical gaze on Janice.

Janice walked to David and placed her hands on his shoulder. "I'll be fine. I'm feeling better, and if I remember something it will hold until you return. Go. Please. I don't want another spoiled day on my conscience. This is your last chance to enjoy yourselves and I insist that you do." She smiled at David and kissed him on the cheek. "Thanks for all you've done. I don't know how I would have made it this far if it hadn't been for you and Yvonne." She released David and gave Yvonne a hug in turn.

Janice agreed to let Yvonne order soup and crackers sent up to the room for her lunch before they left.

They found a cozy café in the Monastiraki shopping district. David admired Yvonne's simple off-white dress accessorized with brown beaded necklace and matching bracelet. He was pleased to notice she was wearing the topaz earrings he'd given her. Never before had he noticed the small details on any woman the way that he did with her. It pleased him to think he might have found his soul-mate.

Yvonne squirmed under his scrutiny. After ordering salads and white wine, they sat quietly and enjoyed being together. "I'm feeling a bit sad that the tour ends tomorrow. In spite of all the crazy things that have happened, I met you, and getting to know you has been good for me." Yvonne pushed around some feta cheese left on her salad plate. "I must say though, it will be good to see my daughter again. I've never been away from her for this long—I feel like part of me is missing."

"I hope when we return home you'll continue to let me spend time with you. I'd like to meet Christy." David's serious look pierced Yvonne's heart, but she couldn't bring herself to answer him.

"Are you ready to go?" He gestured to the waiter to bring his bill.

As they rose to leave the restaurant, David asked, "If you don't mind, I'd like to pay one last visit to the Maverickos Antique shop to say goodbye and thank them once again for their hospitality."

"Of course." Yvonne linked her arm in Davids.

The Maverickos' store was within a block's walking distance. They walked slowly, holding hands. After they crossed into the next block, they encountered Damian following the Fontinellis. They watched dumb-founded as Rosanna and Nicholas went into the Maverickos Antiques and Jewelry Store. Damian did not enter but crossed the street to find a vantage point where he could watch unobserved.

"Now what do we do? What in the world is going on? Why would they be going in there? Is it just a coincidence?"

David stopped walking and held onto Yvonne so that she would not proceed. He pulled her into an entryway to the corner drugstore to watch and think.

"Let's go ahead. Maybe we can get an idea of what, if anything, is going on. Maybe they're just browsing. Anyway it's a free country and we can go wherever we please." David, satisfied with his reasoning, stepped out of their cover.

"Wait!" Yvonne pulled him back. "Let's think about this. We can't just show up there. They might think that we are following them."

"Well, we're not, are we? We're there to say good-bye to my partners' family."

"True, but, David, don't forget Damian is watching across the street. He'll tell Inspector Trakas. He'll think we've been following the Fontinellis and he'll be furious."

"Too bad. We have every right to be here." David stepped out again and Yvonne followed. When they arrived in front of the store, they looked casually inside as if they were window shopping. "Funny—I don't see them anywhere. I wonder if there's a back exit—one that I didn't notice when I was here before?" David held the door open for Yvonne.

As a bell chimed, Alexis Maverickos entered the room from the back of the store and greeted them. "David, how nice to see you again. I did not expect this pleasure."

"Alexis, we returned from our tour and are leaving for Florida tomorrow, so I wanted to have one more chance to thank you for your hospitality and to say good bye." David saw Alexis stare at Yvonne. "Forgive me. This is Yvonne Suarez, my friend, our tour leader."

"It's very nice to meet you, Ms. Suarez." Alexis offered Yvonne a limp hand.

"It's nice to meet you as well." Yvonne shook the outreached hand.

"Alexis, I thought we noticed some friends of ours enter your store a few minutes ago, but they don't seem to be here. Do you have a rear exit perhaps?" David looked toward the hallway where Alexis had entered.

"I don't know what you're talking about. No one has entered here in the last half hour other than you and your friend, of course."

"Maybe I could just check through here." David stepped toward the hallway.

"David, you mustn't go back there. It's our private offices and the public is not allowed." Alexis cut David off before he stepped through the opening.

"What harm could there be in checking? Maybe they're in the back alley."

"Now why would anyone wish to go into our back alley? That doesn't make any sense." Alexis slipped her arm through David's and turned him around leading him back out in front of the nearest cluttered counter that obscured his view of the back. "Maybe you thought they came in here, but, in fact, they may have entered the store next door or another one further down the street."

"Sure. That's probably what happened." Yvonne smiled at Alexis and linked her arm through David's other arm.

"David, now that you've said goodbye, I think we must return to the hotel. I have some final arrangements that need to be made before we leave tomorrow morning." Yvonne tugged on his arm.

"Yes. Well, goodbye, Alexis—but—what about your husband and George, are they here? I would like to say goodbye to them also."

"No, I'm sorry, it's only me. Loukas and George are not here at the moment. Don't worry. I will extend your goodbyes to them later this evening. Have a nice flight home, David, and please give Demetrius our love and tell him to write to his mama."

They exited the store and turned to go further up the road, holding hands like lovers who were window shopping. "Let's go to the end of the street and find a spot out of Damian's range of vision where we can watch them exit from the front or the back." Yvonne whispered these instructions into David's ear and laughed as if they shared an intimate joke.

David put his arm around her waist as they walked and tried to slow his gait to look normal, though he wanted to hurry. When they got to the end of the road, Yvonne said, "Turn here, David. You can wait around this corner to watch the front and I'll jog up to the other corner and see if they exit from the rear of the shop."

"No, Yvonne, you watch the front. I'd rather watch the alley way. It could be dangerous and I don't want you to be the one to meet up with them first. How will you signal me if you should see them leave from the front?"

"Better yet, what are we going to do if we see them exit? Confront them? This is crazy." Yvonne leaned against the buildings outer wall. "What is this going to accomplish anyway?"

"We don't have to confront them, but at least we'd know whether or not Alexis was lying about them being there? We know what we saw. So why did she lie about it?"

"David, there they are." She pointed to the alley where Rosanna and Nicholas were coming around the corner walking at a fast pace. They stopped short when they saw Yvonne and David standing at the end of the street. Yvonne grabbed David's hand and held it tightly. "Now what do we do?"

The Fontinellis began walking toward them. David smiled and walked toward them with Yvonne in tow. "Fancy meeting you two here."

"Are you out for an afternoon stroll?" asked Nicholas.

"Yes we are. What about you? What's so interesting in the back alley?"

Rosanna pulled out a gun and pointed it at the two of them. "I think we've had enough of the two of you and your interference in our business."

"And what business would that be?" Yvonne stared at the small gun in Rosanna's hand.

"You see what I mean, Nicholas. She's too damn nosey."

"You're right, my dear, but what are we going to do with them?"

"We're going to see that they don't interfere in our business any-more. Turn around you two." Rosanna shoved Yvonne in the direc-tion of the alley.

David grabbed Yvonne's arm and turned her around. "No. We're not stupid enough to follow you down a quiet alley. Come on, Yvonne, let's go this way."

They turned their backs to walk away.   Rosanna took a step for-ward and hit Yvonne with the butt of her gun knocking her to the ground. David caught the movement and watched Yvonne fall to the ground. "What the hell? Are you crazy?" David screamed at Rosa-nna and bent down to help Yvonne. Nicholas took his best shot and kicked David in the head. "Quick, Nicholas, grab David and I'll get Yvonne. Let's get them back to the shop."

Rosanna pulled Yvonne to her feet and shoved the gun into her ribs, forcing Yvonne to stumble ahead. Nicholas twisted David's arm behind him and prompted him to follow.

They arrived at the back entrance to the Maverickos Antique and Jewelry Shop. Rosanna knocked loudly with the butt of the gun, and they were let in by Alexis.

"What have you done? Loukas! Come here quickly."

Loukas entered the back storage area. "Rosanna, Nicholas, what happened? Why did you bring them here?"

"That's a very good question." David looked around the back room noting hundreds of various size boxes stacked to the ceiling. He couldn't think of a better way to hide stolen property than among such a disorganized mess of boxes.

"They were waiting around the corner, and this one—she has done nothing but cause problems." Rosanna pointed the gun at Yvonne. "We had to bring them somewhere, and this was the quickest way to get out of sight." Rosanna waved the gun from Yvonne to David. "Loukas, tie them up. Start with him."

"Now, Rosanna, is that really necessary?"

"Not unless you'd like me to shoot them right here, right now, and leave them for the two of you to dispose of. Now get them tied up so that I can think of what to do next." After a moment, Rosanna asked, "Where's George?"

"He's not due back until tonight." Alexis took a step closer to Loukas while he dug through a drawer for some rope.

"We need to return to the tour so that we don't arouse suspicion. When George returns this evening, have him eliminate these two and dispose of their bodies. The tour will have to continue without them."

Thinking Rosanna was distracted, David lunged for her gun. She caught the movement out of the corner of her eye and sidestepped, giving Nicholas a chance to jump on David and knock him to the floor. Yvonne screamed and Rosanna pointed the gun at her. "Shut up or I'll shoot you now." For good measure, Nicholas grabbed David's head from behind and banged his forehead hard against the floor. "Loukas, give Nicholas the rope. Nicholas tie him up, then tie up the other one." Rosanna nodded her head toward Yvonne while holding the gun steady on her.

"Can't you dispose of them yourself? We don't want that kind of trouble." Alexis glanced nervously at David.

Rosanna gave Alexis a sly smile. "George can do it. He's a big boy. I don't care how he kills them, but I might suggest that he dump the bodies at the reconstruction site of the new stadium for next years Olympic Games. They'll be hard to locate there. Perhaps their bodies will strengthen the concrete helping to hold up the seats. Give them a purpose in death that they don't have in life. They will be immortalized for the next millennia." She stared at Yvonne and chuckled at her own cleverness.

Nicholas joined in her levity. "Brilliant idea, my dear."

"But how will you explain their disappearance?" Alexis wrung her hands in desperation.

"We won't need to. We'll be as curious as the rest of the group when asked, and by tomorrow we'll be on our way home—with the art, of course." Rosanna returned her gun to her purse.

Yvonne thought hard. She needed to buy them some time. A delay might bring help. It worked in the movies, why not in the real world? Maybe she could pit them against each other. She grounded herself by taking a deep yoga breath and spoke in a casual tone. "Since you're planning to dispose of us anyway, do you mind answering a couple of questions?"

Yvonne's easy tone annoyed Rosanna. "That depends. What do you want to know?"

"Was it you that pushed Janice down the steps at the Acropolis? Do you know who ran Beverly down with a car?"

"Yes. And yes. We're out of time. That will be all the questions for now."

"But why push Janice and hurt Beverly?"

"You don't need to know the minor details. I said that will be all the questions for now. Come along, Nicholas, we must return to the hotel. We want to be there when they notice Yvonne and David haven't returned from their afternoon outing." Rosanna turned to Loukas and Alexis. "Make sure you keep a good eye on these two and that George understands how important his task is."

Rosanna and Nicholas opened the back door to find Police Inspector Trakas pointing his 9 mm SIG Sauer at them. She reached into her purse, but before she could pull out her small handgun, his fellow officer had placed handcuffs on her. Nicholas threw up his hands in surrender.

"Thank heavens, you got here in time. They were going to kill us if we didn't follow their instructions to eliminate these two." Alexis pointed at Yvonne and David, seated against a row of boxes with their wrists and ankles tied.

"That's right," Loukas took a step to stand next to Alexis in unity.

"Don't believe it, Inspector. They are part of this scheme." Yvonne squirmed trying to sit up straighter.

"Here you are, Ms. Suarez and Mr. Ludlow, in the thick of things again. Did I not warn you to stay out of trouble and mind your own business?"

"We tried to do just that. We had no idea they were involved with the Maverickos Family. We only stopped by so David could say good-bye to them."

"Why would Mr. Ludlow have to say good bye to the likes of them?"

"Well you see, Inspector, they are the parents of my business partner, Demetrius. I just stopped to say hello to them on his behalf when we arrived in Athens last week. They invited me to dinner. I had no idea they were part of an art smuggling ring until a few minutes ago when they tied us up here."

Inspector Trakas scratched his head. "You are partners with their son?"

"Yes, that's right. He helps me run our software company in the States."

"That's very interesting. And what do you know about this son of theirs? Is he in communication with his family?"

"I would say they communicate on a regular basis. At least I think so. I've never really paid much attention."

"Why are you really here, Mr. Ludlow? I don't believe in co-incidences."

David gave Yvonne a guilty look. "I suspected Demetrius of embezzling from my company but had no proof. Before I go on, do you think you could untie us?"

Inspector Trakas gave orders to an officer standing nearby to un-tie Yvonne.

David continued his story while waiting his turn to be untied. "I thought if I could see where Demetrius came from, meet his family, it might give me some indication if he was a real problem or if I might be imagining things. He is in charge of my company's finances. I am the one who designs and sells the software programs to banks and other similar institutions, so I don't have time to watch him as closely as I'd like. When I noticed the money wasn't adding up from the new accounts, I began to wonder if he was stealing from the company."

Yvonne had heard enough. "Do you mean that you were using this tour to spy on your partner's family? Do you even have a heart condition? Have I been worried about you for nothing?"

"I'm sorry, Yvonne. I really did need this vacation due to stress, but I did combine it with my desire to check up on Demetrius and his family. I'm afraid that my heart is fine."

"Oh—you—liar, how could I have fallen for your smooth talking? I should have known you were too good to be true."

"You've fallen for me. I knew it!" David grinned.

"I'm sorry to interrupt this lover's quarrel, but can we continue with my inquiry?" Inspector Trakas turned back to Yvonne. "You may thank Damian for coming to your rescue. He was watching when they overpowered you and brought you here. You are very lucky that you weren't killed before we could rescue you.

"You will come with us to the station and make a statement. I'd like to find out if either of you know anything that will help us keep them behind bars."

Yvonne rubbed her wrists. "Rosanna admitted to pushing Janice down the steps at the Acropolis, and she knows who ran over Beverly Nystrom."

"Ah, Ms. Nystrom, I'm glad that you mention her. She will be returning to your group in the morning to make the flight home with you. She has a broken leg and a broken arm, but with help she will be able to travel. She has given us as much help as she possibly could with the case."

"She has? How did she do that?" Yvonne glanced at David.

"It seems she happened to overhear part of a conversation at the New Modern Museum on Andros Island the day before the robbery. She was able to confirm our suspicions that they were involved in the robbery of the Tedeschi painting."

"But, I thought she didn't see who ran her down."

"She didn't, but she was scared enough to know who was behind it. She knew better than to try and identify them. She was right to be scared, but we convinced her that her only chance for a safe future would be to help us put them behind bars. She's a lady with too much nerve for her own good. She confronted Bill Armstrong after the robbery and threatened to blackmail the three of them if they didn't share the proceeds with her. She defended her actions because she sought a way to pay for law school. She thought the end justified the means. Blackmail is illegal. Her poor judgment and lack of ethics indicates she's not the kind of person who should be going into law."

"Inspector, do you have any idea who ran her down?" Yvonne ignored David's attempt to help her stand. She stood up easily on her own and wiped the dust from the floor off the back of her dress, checking to be sure it was falling in a straight line.

"My guess would be George Maverickos. He was on the island at the time, and is involved in the smuggling up to his eyeballs. We are on the lookout for him and will pick him up as soon as he returns to the shop or his home."

— • —

George watched as Nicholas and Rosanna forced David Ludlow and his travel agent into the back of his parents shop. Rosanna had a gun aimed at the couple. What were those crazy Americans thinking? What had he gotten his parents into? There had been little risk of them getting caught smuggling, but hurting people and getting away with it was quite another matter. He parked away from the shop so that no one could connect him. If he doubled back on foot, he could size up the situation.

As he walked to the end of the street, he noticed more movement in the alley. A police official and officers entered the rear door of the shop. Within ten minutes, the door opened and he watched as police officers took his parents and the Fontinellis away in police cars. Finally the official exited the building and instructed two more police officers to guard the door as he, David Ludlow and the woman departed in another police car.

— • —

During Inspector Trakas' interrogation, Yvonne explained her theory that Bill had killed the airport maintenance employee and had probably taken possession of the stolen statue of Hera and jeweled dagger. She told him Janice believed Bill's abusiveness was tied to guilt feelings over getting mixed up in the art theft. The inspector questioned Yvonne and David repeatedly for several hours until he felt they had told him everything of value.

Later, when they returned exhausted to the hotel, with the exception of Janice, the rest of the group was gathered in the lobby bar area waiting for last minute instructions from Yvonne.

"I have some bad news and some good news. Which would you prefer to hear first?"

"The good news," most said in unison.

"The good news is that Beverly Nystrom will join our group in the morning for the flight home. She will need our assistance to make her as comfortable as possible. She will be wearing two casts." Yvonne sat in one of the lobby chairs. She lowered her voice. "The bad news is that we will be short two more members tomorrow. Rosanna and Nicholas Fontinelli have been arrested as part of an art-smuggling ring that operates in Europe and America."

No one spoke for a moment. Then questions were fired at her from all directions. Yvonne sunk further in her seat.

David took over. "Yvonne is a hero. She helped with the capture of these two criminals along with two other culprits who were in on the deal."

"No, David, I'm no hero. If anything, you're the one who's been around to help out whenever needed."

"Don't be so modest, Yvonne. Come on, give us the scoop." Mark's eyes sparkled with excitement.

"Well, I did put a couple of things together that helped clear up some of the confusion. Right now, however, I need to talk to Janice because, unfortunately, Bill was also involved in the smuggling ring without her knowledge, of course. She's going to need our support more than ever."

"Would you like me to go with you?" David began to rise from his chair.

"No."

"Are you so sure that Janice was kept in the dark about all this?" Cynthia, seated between Ari and Mark on the sofa, peered at the rest of the tour group with a look of distrust.

"Yes. I'm sure. She was kept out of the loop but not out of danger as it turns out."

"Yvonne would you like me to come with you?" asked Evelyn.

"No thank you, Evelyn. I'm sure she'd appreciate your concern, but I think that she'd be less likely to open up. She's been embarrassed about much that has happened."

Yvonne stood. "Shall we dine at the rooftop restaurant? This is our last night. If you all agree, I'll make reservations for us before I go see Janice. How many are in for dinner?" Everyone's hand went up as they were eager to have one last view of the Athen's night sky and get all the details about the latest scandal. She left them seated in the lobby bar, and went to the concierge to reserve their table for dinner, then took the elevator up to the fifth floor to Janice's room.

"Janice, it's me, Yvonne. May I come in?"

Janice opened the door. "Come in." She returned to bed and propped up some pillows so she could sit up. Still groggy, she tried to listen intently.

Yvonne took a seat in the side chair. She hesitated not sure what the impact of her words would be. "The police arrested Rosanna and Nicholas along with some locals as part of an art-smuggling ring." She waited patiently for the information to sink in.

Janice started to cry. After she calmed down, she asked, "Was Bill part of it too?"

"Yes, but if it's any consolation, the police think that he was not a major player like Rosanna and Nicholas are. They think he was targeted for his trusting nature."

"It's nice of you to say that, Yvonne—but I know that he—he was whole-hog into it and he got greedy."

"Have you remembered whether you took the sleeping pills of your own accord? Honestly, I'm a little worried about you."

"That's just it. I do remember. When I woke from my nap this afternoon, it all came back to me. Rosanna had stopped by my room to see if I was sleeping okay and offered me more of her sleeping pills. I told her, 'no thanks,' but she set them down on the bedside table anyway. 'Just in case,' she said. I didn't buy her sympathy. I confronted her about her relationship with Bill and instead of denying it she laughed at me, and said, "How could anyone love such a mouse. Bill wanted a real woman one that would give him some excitement and thrills." After she left, I saw the sleeping pills sitting there. I knew she left them hoping I'd take them—maybe kill myself. At that moment I thought she was right—I'd be better off dead. I guess I hoped that I'd implicate her in my death, so I swallowed a handful, but nothing ever works out the way I plan it. Yvonne, promise me you won't tell anyone else why I did it. I was crazy to pull such a stunt. I'm so ashamed. Please forgive me."

"No need to apologize, you were under too much stress. Just promise me you'll get some counseling when you get home and that you'll never try to hurt yourself again." Yvonne gave Janice a hug. "I won't say a word. Besides, Rosanna and Nicholas are the real villains here. They are the ones who deserve punishment.

"Thanks for understanding, Yvonne." Janice wiped at the tears in her eyes.

"You are free now to go and do whatever you wish from now on. It would be awful if you let an opportunity like that slip by you. I know it will take some time to come to terms with the loss of Bill and the way that he died, but you have friends and people who care about you. They will be there to help get you through this."

"That's nice of you to say, but I really don't have that many friends. So much of our lives were tied up with Rosanna and Nicholas. Bill pretty much shut out everyone else from my life. I suppose I could reconnect with my sister, and in time I may earn back some of my old friends. Maybe I could count you as my one good friend."

"Absolutely, consider me your best friend if you wish. I will be here for you now and in the future.

"I should get back to the group if you think you're going to be okay. I won't insist that you join us for dinner. I'll understand if you need a little time to yourself, but you're more than welcome to join us." Yvonne gave her another hug.

"Thanks, but I'm not up to facing everyone. But, you go—enjoy your dinner. I won't do anything stupid. I promise." Janice sighed.

When all but David had left the dinner table, Yvonne gave him a smile. "Finally, we can breathe a little easier. I meant it when I said I wouldn't have known what to do if you hadn't been there for me."

"I'd like to continue to be there for you when we return, Yvonne. Face it. We make a good team. Heck. We make a great team." The waiter refilled their wine glasses for the third time that evening.

Yvonne fidgeted with her napkin for a moment, and then placed it with emphasis next to her plate. "What about the fact that you lied to me? You can't expect me to just forgive and forget."

"I couldn't tell anyone the truth, not until I knew what it was myself. Even now I'm not sure what role Demetrius played in all this. I didn't want to put you in an awkward position."

"Except that's exactly what you did, isn't it? I don't know what part of your act to believe. Maybe none of it, maybe I was just a means to an end."

"Yvonne, you know better than that. I have never lied about my feelings for you. Why do you think I wanted to be there with you every moment? I was worried sick that you might get caught up in this and be hurt. My worst fears almost happened."

"Now that the others have gone back to their rooms I feel like I can relax for the first time since this whole trip started. Let's walk outside to the balcony. I want to take in a last look at the city of Athens by moonlight."

David signed the check. "Let's take our wine." He took her free hand and they carried their wine glasses with them to the balcony. A balmy breeze caressed the night, and the world sparkled with lights that encircled them. Absorbed in thought about the wonders below, Yvonne set her wine glass on the concrete railing. David followed suit. His arm went around her shoulders, and they continued to gaze at the view. The Acropolis was an eerie sight to behold. At that moment he knew what it felt like to be a Titan at the top of the world with the goddess Hera by his side. He wondered at the myths that had been written about such things. Remembering the adventures he had encountered on this tour, he understood how these larger-than-life stories had come into existence.

"Yvonne, let me take you back to your room and make love to you. Let me prove to you that I'm sincere, once and for all. Let me treat you like the goddess you are."

"Mmm. Being treated like a goddess—once again it sounds too good to be true. I'm sorry, David. I can't." She turned abruptly and left him standing there alone.

All the pretty words scared her. They reminded her of the times that Gino had lied to her. No, she wouldn't put herself or Christy through that again.

DEPART ATHENS

DAY 16

I'm going to miss this group, especially Cynthia, thought Ari. She wants me to visit her in Fort Lauderdale. Everyone invites me to visit, but they are only wishing to take home more than just photos to remember their good times. Cynthia, she's different. She's fun and adorable. We could have a great time together.

This had to be the worst tour ever. Staying on track was impossible. All the horrible accidents, I don't know how we managed to complete the whole itinerary. I must admit, though, I like these people. Ari smiled at Yvonne. Light conversation was all he could muster on this last day of their tour. "In spite of everything, I hope each of you has enjoyed your visit to Athens and the Greek Islands, and that you'll wish to return in the future."

"We're going to miss you, most of all." Evelyn's eyes were moist. The others nodded in agreement.

Ari got a lump in his throat. "I'm glad to represent my country in this way."

Their bags were checked. They had passed through security, and passports were reviewed. The long walk to the gate seemed to energize them. Sad at first, they were beginning to feel excited about heading home. Upon arrival at the departure gate, they found Beverly seated uncomfortably in a wheel chair near check-in. She mustered a weak smile for her travel mates but barely glanced at David and Yvonne.

Evelyn spent her waiting time writing notes in her journal while Richard read some of the museum books she'd urged him to buy.

205

Missy thumbed through her new Fortune magazine, and Todd was busy reading the latest John Grisham thriller. Cynthia and Mark gossiped about how they would embellish their romantic escapades once back in the hair salon. Yvonne watched Beverly fidget in her wheelchair trying to get comfortable and wondered if she would ever book another trip for her. She studied Janice who stared into space like a zombie, and she hoped that being home would help heal her emotional wounds. Seated next to her, David typed endlessly on his laptop.

Yvonne was jumpy. She couldn't shake a weird feeling. A flashback of two weeks before at the airport in Ft. Lauderdale, and Bill Armstrong asking about security and travel delays made her sad.

Missy came out of her seat and rushed past Yvonne heading for the restroom. Yvonne reached for her carry-on luggage and followed Cynthia.

Yvonne could hear Missy, locked in the last stall, vomiting. She dampened a paper towel with cool water and waited. After Missy was spent, she came out white-faced and shakily leaned over the bathroom sink. Yvonne reached out with the cloth and placed it on her forehead.

"Thanks. I feel better now. It must be something I ate." Missy cupped her hands and filled them with water. Carefully she sipped the water from her hands to rinse out her mouth.

Yvonne waited. "Are you going to be okay? Maybe some crackers would settle your stomach. I may have some in my purse. I saved them from the meal on the plane coming over. They're crushed up a bit."

"I'll take them for later. Thanks." Cynthia exited the restroom.

Yvonne refreshed herself quickly, the smell of vomit wreaking havoc with her own stomach. She smiled to herself. I wonder. Could it be morning sickness?

As she stepped out of the ladies room, David was coming out of the men's room. Close behind him was a man who looked familiar. He pushed David in the wrong direction. David walked stiffly as if not sure which way to go. Yvonne knew something was wrong. The man had a coat loosely draped over his extended arm. Her intuition said this strange man had a gun pressed in David's back.

Ay, Dios Mio. Que lagrima! More trouble? They'll be calling us to board the plane any minute. I'd better follow them. "David, what's going on here? Don't you realize, I've got to get back home to Christy?" Before arriving back at the security check point, the man pushed David through a heavy metal door.

Now what? I need to get help, but if I leave to find security guards, it may be too late. She pushed the door open a crack. She could hear footsteps. The room led to a stair well. She heard footsteps climbing the stairs. The door made a scraping noise on the cement flooring, so she squeezed through the small opening and followed as quietly as possible. From above, she heard another door open. The noise of machines drifted down to her. Where had they gone? She tried to think. What could be up there? The roof? Why was it so noisy? Did she have anything in her carry on luggage that could help to fend off an attack? By now she had no doubt David was in serious danger. She remembered the Greek bust of Plato that she'd bought as a souvenir for her parents. She refused to pack it in her suitcase for fear it would be damaged. It was the only thing heavy enough to hit someone with that might slow him down. She kneeled down and unzipped her rolling carry-on. Next she removed the clothes she'd stuffed around Plato for padding. She grabbed the bust firmly and lifted it out of the bag. She left her bags on the stairwell and removed her shoes stepping cautiously until she found the door they'd gone through.

The room was noisy. Yvonne was confident no one had heard the door open. She peeked inside taking in the immense air conditioning units that serviced the airport. The loud mechanical noise hurt her eardrums. She stepped inside and listened intently. Her heart thumped when she heard the sound of metal hitting the ground. Without thought, she sprinted in the same direction. David and the man were rolling on the floor, struggling to retrieve the gun that David had apparently knocked out of his hand. The man latched onto the gun, and David grabbed the barrel. David wrestled with him trying to get it out of his grip. Yvonne came up behind the man. She raised Plato and slammed the bust down with all her strength on the man's head, just as the shot rang out. He fell on top of David. She grabbed the gun out of his limp hand and shoved him off. Blood oozed from David's chest.

"Oh no, David, please! Hold on—I'll get help.

Yvonne ran down the stairs straight to the security station. She slammed the gun on the counter but did not let go of it. "Help, My friend's been shot! The security guards seeing the gun grabbed Yvonne and took the gun away. "Please call a doctor. He needs help. He's bleeding." She pulled away from the guards grasp and ran back toward the door that led back to David. The guards chased after her. She stopped at the door and screamed at them. "Go—call the police and an ambulance we need help. He could bleed to death."

"What about the man you say shot your friend? Where is he?" The guard held the door to prevent her from going through.

"I knocked him out with my parents' bust."

"Excuse me? Your parents' bust?"

"You know—a bust, Plato, a souvenir I'm taking home to my parents. Don't you see, we need to hurry... that man had the gun ... he could wake up at any moment."

"Fine. Stay here and we'll help your friend. You stay over there by the counter. They will call an ambulance."

Yvonne waited for what seemed like hours for the paramedics to arrive, and the security guards to return from the noisy room.

David had lost a lot of blood and was unconscious when they rushed him to the hospital. The police refused to let Yvonne go with him. She had to give them a statement before they would allow her to leave. They searched but did not find the mysterious man who shot David. Yvonne missed her flight home but insisted the others leave as scheduled.

The bullet missed David's heart by a fraction. The doctors said he was lucky to be alive but would recover completely. Yvonne stayed by his bed at the hospital until he was conscious and she knew he would be all right. When she called her mother to explain that she couldn't leave this man who had helped her so much, her mom understood but insisted she hurry home regardless. They were worried about her safety. "Mom, Dad, don't worry. I'm fine. I miss you all so much. Please kiss Christy for me and tell her I'm sorry I've been away so long. I'll be home as soon as David can travel safely."

"Mr. Ludlow, I thought we'd seen the last of you and now this."

"Believe me, Inspector, I'm not the least bit happy to see you either."

"Did you see the man who attacked you?" Athens Police Inspector Trakas asked his first question.

"Yes, Demetrius Maverickos, my business partner." David tried to sit up but the pain in his chest forced him to lie back.

"Are you sure? Did you get a good look at him?"

"I know him well, Inspector. I was in the men's room washing my hands. I looked up and he was standing there with his gun pointed at my back."

"Do you know why?"

"He said I'd ruined his family's business and his plans to steal millions of dollars from our customers."

"How did you do that?"

David looked at Yvonne "We helped capture his parents and the Fontinellis who were part of the art smuggling ring behind the museum thefts."

"What about your customer's millions of dollars?"

"I figured he was crooked like the rest of his family. Their arrest confirmed my suspicions that he was embezzling from our company. My biggest concern, however, was the codes I'd created as part of the ATM software provided to our customer banks throughout the United States and Europe. He could steal millions with that information. So before I left for this trip, I moved all the coding information to a secure safe deposit box that he knew nothing about. When he realized I'd hid the codes, he became angry and flew here to force me to disclose their location."

"Inspector, David needs his rest. Shouldn't you be looking for Demetrius and his brother George? What if they decide to go after David here at the hospital?" Yvonne stood face to face with the detective.

"We will assign a guard to protect him until he's released and safe aboard his flight home. In the meantime, I assure you we will do all we can to apprehend the Maverickos brothers." Inspector Trakas nodded toward David. "Mr. Ludlow is a lucky man to have a fierce woman like you by his side."

Yvonne smiled. "Good bye, Inspector, and good luck. You will let us know if you learn anything, right?"

"Of course." Inspector Trakas turned and left the room.

"Yvonne, you're exhausted. You haven't left my side. Have you booked a hotel room anywhere? I'm sorry you missed your flight." David winced when he tried to reach out to Yvonne.

She grabbed his hand. "Stay put. Don't worry about me, I'm fine. I booked a room nearby. I certainly need a shower and a good night's sleep." Yvonne called the Pinkerton Agency and was reassured that the tab would be covered by the agency's insurance since their client had been hurt while on the agency's tour.

Yvonne visited David every day bringing him magazines and outdated New York Times. She read short stories to him, and together they'd work the daily crossword puzzle. She enjoyed the silly banter back and forth about his future plans to date her. His nerdy side would appear when she questioned him about his company. She enjoyed those moments too.

David worried about his company. He depended on one secretary to hold things together while he was away. He called her daily to check in and give advice in dealing with his customers.

Yvonne received several calls from her parents and Christy telling her they missed her and anxiously awaited her return. No call came from Inspector Trakas saying he'd caught the Maverickos' brothers. Before they knew it, a week had gone by and the doctors released David to travel.

On the flight home, Yvonne thought about all that had gone wrong on her tour, and all she'd need to answer for when she talked to her boss. Would they blame her for endangering her client's lives? Had she jeopardized her job staying away so long? Even though she really liked David a great deal, was she ready for a committed relationship? David had his company to save, and she had her life to return to. Christy was her first priority, and her ex, Gino, was still a problem. She was sure he'd view David as a threat to his relationship with his daughter.

David knew what he wanted. He wanted to continue seeing Yvonne. He appreciated her loyalty to her daughter and her family. He had always wanted a woman like her. He was proud of the way she'd gone after him when she thought he might be in danger. It took a lot of guts to do that. He wished he could convince her that she was stronger than she gave herself credit for. In time, he would convince her.

EPILOGUE

Yvonne's reception at the agency was a surprise. The Monday morning of her return she was hailed as a hero. All the agents wanted the details of her adventure. There had been a write up in the local newspaper. Local Travel Agent Helps Crack International Art Smuggling Ring.

On her next day off, Yvonne drove Christy to her friend's house for a play date. She took the free time to visit with Janice. "How are you really doing?" Yvonne wanted more than the automatic response.

"Very well. My sister and I have renewed our relationship and we are busy trying new things. I'm enjoying the freedom to come and go as I please without answering to anyone." Janice spoke with an enthusiasm Yvonne had not heard before.

"What else? I sense you aren't telling me everything." Yvonne watched Janice try to remain composed.

"It was funny, really. When we arrived at the airport, I arranged to send Bill's body directly to the funeral parlor. Well, he was still stirring things up even in death." Janice giggled. "A big commotion was made when the attendants removed his body from the transport casket. They found a jeweled dagger, a small museum quality painting and the golden statue of goddess Hera all hiding with his body. Fortunately, the funeral director is an ethical man. He called me to see if I knew what they were doing in there, and I called the police. They have since gotten in touch with the Athens police, and best of all, the museum is paying me a small reward for returning the art."

Yvonne wondered if she would hear from Inspector Trakas. Had he found Demetrious and George Maverickos or were they hiding out somewhere in Europe until the heat was off and they had an opportunity to continue their life of crime?

Yvonne received thank you notes from Cynthia, Missy and Evelyn. Cynthia informed her she was expecting a visit from Ari and would bring him by the agency to say hello when he arrived. Missy announced she and Todd were thrilled about having a baby. Evelyn asked her to keep her eyes and ears open for a deal on a cruise to the Caribbean after thanking her for getting them home safely. Now that Richard was retired they wanted to see the world.

A week after her return from Greece, Yvonne received a large bouquet of her favorite yellow "Peace" roses. The card read: How about a date Saturday night?

ACKNOWLEDGEMENTS

Hera's Revenge is the first in a series of travel mysteries featuring Yvonne Suarez. Her character has been created from a combination of spunky travel agents that I have known. The major influence comes from travel agency owner, consultant and travel agent extraordinaire, Yvette Fragetti.

Many thanks to the High Country Writers whose numerous members were always available with programs and inspiration to keep me plugging away at my writing until complete.

To the members of my small critique group, Chloe Coleman, Marcia Cham, Merle Guy, Sandra Horton, Linda Jencson, Ingrid Kraus and former members Judith Banks and Carolyn Wilder, I could not have done it without you holding my feet to the fire to see that I worked hard and continued to improve my writing skills in every aspect.

I'd like to acknowledge my children, Greg, Kelly and Christine; my step children, Lori and Leigh; and my sisters Pat and Tracy who believed in my ability to write. A special thanks to sister, graphic artist Tracy Arendt for her countless hours of help and design work, and to my esteemed editor, Sandra Horton who has helped me to make my story stronger.

Last but not least, I'd especially like to thank my husband Walter who has always encouraged and patiently waited for me to complete my first novel.

The following works were most helpful to me in preparing this novel:

Mythology: Timeless Tales of Gods and Heros by Edith Hamilton, A Mentor Book from New American Library, New York, NY 1969 **Hera's poem is attributed to an anonymous ancient poet in this book.

Greek Horizons by Helen Hill Miller, Charles Scribner's Sons, New York, NY 1961

Treasures of Greece by John S. Bowman, Crescent Books, New York, NY 1986

Ancient Greek and Roman Religion by H. J. Rose, Barnes & Noble Books reprint from 1940 edition, New York, NY, 1995

New LaRousse Encyclopedia of Mythology Paul Hamlin Publisher, New York, London, Sydney, Toronto 1968

The Archaeological Museum of Delphi by Marilena Carabatea Adam Editions, Kato Halandri, Athens – Year unknown

Greece Past and Present by S. Lombardo, Barnes & Noble Books reprint from White Star, Vercelli, Italy 2000, New York, 2004

Insight Guides to Greece Editors, Maria Lord and Brian Bell, Langenscheidt Publishers, Inc., Long Island City, NY 2003, updated edition 2005

Insight Guides to Greek Islands Editors, Jeffery Pike, Emily Hatchwell and Brian Bell, Langenscheidt Publishers, Inc., Long Island City, NY 2003, updated edition 2005

Athens Editions, G Gouvoussis, Ratzieri, Athens, Greece – Year unknown

Smithsonian Magazine, February 2008 Article, The Parthenon: Secrets of the Ancient Temple by Evan Hadingham, Washington, DC

ABOUT THE AUTHOR

Wendy Dingwall owned and operated her own travel business in South Florida for over 12 years. In 2001 she moved to the mountains of Northwest, North Carolina. Two years later she began working for a local book publisher, marketing authors and their books, and began writing her first mystery novel, fulfilling a life-long dream. In July 2009 she opened her own publishing company and in the spring of 2011 will have published 13 books by various authors. She continues to work on the second and third novels in her Yvonne Suarez Travel Mystery series.

She currently resides on a 50 acre farm near Boone, NC with her husband, Walter, their 2 maltese dogs, 1 cat, and miscellaneous wildlife.

CPSIA information can be obtained
at www.ICGtesting.com
Printed in the USA
BVOW03s1803150117
473543BV00001B/95/P